*For Vickie,*

*"See those two shooting stars? That's us."*

Radiant Publishing House Inc.
P.O. Box 379
Walden, NY 12586
www.radiantpublishinghouse.com


Paperback
ISBN-13: 978-0-9991857-8-0

# **Index**

All bolded words may be found with further definition in the Tome of Insights on page 268.

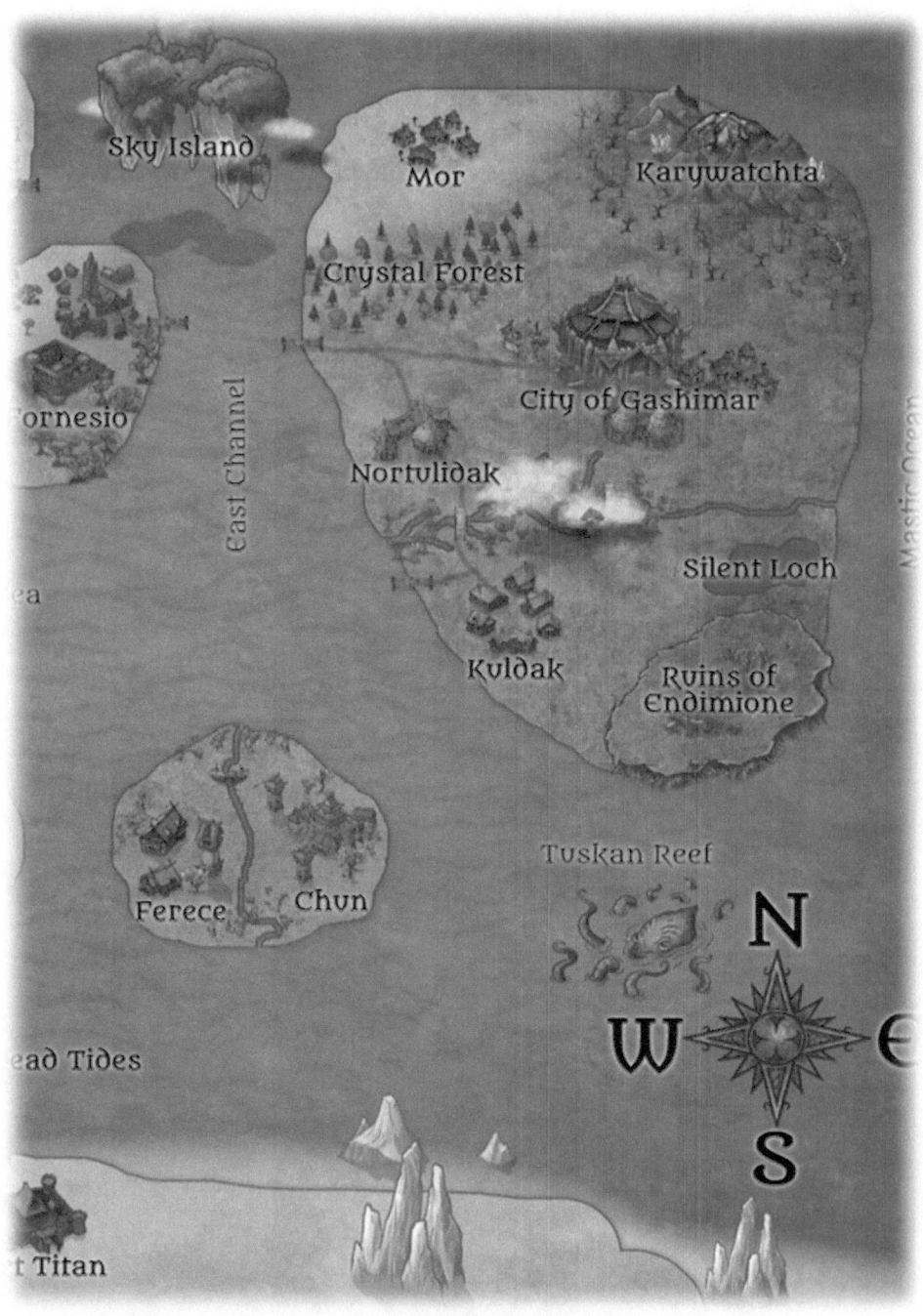

M.C. Grimm

# Radiant Heroes

## Episode II: Beyond Horizons

## By M.C Grimm

M.C. Grimm

# I

## Life Lessons

*"Never underestimate one who can find victory in defeat; that is the making of a true master."*
*The Wayward Warrior - A Tribute to Solihart*

The winter frost covered the windows, obscuring the view of carriages and people walking past the clinic. The room had a dry heat that carried a scent of burning logs from the wood stove. Lee was on his knees, digging into the cushion of the chair and staring at the figures blurring past. He lifted his finger and traced a small circle into the frost; leering a squinted eye to view the world.

"Pay attention, boy," Lavi scolded as he swatted at Lee's head, "I am trying to teach you something, **Maker** knows you won't learn it on your own."

Lee fixed his thin black hair and stood up from the chair, "I'm sorry father," he began following Lavi into the treatment center as his robes flailed behind him.

"Best not to let it happen again," Lavi commanded. "I am going to teach you something rather different today. I need you to take note of everything I do because I will only do it once. After I finish, you will have to show me what you've learned. Do you understand?"

"I understand and I'm ready to learn," Lee said excitedly.

"Wipe the smile off your face, boy. I'm here to teach you, not amuse you; take this seriously."

"Okay," said Lee.

"Good. Now, do you remember the Dinsley family from the **Northern Villas** on Emerald Avenue? The **reptilians**?" Lavi asked.

Lee shook his head.

"Recently their daughter was kidnapped and held for ransom. Apparently, some *delinquent,* a **half-breed**, came to the **Dinsley Clinic** and feigned an injury. While Mulag was readying a gurney, the man grabbed young Drakas and ran out."

Lee became rigid, "Just like that?"

Lavi knelt down and peered into his eyes. He spoke very deliberately, "Just - like - that." He snapped his fingers and Lee jumped in place. "That is what inspired this particular lesson I have for you today."

"Didn't Mr. Dinsley- " Lee started.

"*Master* Mulag Dinsley," Lavi corrected.

"Didn't Master Dinsley go after her?"

"He did, but the half-breed was much quicker than he was. The next day he discovered a letter stuck into the door of his own clinic with a dagger. The delinquent demanded five thousand gold pieces to have get her back."

Lee was anxious, "He paid it, right? Was she okay?"

"Yes, yes," Lavi waved his hand in disinterest, "he paid it, and Drakas was fine. She was never hurt and was always fed—it was the best of a bad situation. Mulag didn't-"

Lee interrupted him with a snicker, "Master Mulag."

Lavi did not find Lee amusing, and his face flushed with red. He quickly began reaching into drawers of his procedural cart as if searching for something, "Let me tell you something, boy; a Master may call another Master by their first name. You are certainly no Master, you are a foolish eight-year-old boy," he scolded. "I would be relieved if someone stole you away, but your mother - she insisted I talk to you."

Lee hung his head.

At this time, Lavi was knotting some short ropes atop the gurney, "She told her father that the half-breed would go out for hours at a time but would tie her up so she couldn't escape." He began wrapping the ropes around his wrists and put them out before Lee, "Pull that one there - no, the other one - yes." He pulled at his wrists to show the binding was tight.

"What are you doing?" Lee asked.

Lavi sighed, "What I am trying to tell you is that being a **cleric** is a rewarding profession, but it does have its risks. We earn good coin and because of that, we have something worth stealing. We are worth robbing, boy. Now, there are many ways you can do this, but pay attention because I am only going to show you this once."

Lee nodded.

Lavi twisted his wrists within the rope, showing that his hands were completely restrained. He first attempted to slip out of the knot, but the bulge of his thumb was too large. Then, he attempted to pull his arms outward and let out a strained groan. He released, took a breath, and then followed up with a second failed attempt. He was slightly out of breath as he spoke, "A good knot can't be slipped. A quality rope won't snap easily."

Lee was now sitting on top of the gurney, looking on in fascination, "Then, what do you do?"

"We are clerics, boy, so we will play to our strengths," Lavi replied.

Lee looked at him, intrigued, and asked with a giggle in his voice, "How can *healing* get you out of rope?"

In that instant, Lavi slammed his bound hands against the underside of the gurney with all his might. The bed was lifted from the floor and crashed backed down on its legs with a wobble. Lee was tossed forward in shock but was able to catch himself from falling by grabbing onto a medical cart.

He turned back and his eyes widened in horror - both of Lavi's hands were covered in blood and they were contorted. A thin white shard of bone was piercing out from the base of his thumb with a strand of torn skin loosely hanging from the tip.

"Father!" Lee shouted, taking a quick step towards him.

"Stop," he commanded, "just watch." Lavi twisted his wrists together. The knuckle beneath his thumb was clearly shattered from the force of hitting the gurney. To Lee's surprise, this allowed his hands to squeeze further under the rope. While that only made a slight difference, the blood from his wound seemed to lubricate his skin and helped him slip the rest of the knot.

Lavi looked to Lee with a grin. He held his mangled hands before him as blood began to shine in a pool at his feet. A familiar green glow began to pulse from his wrists, wrapping and enfolding around his palm and fingers. The bones made an audible snap as they shifted back into place. The fresh blood that had yet to drip chased its run back under his skin until at last, the flesh itself seared back together—completely and perfectly mended.

Lee stared at Lavi's hands in shock. He was also in awe—as he often found himself while watching Lavi's masterful healing magic.

"Do you see now how I was able to heal out of rope?" Lavi questioned.

"Yes," Lee nodded excitedly, "that was incredible! Did it hurt?"

"What a stupid question to ask," he snapped. "Do you think it hurts to shatter both of your hands?" At this time, Lavi shifted back to the gurney, and began tying knots in the shorter lengths of rope.

"I would think it does?" Lee mumbled. "But you didn't even scream - you didn't cry at all."

"I have been around blood and broken bones my entire life and trained myself to be strong with the skills that I have. Pain is nothing new to me, and if you wish to become a master cleric someday, you will have to accept pain as a part of life." Lavi stepped towards him. "Put out your hands."

"What?" Lee blurted out.

"Give me your hands, boy," Lavi scolded.

Lee came to the realization of what Lavi wanted and shivered, "I don't want to do that. I don't want to break my hands."

"I told you that you would have to repeat this lesson before we even began," Lavi's eyes glared at him, "It only hurts for a moment."

"I can't heal as well as you," Lee explained as he stepped back, "and I don't want to hurt myself."

"When the time comes you won't have a choice. This is going to make you a better cleric and a stronger man someday. This might be the difference between life and death!" Lavi shouted and moved towards him, "I promise you, that if you were taken like Drakas, I would not be paying any half-breed. You have to take care of yourself and this is how you learn."

Lavi had taken two quick steps and was looming over Lee. He knelt down and held his small hands together, binding them tightly at the wrist. After the knot was tied he gave, as Lee felt it, a crushing twist to be sure no slack was left in the rope.

Lee squirmed, "It's so tight. I can't even feel them."

"That's good," Lavi replied, "then it won't hurt as much."

Lee wiggled in place and writhed his body in a jerking motion. He began spinning his hands around one another and biting at the rope. He lifted his head to spit small fibers from his tongue.

"I can't get out," he muttered.

"That's a good knot tied in quality rope. Do as I just did; *you* won't figure out a better way," Lavi instructed.

Lee approached the gurney and looked over to his father, his eyes searching for concern and hoping for a change of heart. What he found was a cold stare, glaring back at him impatiently.

"On with it, then," said Lavi.

Lee lowered his wrists, shut his eyes, turned his head away, and thrust his hands quickly upwards. They met the rail with a heavy smack and the bed shifted slightly. He felt a throbbing in his thumbs, but it may have just been from the loss of circulation. There was a split down his nail bed, but his thumbs were neither broken nor bleeding.

"Again," Lavi barked, leaning closer.

Lee looked down, focused on his father's example, and repeated, this time with a more powerful thrust upwards. The gurney raised up an inch and met the floor with a bang. He could see his left thumb was clearly dislocated while the right was just beginning to swell. He threw his hands upward again, and again, and let out a soft sob in protest.

"How many times do you want to have to do this?" Lavi questioned. "Do it as hard as you can."

"I'm trying," Lee felt tears streaming down his face.

Lavi was unmoved by Lee's pain, "If you were *really* trying, you would be free by now."

A silence fell over the room as Lee wiped the tears from his face. His eyes fixed on the gurney and he let out a child's version of a barbaric yell as he wound up and hurtled his hand onto its underside. The bed toppled over as Lee was thrown off balance and onto the floor. His right thumb was now broken and his left dislocated.

As satisfied as he felt to do as his father instructed, Lee was in the worst pain he had ever felt. He was focused on understanding his father's lesson, but couldn't help asking himself why he had just broken his own thumb.

"Now, slip out," Lavi muttered.

Lee twisted his wrists again. The blood was pulsing out of his nail bed and he could feel the braid of the rope sliding with ease. He pulled one hand forward while shifting the other back. The nub of each broken thumb slipped beneath the knot. The rope fell to the floor with a singular wet flop. He had escaped his binding and stood, for a moment, triumphant.

Lavi looked on, unimpressed, "You're almost done."

His broken thumb was throbbing, and blood was still streaming down his nail bed - leaving small drops on the floor. Lee was dizzy but held his hands out before him and focused. He could feel the warmth of his energy building in his chest and pushed it out through his arms. He waited for the green aura to radiate into his hands and mend them, but it stopped at his wrists. He recomposed himself, standing firm in the center of the room. Again, he couldn't focus his energy into his hands.

"Focus, boy," Lavi ordered. "You have to move the energy out from your core. First your wrists, then your hands."

Lee was beginning to panic, the throbbing was becoming unbearable and he felt exhausted, "I can't!" He cried.

Lavi stood in front of him, "Try again."

Lee closed his eyes, centered on the warmth in his chest and rushed it through his shoulders and down his arms. He focused on the pain in his thumb, and his essence was choking at his wrists—pushing, but not healing, "I just can't, it hurts too much."

Lavi scoffed, "You have every advantage. You have received better instruction than Drakas, you have more maneuverability in the room than she had, and yet, your small child mind stops you. Perhaps necessity will teach you how to focus since I cannot." He stomped towards him in anger and grabbed Lee by the back of his collar.

Lee was dragged backwards, his hands held up delicately as he struggled to get his feet beneath him, "What are you doing, where are we going?"

Lavi flung the closet door open and threw some garments out into the room. Lee began to crawl away on his forearms, but not before Lavi had again grabbed the back of his neck and tossed him onto the dusty closet floor. There was a shriek of pain as Lee instinctively broke his fall, landing on his dislocated thumb. The light retreated beyond the door as it slammed behind him. He could hear a chair quickly dragged across the floor and wedged outside.

The darkness left no wonder to the warm liquid running down his forearm, and the throbbing in his hands.

"You won't be coming out until you have mended your hands," Lavi said calmly. "Take all the time you need, boy."

Lee rolled onto his back and sobbed quietly. Between bouts of crying, he would attempt to channel his energy beyond his wrists but was unsuccessful. The pain was somehow softer now, and his nail stopped bleeding. Hours passed between tears, attempts, and failures. Lee was beginning to fall asleep.

Footsteps approached the door, and his father's voice echoed within, "Have you fixed your hands?" His voice lacked concern.

As if no longer tired, Lee opened his eyes and fixed them on the shadows beneath the door. He remained silent.

"I asked you a question. Have you fixed your hands?" Lavi repeated.

Lee rolled onto his knees, clenching his broken hands into contorted fists. He remained silent.

"If you don't answer, I will make you regret it," Lavi said with authority. "Don't make me ask again."

As if no longer afraid, Lee mumbled, "I hate you."

"*What* did you say, boy?"

He heard a quick movement as the chair scraped the floor and smashed into the wall across the room. Pieces bounced and rolled with heavy wooden thuds, accompanied only by the rapid stomps moving closer.

"I hate you!" he shouted.

The knob twisted and the door was thrown open with a crash. The light in the room was blinding to his darkness-attuned eyes and the blurred silhouette reached down for him maliciously. Fear and anger overcame him, and then—darkness.

*A blurry silhouette.*

*Throbbing pain.*

*Darkness.*

Lee's eyes began to focus as if waking from a dream. Everything before him was still blurry. The last thing he remembered was being at a festival with Marlow.

His senses began to awaken and the smell of fire and a salty mist were carried in the breeze. He was perched upright on his knees with his hands in front of him. Was he tied up? How did he get tied up? Oswald, the magic show; it all came rushing back to him, as detailed as a novel. He turned his head and could see a large bonfire with dozens of figures standing around it. Lee didn't notice the figure until it walked inches past. It came from behind him and approached the fire. The figure was a man, and he leaned over to speak with one of the other blurred figures. Then, they both started towards him. Lee twisted weakly, still in a daze, but only managed to topple himself over.

One of the figures knelt down in front of him patiently while the other came around him from behind and pushed him back onto his knees.

The figure in front of him spoke with a gentle, deep voice, "I'm sorry they had to rough you up like this, but I heard you gave my guys a bit of trouble back there, kid."

Lee blinked quickly and the man came into view. He was a tall human in brown leather armor that accented his chiseled features. Down each of his legs were holstered several small hatchets, and from his back protruded two long handles to more elaborate axes. His skin was pale, and he had numerous scars clearly from battle. Long gray hair peeked from under his hat, and a matching goatee moved as he spoke.

He reached for his canteen and held it out to Lee, "Water?"

Lee slowly grasped the canteen and removed the cork. He took a small sniff and then, realizing there wasn't any venom or poisons, downed the entire canteen. He chugged it too quickly and let out a cough, "Thanks."

The man took the canteen back, tipped it over to show not a single drop was left, and with a glance at Lee, he scoffed. He threw it to one of the other men, "Refill that."

The soldier ran off at once, as ordered.

The man stood and took a few steps towards the bonfire. He was centered with his feet shoulder width apart and his arms crossed.

Lee took these few minutes to study the man as he was looking away. He took note of his excessive weaponry. Fourteen hatchets, two axes, and a small hand crossbow. Along his belt, Lee could identify three potion vials: two **healing potions** and one minor **antidote**. Luckily with his alchemy skills he could tell the difference between the crimson of a healing potion versus the maroon of a **flame nest**. The pale green of a minor antidote is recognizable, even by beginner alchemists.

The man was facing away the entire time, but his boisterous voice was carried on the breeze, "Didn't your parents ever teach you that it's not polite to stare?"

Lee was startled, "I... how did you know I was looking at you?"

"I don't need my eyes to see," he turned on his heel and came to crouch again in front of him. "Your name's Lee, isn't it?"

"Yes," Lee nodded. "Who are you?"

"I've gone by many names over the years, but nowadays I'm called the Axeman," He replied.

Lee looked at him confused, "The Axeman? Is that why you carry all the axes?"

He shrugged, "I think it's because I carry all these axes that I'm called *the Axeman*, but who can tell with titles anyway? Seems unoriginal altogether." His laugh carried over the ridge.

Lee felt calm but wasn't sure why. He felt like he was having a casual conversation. Then, he looked down at his bindings, "Why am I here?"

His captor's laugh was cut short and his smile faded, "I need your help with Prince Stein."

"What do you want with Stein?" Lee asked.

"I think I'll save us a lot of questions if I help you understand something broader; what do you do for fun, Lee?" asked the Axeman.

"I eat, go to the park, I draw with my mom's pastels. There's a lot that I do. What does that have to do with anything?" Lee said.

"How does it make you feel when you draw with your mom's pastels?" he asked.

"I feel like I'm with her again, and like she never left. It makes me happy. Some of the pastels still have the indent from where she held them in her fingers; I try not to use those." Lee hung his head.

The Axeman grinned, "I know how you feel, Lee. I can relate to holding on to a feeling, wanting to relive it over and over and never let it go. You have a few things that you do for fun, a few things that make you feel alive... that's how they make you feel, right? Alive?"

"I guess so."

He set his eyes to the stars, "For me there is only one thing that makes me feel that way; one thing that makes me feel alive. It's the rush of a challenge, that feeling when you push yourself to the limit and feel your body almost break. I feel alive when I am fighting for my life, one wrong move away from death. I only seem to get that through dueling someone who's as tough as me. That's why I need Stein."

Lee smiled, "You took me so that you could fight Stein?"

"Yes," he said shortly.

"That was pretty dumb; he's going to be angry." Lee said, "He's going to kill you."

"That's the point."

"No," Lee explained, "he's not going to come and just duel you. He's going to come and really kill you - a lot."

"I'm looking forward to it already," the Axeman grinned with satisfaction. "The reason I needed to tell you this was simple: there are rules to dueling that I need your friends to follow. If they don't follow them," he stared intently at Lee, "I will have to kill you. If you try to escape, I will kill you. If everything else goes well, you'll get to walk out of here or even join my crew if you want."

Lee laughed, "No thank you, I'll be leaving with my friends."

"You seem confident - you are really building up Stein for me. I hope he doesn't disappoint." He began walking back towards the bonfire.

"They won't be afraid of you and your little hatchets!" Lee yelled.

In a flash, the Axeman turned to face a line of trees, and stood with an arm outstretched. Lee looked over and saw one of the long axes buried deep in the trunk of a tree. He moved so quickly that Lee didn't see him turn, draw a weapon, aim, or throw it. But there it was, centered in the shaft of the tree. There was a soft creaking sound that built up and finished with a violent crack as the trunk split in half, falling into two separate pieces with the hatchet resting on the ground between them.

The Axeman continued his stride and laughed, "They won't live long enough to *feel* fear."

# II

## <u>Tension</u>

*"Madness; chilling as ice, foreboding as death, intense as flame, indiscriminate as lightning - the most powerful and all-consuming element in the cosmos."*
*The Chill of Death - A Tribute to Crowlastte*

The party was navigating through the streets of **Vian** under the cover of darkness. Dense clouds bellowed overhead, obscuring the light from the two moons hanging full in the sky. There was an unusual, foreboding stillness, as if the walls were previously held up by the sounds of life and the enduring quiet would bring them crumbling down.

The city remained shut down as guards scrambled about, seeking the taken Queen Sana. Other than the periodic, rapid marching of the patrolmen, there was little stirring throughout the city. People were forced to return to their homes. Many were still drunk or riled from the festival, both citizens and guards, which made the efforts that much more challenging.

Stein, Drogon, Marlow, and Gwynn were making their way towards the north ridge. Although most the group moved silently, Marlow was dragging his injured leg. His other leg stomped heavily as he forced himself forward to keep pace with his allies.

On more than one occasion, did they narrowly avoid discovery, and turn to him with a damning stare.

After the latest close call, Stein stepped towards him quickly and with authority he whispered, "I think you've done enough - you should go back to the *Yoshi*."

"No," replied Marlow.

They stared each other down, neither moving a muscle.

"No," Marlow repeated.

Stein turned away. "Do what you want, but I will leave you behind if I have to."

"Stein, you aren't the only one who cares about Lee," Drogon said. "We are in this together, and if what Gwynn says is true, then we must work together to help him."

"It's true," Gwynn added.

"We won't be able to help him if we get caught by Vian guards before we get there - now will we?" Stein continued.

"You need to focus," said Drogon. "Normally, your strength and your anger are enough, but this Axeman is a renown duelist - he will be focused."

"I don't care what he is!" Stein erupted, "I'll kill him for taking Lee."

Drogon moved towards him and rested a hand firmly on his shoulder, "Then you need to live, and to do that, you'll have to push aside your emotions and focus. When studying the **Gallant** fighting styles...what is it they teach you?"

Stein sighed, "**Centbre**."

"There's a reason that centbre teaches to be centered and focused, you know. There may be other fighting styles that favor a scythe wielding maniac." Drogon laughed, "I think your best bet for this fight is to stick to what you've mastered."

Stein calmed, "Thank you, Drogon."

"You say it like you've learned something," he scoffed as he continued walking towards the ridge. "I'll have to remind you not to lose your mind at least one more time—tonight alone."

Stein looked towards Gwynn and mumbled, "Probably," before continuing after Drogon.

The silence of the city was eerie. Even their stealthy footsteps made an audible sound of sand grinding on the stone path. For a moment, Marlow and Gwynn were behind, and out of earshot of Drogon and Stein.

"I'm sorry I dragged all of you into this," said Gwynn.

Marlow looked to her, "Nothing to be sorry about."

"I feel like there is. I wasn't entirely honest about the Axeman or Porbella, and because of that, I put Lee in danger. Now, to top it off, I'm pretty sure Stein is going to *try* to kill me once we get through this." She let out a deep exhale. "*If* we get through this."

"We would help them either way. Doesn't matter if you tell us before or tell us now. We would help, so you don't need to be sorry," Marlow explained. "Stein is *Toren*."

"Toren? What does that mean?" Gwynn asked.

"In minos, Toren is when you fight because you are broken," He responded.

"Broken how?"

"Not my place," Marlow turned away.

Gwynn stared at him a moment before nodding with appreciation, "Thank you."

They reached the base of the small mountain on the coast. The mountain seemed as if cut in half on the side facing the sea. From where they stood, the landmass blocked their view of the water, but they heard the violent crashing of waves on the other side of the ridge. They began their deliberate ascension. It was a hundred feet high with a flat summit and a steep incline—this was the North Ridge. If it weren't for grappling on small trees and embedded rocks, this climb would require special climbing gear. As they grew closer to the peak, they could smell the fires that they had watched from the port.

Stein led the climb with Drogon mere feet behind, then Gwynn, and finally Marlow. While there was no longer fear of Vian guards, they were aware that The Axeman and his followers were atop the summit and possibly scouting nearby. This awareness made them climb at a less strenuous pace to save their strength.

When they were halfway up the ridge, an unfamiliar voice carried down from the summit. They couldn't hear it at first and were forced to come to a stop to make out his words.

"Oye!" A man yelled in a frustrated tone. His voice carried on the wind with a soft accent.

"Hello?" Drogon responded.

"How goes the climb?" he asked modestly.

Drogon looked up to Stein as if confused, "Fine?" he shrugged.

"Aye, good. Can I throw you down a canteen or anything?" he said.

Stein peered down, "Gwynn, what is this?"

She reassured them, "I know, it sounds crazy. He's a duelist and wants you to be fit to fight when we get up there. It won't be poisoned or anything, but I do have water if anyone has need of some."

"That's..." Stein was lost for words.

There was a brief silence.

"No, thank you," Drogon shouted up the ridge.

"Are you sure? We also have some cooked pork and fresh pears. Can I interest you in some of that?" he asked.

"Pork," Marlow said.

"No," Stein erupted, "all we want is to bleed every last drop from the one up there who calls himself the Axeman, take back our friends, and go back to our lives while your corpses rot up on that summit!"

There was another silence, longer this time.

"Give me a second, I'll be right back," he said.

Stein continued climbing and the rest of the party started behind him. Suddenly, Drogon felt something soft bounce off his head, and he quickly caught it in his hand. A white cloth was wrapped around something warm. He unraveled it to find a piece of pork.

Drogon laughed, reached down, and stuck it onto Marlow's horn, "I guess this is for you?"

"Must be," Marlow threw the cloth to the wind and devoured the pork.

Stein was looking down towards him, "Seriously, Marlow? It could be poisoned."

He snarled in response.

"Oye!" the man up top yelled again.

"What now?" Stein asked.

"The Axeman told me to try to be accommodating for you, but I wasn't sure what to do for the 'bleed out every drop' bit, so I had to ask him. He said I should drop some of these here rocks down at you and see if you're worthy to finish the climb," he said and then waited for a response.

"Why are you telling us?" asked Drogon.

"Aye, The Axeman said I should only drop them at Stein, since the rest of you have been decent folk. I'm not quite sure how to do that - it's not like I can see you, yet."

"You'll see me—very—soon," Stein promised.

"See that? I should be dropping a rock right now, but I don't know where to drop it," the man said, "Oh well, I won't drop any rocks yet, then. Hey, who was it that asked for pork? Was that the half-breed? It didn't sound like that Moonstorm fellow."

Drogon and Stein looked towards one another.

Drogon whispered, "They still think Tholden is with us. Maybe they had eyes on us, but that would mean we lost them back in the *Radiant Empire*."

"Gwynn has been with us since we left the empire," Stein said. "We never lost them."

She leered at him, "I'm not reporting back to them. I've apologized, and told you this wasn't my intention, yet you insist on being selfish and thinking you're the only one with family up on this ridge."

"He wouldn't be there if you thought about anyone else - tell me how selfish I am?" Stein said.

"I was only *ever* thinking about Porbella," she replied.

Drogon raised his voice, "Enough!" He took a recomposing breath, "We have to stay focused and not fight each other off the side of a cliff. Stein, Gwynn made a mistake. Gwynn, Stein feels betrayed," he addressed before reasoning their situation. "Once we reach the summit, we will have no choice but to work together to make all of this right again. For Porbella and for Lee. Can you handle that?"

They each looked to Drogon, then to one another. They said nothing but continued the climb with a silent understanding.

As they reached the peak of the ridge, the man atop offered a firm **dwarven** hand to help them up. He wore fitted brown and black leather armor that complimented his ponytail and long braided beard. He had a small fire burning near the cliff and seven cushions circled around it. This small sitting area was a short distance away from a line of trees that seemed to separate them from the main encampment and the larger part of the summit. He gestured for them to sit with him, but they remained standing, peering into the tree line impatiently.

"Aye, friends, my name's Edgar, and I am a *bronze* to the Axeman aboard the *Splinter*. Before I bring you over, I need to go over some rules. Please sit," he said.

Gwynn stepped forward and turned towards the group. "I know this isn't what you're used to, but he is a true duelist. There won't be any surprises."

They each slowly sat, keeping their weapons ready and attentive to their surroundings. The noise from the main encampment was that of excitement and celebration. It was almost as if they had no care that the group was even present.

Edgar spoke softly, "First, on behalf of the Axeman, thank you for making the trip-"

He was immediately interrupted by Stein, "A lot of choice you gave us, kidnapping children."

"Yes, it is unfortunate that in pursuit of great challengers we must sometimes give incentives to those who might otherwise ignore our requests," said Edgar, "I assure you that Lee, Porbella, and Sana are all in good health. After your duel, even should you lose, your loved ones will be released. The only thing that will bring them harm is your actions."

"You mentioned Sana, as in Queen Sana?" Gwynn asked.

"Yes," he answered.

"Why the queen?" she continued.

"We had suspicion that you might not understand how she fits in. Any ideas?" Edgar replied.

"She is the Queen of Vian?" Stein said. "Where we just made an agreement to fight against Donahay, and you, stupidly; wanted to give us more *incentives*?"

He smirked, "No. Any other guesses? How about you, Drogon?"

"I would have to agree with Stein. Your motives seemed fixed with getting us up here," Drogon said.

Edgar laughed. "Oh, I knew it, you have no idea! Aye, so let me ask you something, what can you tell me about Merelda?"

"My mother?" said Drogon.

Edgar pulled at his beard with a grin, "What is she like?"

"She is kind, what does she have to do with anything?" Drogon stared intently, his eyes tensing with anger and concern.

"You really aren't getting it, so I'll just ask you, is she **dragonkin**?"

The party was now looking to Drogon, confused.

"She is a *dwarf*," Drogon said.

"That's unusual isn't it? Even half-breeds take after their mother, don't they? Why- one might think you were left orphaned or rather—adopted by the *kind* Merelda, don't you think?"

Drogon was silent as the realization came over him.

Gwynn continued, "Are you suggesting that Queen Sana is Drogon's mother?"

"We have a winner!" Edgar applauded, "Congratulations, it's a boy."

Stein reached over a hand to Drogon's shoulder; no one was certain if it was sarcastic or supportive.

Drogon's eyes were affixed to a point in front of him, widened with shock, "But, my mother never... Merelda never told..."

"Wait, I apologize, we have gone very much off topic here." Edgar repositioned himself on his cushion. "The rule of the duel—each duel is one on one. Should anyone interfere - so shall the crew of the *Splinter*. Every duel is to the death; however, should you prove yourself worthy. The Axeman may offer you to join his crew in exchange for your life."

"Is that what got you here?" asked Gwynn.

"That's the entire crew. Fame seeking duelists, powerful warriors, far more formidable than **corrupted**—that's for sure," Edgar answered.

"What about when we win?" said Stein.

"No one has defeated the Axeman in a duel before, but if you win, you inherit the *Splinter* along with the loyalty of her crew and treasures she holds," he answered.

Drogon shook his hands in front of him to disrupt the conversation, "Wait - may we please go back to Queen Sana being my mother? How do you know this?"

Edgar sighed, "I didn't think this was going to be *that* big of a surprise to you since it would've been obvious to anyone else that the dwarf, Merelda, isn't your birth mother. Let us just say that Queen Sana is your mother, but King Connero is not your father. In fact, Connero ordered both you and your actual father's execution out of pure rage. Needless to say, he was able to flee with you to the **Radiant Empire** where he knew Connero wouldn't follow during all the tension at that time. Aye, if he knew who you were, he may have killed you earlier today on principle."

"But how do you *know*?" Drogon glared.

"There are records of the affair, child, and execution order in the military records of General Krain. You can find it in the private royal records—somewhere around the *treason* section," Edgar replied.

"General Krain was my father?" Drogon probed.

"I really don't want to spell out your family's history right now," Edgar said. "We happened across it by mistake, *treason* is filed just before *treasure*. It made sense to use her in case you or Krain would come looking for her."

Drogon hung his head, "Merelda never spoke of this."

Edgar shrugged, "Can't really help ya with that."

"However you came into her life, it sounds like she took you in as her own," Gwynn explained.

Stein stood, "I'm sorry Drogon, we can deal with this later - are we done here?"

"There is one last thing," Edgar added. "The Axeman initiated the duels, so he will pick who he wishes to challenge first. You will have to respect his choice, or it will be treated as breaking the rule of the duel. Any final questions?"

"I've heard enough of this nonsense," Stein looked to each member of the party, "good?"

"Go," said Marlow.

They stood after their short rest, feeling eager and ready. Following Edgar through the tree line, they could see the dancing fire illuminating the encampment. A dozen tents circled around a large bonfire where two dozen well-equipped soldiers waited while drinking and cheering.

Sitting on cushions beyond the fire they could see Lee, a youthful blond **elf** that Gwynn identified as Porbella, and an elegantly dressed dragonkin that they recognized to be Queen Sana.

Lee perked up as soon as he saw them being led towards the bonfire. He smiled wide and leaned towards Porbella. While they were too far away to hear what he said, the party could see Lee mouth, *"we're saved,"* as Porbella smiled hopefully.

Before them stood a tall human man with fitted brown leather armor. It accented the tone of muscles on his body and had intentional gaps in the coverings. He stood with his back to them, displaying two jeweled and worn, yet well-maintained axes. Down each of his legs were a dozen equally crude hatchets.

"Line up," he said in a near whisper.

The crew was immediately silent and circled around the encampment like fans in an arena. They were patient and composed, but all appeared excited. While some were still holding their tankards and canteens, they each were ready to draw a weapon at a moment's notice. It was clear this was routine for them, and they were looking forward to it.

The Axeman turned slowly to face the party, "You too, please."

Edgar gestured for the party to form in a line and waved them farewell as he made his way into the circle.

Stein, Drogon, Marlow and Gwynn stood still. They were encircled by the two dozen crewmembers atop the summit of the northern ridge. Lee, Porbella and Queen Sana were sitting beyond the bonfire, beyond the Axeman.

Gwynn peered to her sister, concerned.

Marlow limped and snarled.

Drogon stood, unwavering.

Stein pulsed with rage.

And the Axeman smiled.

# III

## The Rule of the Duel

*"Roar loud, so Tauros might hear you!"*
*A follower of Tauros.*

The party slowly shifted into a line facing the Axeman, who kept still as his eyes wandered eagerly. Then, as if routine, the crew of the *Splinter* widened their encircling formation to give room for the battle to come.

The Axeman spoke softly and deliberately, but his voice seemed to bellow across the summit, "Your loved ones go free when we are done here," he paused. "If you force me to kill them," he paced in front of Lee, "I won't lose sleep over it."

Three soldiers moved around the circle to position themselves behind Lee, Porbella and Sana, then, they drew their weapons. Lee and the others squirmed nervously in place and looked through the flames towards the circle. With that, the realism of their dire situation became alarmingly more apparent.

"Not a wink." The Axeman continued, "Let's begin and *do* try to have some fun. Gwynn, it is only fitting that you and I have this first moment. Come." he moved into the circle.

"Gwynn brought me here to fight in her place," said Stein.

"That was our original deal," the Axeman replied. "A deal between her and I. She didn't deliver you *when* she promised. So, now she can fight for herself."

"Why not me first?" Stein considered that the duelist might defend his pride and insisted, "Are you afraid to fight me and die in your first round?"

The Axeman grinned, "You should limber up, as well," he stopped once he reached the center of the circle. "Come Gwynn, this has been a long time coming."

Gwynn looked to Stein, "It might not mean anything to you, but I am sorry to have dragged Lee into this. Even if you never forgive me, I want you to know, I do care for him - and for you." She looked at him, hoping he would say something, anything. After a few seconds of silence, she said, "Look after Porbella for me, she's a good kid. She has a lot to learn, but she has a good heart."

"She'll be okay," Stein said.

Gwynn half smiled as a tear fell down her cheek. She gave Stein a nod, wiped her eye and stepped into the circle. Drawing a blue flickering arrow, she readied her bow and stood at the edge of the circle.

"Wait," said the Axeman. "You'll only have the one shot if you're using your bow, and if you miss, this is hardly going to be entertaining."

"This is what I have," she replied, "It'll have to do."

"Maybe one of your friends will let you borrow a weapon to use with your bow?" He added. "It will make this more enjoyable for the two of us."

Without hesitation, Drogon drew Rayne from her sheath and approached Gwynn. He leaned in, "Fight well and make that shot count." With that, he stuck it into the ground at her side and left it to shimmer in the light of the bonfire.

"Whenever you're ready," as his goatee smirked.

A steady inhale filled her lungs. Exhale. Gwynn moved with reflexes of pure adrenaline, raising her bow with unwavering focus and her eyes locked on like a bird of prey. In this singular fluid motion, she had notched, pulled, and released. Before her arrow had time to reach its target, she had thrown her bow to the ground and torn Rayne loose from the dirt to charge.

The blue flicker of light cut through the night air with a whistle. The Axeman watched it as if in slow motion, weighing the most challenging means of avoiding death. He reached up, grabbed one of the long-handled axes from his back, and brought it down on the arrow—splitting it cleanly in two pieces.

It wasn't until the arrow had been split, that he could feel electricity pulsing through his hands and up his arms. The blue flickering arrow held a pulse of pure lightning and the Axeman grinned as he felt the rush of pain surge through his body. He stood, for a fraction of a moment, stunned.

Most of the onlookers saw only the green blur of Gwynn's armor cashing behind the arrow. For the Axeman, this was quite different. The excitement grew as his heart began to race;

paralyzed as a vengeful elf neared him, intent to end this fight in an instant - he loved every fleeting moment. When she was, still three paces away, he felt his muscles loosen and his strength return to him. The thought "too bad" crossed his mind as he avoided a glorious death, yet again.

A quick inhale. She lunged Rayne forward, aiming for where a human heart should be. The lightning emanated off of him and he nimbly spun in place to avoid her. Gwynn slashed upward, attempting to use her momentum to catch his neck. Again, he effortlessly tilted back his head, allowing the blade to miss his throat by a hair's length. She exhaled, shifting her footing to bring her boot up with a somersault. Her heel caught his defending forearm and she leapt backwards, ready to charge again.

He smiled, "At least people can say you hit me."

Gwynn knew he blocked her kick, but for the Axeman to block would mean he couldn't *dodge*. She aimed for next the next attack to be the blade and not her boot to connect.

"That look in your eye says you're overconfident, Gwynn. Don't ruin our moment by letting it go to your head," he added.

"I was just thinking about what people will *actually* say. I think - they will say I killed you!" she shouted, lunging forward again, and reaching with the full length of the blade.

The Axeman flipped back in a handspring, grabbing a hatchet off of his leg mid-flip, and when landing back on his feet, sent it soaring through the air with a swoosh.

Gwynn let out a shriek of pain. She stumbled back towards the edge of the circle clutching at her head. The hatchet narrowly missed her face, severing half of her pointed-elven ear and grazing her scalp. Her long hair was dripping crimson and her hand shook as she stopped trying to press the wound. She took a knee.

"Right to your head," he said with disappointment it his voice. He chuckled softly, "I'm not talking about the hatchet."

Gwynn was attempting to wipe the blood out of her eye, but it was gushing too quickly. She stood, closing her left eye, and breathing heavy with desperation and anger. She let out a barbaric shout as she charged at him with a series of wild slashes. He casually stepped between each swing of her long sword, allowing her to become more and more enraged until her movements became clumsy and presented an opening where he brought up the butt of his axe against her wrist. There was an audible crack as she cried out in pain. Rayne was thrown from her hand and impaled into the ground several feet away. The Axeman capitalized on the moment, sweeping her feet out from under her, placing his boot on her chest with a pound along with his axe at her throat.

Stein took a single step into the circle and all of the crewmen were clutching their weapons, shaking their heads. To further send the message, the soldier behind Lee pressed his blade tightly against his throat, stopping only when he let out a yelp. Stein stepped back.

The Axeman raised his axe slightly, "You have impressed me, Gwynn. I have no doubts that you are both cunning and capable. I could use someone like you on my crew." He paused. "I'll need an answer quickly."

"My sister?" She strained.

"She'll be free to go and live her life. You followed the rule of the duel. You will likely never see her again since you will belong to the *Splinter*. It's the nature of the business to have no attachments; you understand that, of course," he responded. "I need your answer."

A slow inhale. Blood streamed down her face, "Yes."

The Axeman lifted his boot off her chest, stowed his axe on his back, and reached down a hand to help her up, "Take my hand if you are sure, I will only offer a *quick* death once."

She hesitated for a moment, lifted her arm, and took his hand as he lifted her to her feet.

Stein's face flushed red.

"You can't blame her, Stein." Drogon was immediately beside him as if expecting his reaction, "Porbella is safe, and Gwynn's life is her own."

There was a chill in Stein's voice as he said, "Or die like a warrior."

"Sounds like a waste to me," Drogon argued. "Now, she lives; and if any of us beat him, then they are all free."

Stein turned to him, "Leave it to you to make cowardice sound rational."

"And you make living sound redundant," Drogon said, "but I'm sure it wasn't easy for her either. And you know what this means, don't you? It means she believes *you* will kill him."

"Oh yeah? And what do *you* think?" Stein asked.

"I think that Queen Sana might be my mother." He was silent a moment as he stared at her. "She might not be, but either way, King Connero's word and Vian's aid against Donahay may hang in the balance with her life. If we stop here, to think *or* to die, all is lost."

Stein laughed, "Is there ever a time when the whole world isn't going to **the void**?"

"Sure, remember the **vetala**? That was only a city we saved." Drogon smiled.

"Same with the **hydra**, I suppose," Stein said. "You're right."

There was a brief moment of silence between them before Drogon asked, "Am I distracting you from going into a bloody killing spree?"

His face was stern as Stein replied, "Barely."

"Attention all," the familiar voice of Edgar beckoned. "The Axeman has triumphed, and the *Splinter* has gained another member!"

There was loud cheering and hawing as the crew held their weapons to the sky. Many threw about their axes and swords wildly, while others beat their fists to their chests. A scrawny crewman with a medical bag came to Gwynn and walked with her beyond the bonfire. Porbella locked eyes with her and reached out, grazing fingertips as Gwynn was pulled past and into the ship.

"Cut the little one loose," the Axeman ordered.

The crewman behind Porbella lowered his blade from her throat and cut loose her bindings. He lifted her to her feet and dragged her over towards Drogon, releasing with a shove.

She was a twelve-year-old version of Gwynn, long red hair with deep emerald eyes and the same narrow chin that made them unmistakably related. She was wearing tan robes that were caked in dirt and salt. Even though she had a lean elven build, she appeared fairly undernourished.

"What is going to happen to Gwynn?" She asked.

Drogon looked down at her and gripped her shoulder, "She's going to be fine, and so are you."

She looked back towards the ship longingly. There was a faint understanding before a rush of tears in her eyes. She calmed their swimming and then peered up at Drogon, "Can she come with us?"

"Not yet," he replied. "Are you alright?"

She was silent.

Drogon nodded and reached into his pack, "You look hungry, and I happen to have some **cookies**. They're stale, but I'd imagine it's been a while since you've had any."

Porbella's eyes widened halfway through the word *cookie*. The moment he had it out of his pack, she snatched it from his hand and began gnawing away at it.

"Thank you!" She smiled awkwardly as if she had forgotten how. "Me and Queen Sana got to talking - she *is* your mother. She told me herself."

The scales of his face forced a smile, "We can talk about all that later. I think you should just relax for now."

At the center of the encircling crewmen, the Axeman stood before Rayne. He pulled it from the ground and admired it in his hand. "Kind of you to let Gwynn borrow this - such beautiful craftsmanship." He turned it over to study the hilt. "Makes me wish they called me *the Swordsman*."

The crew laughed hysterically and stomped at the ground.

"I'll keep it!" a crewman shouted.

"Nah, it's my turn for loot!" yelled another.

Drogon held up his hand and said in a whisper, "Rayne, come."

At once, the blade soared from The Axeman's hand and guided itself across the circle and to Drogon. The crew fell silent as he sheathed it at his hip.

"It just doesn't have the same ring to it," Stein scoffed.

Across the circle, Lee let out a giggle. Although he was quickly silenced by the crewman, he argued, "Oh come on, that was funny!"

"Be quiet, kid," the soldier said as he shoved Lee to the ground. "Just enjoy watching the Axeman rough up some more of your friends for a while."

"Alright," Stein said shortly. "This isn't working for me."

He moved forward into the circle and the crewman drew their weapons. The soldier by Lee pressed his boot firmly into his back and held the sword to him. Drogon and Marlow readied themselves for a fight and shifted to cover Stein's back.

"Stow your weapons," the Axeman ordered. "We're almost up to the main course, Stein. I'm just starting to have some fun."

"What about this is fun?" Stein shouted.

"The thrill of a challenge, the excitement of a fresh wound making your blood rush - taunting death itself. The finer things in life, Stein. I thought you could appreciate that?" said the Axeman.

"Mostly, yes," said Stein. "I just don't think these are the challenges you're looking for if you want one who can show you a beautiful death. You want a warrior to introduce you to the **reaper** himself? Well, you're as foolish as you look if you can't see it."

"Oh? And what is it that I can't see?" he smirked.

Stein slid back his right foot and held his hands out before him as if he were holding something heavy. The dim light of the bonfire seemed to twist in the very space between his grip, and in a flicker of blackness, a long gleaming shaft appeared. The obsidian metal emanated a sinister, dark energy. At the top of the shaft was the blackened, crooked blade of a scythe. In another flash of bright crimson light, it ignited into flame.

He stood, lowering his grip, and to allow the heat of the scythe to scorch the grass. "*I am* the reaper, and I have come to claim you."

# IV

## Of Blood and Fire

*"The more you know of the mysteries within it; the less you understand the universe. To know it all is to be either divine or undone."*
*Claiming the Heavens - A Tribute to Hosridon*

The Axeman smiled from ear to ear, "You are one for showmanship, I'll give you that. I hope you're more fun than Gwynn."

Stein flung up his scythe, balancing it loosely with his forearm to pivot on his shoulder. He strolled into the center of the circle, "If you can find fun in death, then I'm all the entertainment you need."

A silence came over Drogon, Marlow and the crewmen. They moved further back to widen the circle.

"Ready?" asked the Axeman.

Stein looked up to the night sky, basking his face in the light of the moons. He peered towards the Axeman, "Let's get on with this."

The Axeman dashed forward with ferocity, kicking up dust and dirt behind him. Within his movement he had drawn both large axes off his back, heaved them up into the air, and brought them down toward Stein. There was a clash of sparks as the obsidian steel of his scythe blocked the attack and their weapons locked.

They stared each other down for a moment before Stein lifted his foot; kicking off The Axeman's knee and into a somersault. Midair; Stein twisted his scythe upwards in a quick series of spins. One. Two. Three midair attacks. They rained embers of flame as they met the parry of axes, burning at the Axeman's flesh and armor. As Stein landed, embers were smoking at the dry grass throughout the circle.

Before he could regain his footing, the Axeman advanced. He spun in a tornado of cleaves with both arms outstretched, using the full length of the shaft to compensate for the reach of Stein's scythe. The rapid speed of his attacks was throwing Stein of balance and after numerous devastating spins; he loosened his grip and hurled an axe at Stein.

Stein felt the rush of blood as the axe carved a deep gash through his shoulder. The intensity of this grazing axe carried it beyond Stein and into a crewman's chest who was standing beyond him. The crewman was certainly dead, but for Stein, the pain chilled his stare with fury.

"He's expendable - did I get you at least?" The Axeman asked.

Stein scoffed as blood soaked his robes, "Any non-fatal wound might as well have missed."

The flame on his scythe blazed more intensely and he swiped a wide arc in front of him. The Axeman rolled beneath the swing and sprung up at Stein's side, bringing down a hatchet in one hand and full axe in the other.

Stein had to react in an instant. He dispersed his scythe and caught the Axeman's wrists, leaving only a puff of lingering black smoke in the air. They tussled for a moment before beginning to shift and kick at each other's footing. The elaborate display of footwork maintained their circular movement. The blades swayed mere inches from their faces. Then, as if both of them had the same plan of attack, they heaved forward with a head butt

The spectators let out an audible cringe of pain. Stein and the Axeman had both stepped back and blood was now streaming from their foreheads. No one could tell if either was even disoriented.

They were now several paces away from one another and Stein was without his scythe. The Axeman stuck his long axe into the ground and shook loose his grip. Then, with blinding speed, he began wildly throwing hatchets. Some were straight and direct throws that cut through the air with a loud whooshing sound. Others were thrown at curved angles and were circling around Stein like a boomerang, coming at him from both sides and behind.

Stein ducked under one while sidestepping another. He leapt over two that were arcing up from his feet before spinning past another, where a hatchet was already circling around to intercept him. It embedded deep into the right side of his chest. He stumbled back, which allowed another two to slice into his leg. Stein was breathing heavy and his boots were splashing in crimson pools beneath him. There was still a distant whooshing carried in the night air.

The Axeman nimbly picked up his long axes from the ground and his dead crewman. He turned, focused, and charged in on Stein for a killing blow.

Stein grasped the hatchet in his chest with a soft grunt. He didn't have the strength in him to pull it out. He faced The Axeman who was charging, confident, and proud. Stein stepped forward and swung with his empty hand outstretched while the Axeman was still a distance away. While his sinister grin alerted the Axeman that he was up to something, it was too late for him to react. When his arm was mid-swing, his scythe reappeared with its point centered on his foe and fire roared off the blade.

The Axeman felt the heat of the crooked blade cleaving clean into his gut. His blood was still bubbling from the heat as it splattered onto the ground. Bits of armor and entrails hung loose. His charge slowed and he brought down two weakened attacks that Stein deflected away with ease. He fell to his knees, "Did I," he gasped, "get you?"

The distant whooshing of a hatchet grew louder, and with a heavy thud, buried in Stein's back. His eyes widened as he fell forward onto his knees mere feet from the Axeman.

"Stein!" Lee cried out. He wrestled with his bindings and tried to stand, but was held in pace by a silent crewman. "Get up, Stein!"

The crewmen and the party closed the circle slightly, only to hear every whisper. Both men were still alive, the duel was not over.

The Axeman remained upright on his knees. His breaths were long and deliberate as he leaned slightly forward to spit out a mouthful of blood. He was still smiling as he said, "This was fun. You didn't disappoint. You really lived up to your reputation, Stein."

Stein's hand was shaking as he attempted to wipe the blood from his eyes. He too, was upright on his knees. There was a hatchet sticking out of his back and his chest, with his robes soaked and stuck to his lean build. His expression was serious, except for a grin at the corner of his mouth. "Thanks," he said shortly.

The Axeman struggled to speak, "Come now. Won't you admit you had fun? You're as twisted as I am."

"Not sure it was fun, yet," Stein said. "Still waiting to see if I win."

The Axeman let out a spray of red as he laughed, "Is that so? Well, I'm going to make sure I live long enough to see you die."

"That's interesting. I had the same idea," Stein replied.

"Good luck," the Axeman wheezed.

"You too." said Stein.

They stared each other down, waiting for the other to succumb to their mortality. Both men bleeding, broken, and tattered, too stubborn to let the other beat them. The Axeman, a lifetime duelist who never fled from a fight or feared death. Stein, a leader and champion of his kingdom who claimed the scythe from a reaper, himself. Both remarkable warriors of their time; both bleeding under the Vian night sky and neither ready to let the other have the satisfaction of winning.

After moments, which felt like hours to those watching, both men simultaneously collapsed to the ground. There was a period of silence that was eventually broken by a gust of wind rustling the trees.

"Well, what does that mean?" Edgar asked.

"A draw?" one crewman said.

"Does this mean we're free?" asked another.

"Means I'm captain now!" shouted a fourth.

Arguing erupted from the circle around the two dead men as all the crewmen debated on the future leadership aboard the *Splinter*. Drogon and Marlow attempted to make their way into the circle, but the commotion was keeping them at a distance. In order to not push the entire ridge into chaos, they kept their weapons stowed and attempted to get a word into the shouting, without success.

Lee leapt up to his feet and was grabbed by the back of his neck. Without hesitating, he flung his bound fists up against the crewman's iron helmet, shattering both of his thumbs and knocking loose the man's grip. He hit the ground with a roll and darted between the distracted crewmen. One had spotted him and made after him at a sprint, but Lee's smaller size gave him an advantage in the commotion. Behind him, he could hear Queen Sana attacking one of the pursuing crewmen and shouting for him to run to safety. Lee didn't care who might try to stop him; he was going to get to Stein.

He broke through the circle. His boots pounding at the charred ground beneath him, coming to a slide on his knees in the pool around Stein. With his hands still bound, he forced the hatchet from Stein's back and threw it away. Then, he rolled Stein onto his back, grabbed at the hilt in his chest and tore it loose. Tears were streaming down his face as he thrashed with the ropes around his mangled hands. He remembered how his blood could help slip beneath the ropes. He remembered how his broken hands would give him greater range of motion. Twisting frantically, his yell turned into a boyish but vengeful shout, and pulled his hands free of the rope.

At that instant, a crewman moved toward Lee. He raised up his sword and prepared to bring it down upon him, but a heaving kick from Marlow's hoof sent him flying backwards. Marlow and Drogon moved to surround Lee from the crewmen, neither yet unsheathing a weapon.

"Enough!" Drogon shouted. "We are not animals, regardless of how this man has trained." He looked around the crewmen and observed their hesitation. "You traveled with him because he bested you and now he has been killed. The comradery among you, for a crew filled with strangers that have no singular purpose - it's beyond impressive. By the Maker, the things you could do as a unit if you were to join a cause. Here you stand, free men and women, given another chance to go and live your own life. As a duelist, as a scribe, whatever you want. We don't need to keep this cycle going for the scraps of one man's legacy—*if* you can call it that."

Edgar stepped forward, "I have followed the Axeman for a lifetime, longer than any other. Many here have been here for over a decade. We don't have a home to go back to, or a life to call our own. This is all we know."

"Purpose?" Drogon asked. "Do you seek purpose? Bountiful and rewarding purpose that will truly put you on the just side of history?"

"Yes," said one.

"What is it?" asked another.

"Donahay, a demigod with the power of mind control seeks to conquer the entire world. He already has taken the Radiant Empire. You could join us, and the greatest army that has ever been assembled as we stop him. You could take your talents and put them to use against the forces that look to devour us and with us, we can win."

"I'd love to crush a demigod," said one.

"That's a real challenge," boasted another.

"Who would lead us?" asked a third.

Drogon asked, "Edgar, what say you? Would you captain the *Splinter* and lead its crew against a most powerful sorcerer in this impossible battle?"

He tugged thoughtfully at the long braid of his beard and began to pace. After three paces back and forth, he turned to Drogon, and then to the crew. With confidence he shouted, "If they would have me, then yes, I would."

The crew cheered and hawed. They appeared very happy to have Edgar as their Captain.

At Drogon's feet knelt Lee. Hunched over the lifeless Stein and holding his broken hands out over him. The green pulse of energy stopped at his wrists over and over again. He had to focus, but losing Stein was overwhelming him. Lee told himself repeatedly, "First, fix your hands, then save Stein. First, fix your hands. First, fix your hands. Fix your hands." His mind went blank, and the cheering of the crewmen seemed to fade into silence. He saw his figure as a black shadow before him. A green glow emanating from his chest, spiraling through his torso, and out his arms and legs. He could visualize the breaks at the base of his thumbs and with each pulse; he could shift bones further back into place. With each pulse, a snap followed by a soothing relief. Again, and again, until his hands were completely mended. He smiled with accomplishment, and then said, "Now, save Stein."

He held his hands over Stein and the energy radiated over him with intensity. With each pulse, a slight vibration left a ripple in the blood that was pooling around them. Slowly the pool gave way to currents, streaming back up his chest and legs like rivers, and into his open wounds. It continued flowing back into him, flushing color back into his skin. When most of it had been reabsorbed back into him, the deep gashes over his body filled and with a surgical precision. The flesh pulled back together and seared itself with a green trace of light.

Everyone watched in sheer awe.

Lee rested his head on Stein's chest and listened, "Drogon? He doesn't have a heartbeat."

Drogon knelt down on Stein's other side and listened at his chest. He sat up with a solemn look across his scales, "I'm sorry, Lee. You can heal the body, but sometimes-"

"No!" Lee shouted. "No, he's not dead. I healed him."

"You can't save everyo-"

"I'm not saving everyone, I'm saving Stein!" he argued.

Drogon reached both hands over Stein to rest on Lee's shoulders, "He's dead."

Lee threw Drogon's hands off of him, "No!"

A green aura surrounded Lee and he pressed his hands onto Stein's chest. Then, he raised them up and Stein began levitating off the ground with energy surging through him, causing his hands and legs to twitch. He hovered in the air as his body convulsed, and the entire summit began to glow with a vibrant green hue. After several exhausting seconds, Lee lower Stein onto the ground and over him, and gasped for air.

And if there was an audible sound of heartbreak, you would have heard it. Lee looked down at Stein and painfully whispered, "You promised you'd be there for me. Kill this reaper if you have to, but don't die."

Stein sat up with a gasp, grabbing at his chest and shouting, "You are nothing!" his eyes were wide open as he took some desperate deep breaths back to life.

Lee threw his arms around him with the tightest hug he could muster, "I knew you wouldn't die."

Stein, partially confused, hugged Lee and looked around the crewmen and his comrades. His eyes locked onto Drogon's and he asked, "Who died first?" before passing out.

"At least he's..." Lee fainted beside him.

One of the crewmen leaned in, "They gonna be okay?"

Drogon pointed to Stein, gesturing for Marlow to carry him. Then he turned to pick up Lee himself. "Yes, Lee is just tired; and Stein, well, he's come back from worse."

# V

### Three To Go

*"We often find only our purpose when we have exhausted the will to search for it."*
*A Generous Life - A Tribute to Mora*

A dream?

A reality?

A memory.

"I have come to claim you," said the reaper in a trailing whisper, "your life has ended, and it is time for me to ferry you into your afterlife."

"No," Stein protested; rage burning in his eyes, "I will not be thrown into a hole with the worms before I devour the very heart of those who put me here!"

The reaper hovered closer through the air, embers dropping off the blade and scorching the grayed earth beneath them, "Many feel as you feel, Stein. They feel as if that they have been taken before their time. Victims of life and her great circumstance. You are not alone in thinking this. However, I can assure you; however, unnatural your death—this is your time. It has been foretold by the will of the Maker, and that is how I am here to greet you."

"What of my will?" Stein moved ever closer towards it, "don't you offer deals? What of my soul in exchange for taking my revenge?"

The reaper's voice remained at a whisper, "You are confusing me with a demon of the underworld. I need not barter for your soul, Stein. It is already mine. I am here as a guide, to help you accept your death and then your soul's place among eternity."

"No," said Stein.

"I understand how you feel," the reaper whispered.

"No," said Stein.

"Many have felt the same way," the reaper continued.

"No!" Stein's voice thundered, echoing through this empty place. He leapt up and soared through the air, as if weightless. His single bound brought him to bring down a fist on top of the reaper's head and pound it from its hover to meet the ground below with a stumble.

Its feet slid and braced it to a stop. The hood was flung back from the momentum and peering back was an off-white skull, cracked through a hollow eye socket and emitting a red glow. Sliding back its left foot and taking a stance, it beckoned him, "Your soul is mine, to claim or destroy - what do you prefer?"

Stein's face twitched. His eyes glared, his teeth snarled, with his mind fixated not on life or death, but the most gruesome revenge. There were no other thoughts, no doubts, or fears, or possibility of nonexistence as he charged at the reaper again.

Below deck on the *Yoshi,* Drogon pressed his hands firmly onto the table as he looked over a map of the lands. *Rayne* was laid across one side, and her sheath on the other, holding down the curved edges open before him. He angled his compass from *Vian* to *Fornesio.* Then, from *Fornesio* to *Vishnin.* He continued from *Vishnin* to *Gashimar.* Finally, back from *Gashimar* to *Luray.* He let out a frustrated sigh and shook his head.

Next to the map, he picked up his tankard and pressed it firmly to his lips. His eyes fell onto the coin purse resting on the table. He put down the tankard and lifted the sack of gold. It didn't jingle with the happy sound it used to, but instead, its contents clunked.

"No," he mumbled, "no, no." Drogon unclipped the sack and dumped it out over the map. Wooden circlets, the size of a coin, rolled out over the table and dropped onto the floor. He sneered, "Tholden, you must think you're so smart."

The second door off this main room opened. Stein was standing in the doorway to his bedroom, sewing up tears in his robes, "What's this I hear about Tholden?" he asked.

"Have you checked your coin lately?" Drogon asked. "Looks like he dispelled the charm that was funding our journey. Now, it will take us even longer to travel if we have to earn gold along the way."

"Maybe this is a good thing," Stein smiled. "This could mean he's dead, right?"

Drogon was not amused, "No. If he were dead, his charms would remain; only the essence in his physical body would return to the Maker. This proves not only that he is alive, but also that he is mocking us. I wonder why he would want to see us fail?"

"I have a feeling we'll be seeing him again," Stein said. "By the way, I must have been out for a while, where are we?"

"We're still in the port of *Vian*." Drogon replied. "You blacked out soon after Lee healed you. He passed out too, but he's still asleep. Queen Sana made it back to the castle, and the *Splinter* is waiting to meet with us on the south side of the island. Last night was a big win for us."

Stein peered down at his robes, "It didn't feel that way to me."

"Well no, but you were the one who went to meet the Maker. You're lucky Lee was able to bring you back," Drogon said.

"I didn't go that far," Stein trailed off.

"What?" Drogon probed, "What do you mean? What did you see?"

"It was just like the first time. I was still there on the ridge, but it was hazy and dark - like all the color had been drained away, leaving only shades of gray. The Axeman was also there, and he made a comment over missing who died first," he paused for a moment, "then, two reapers appeared. They stretched in from a shadow and floated towards us. Surprising, I was still able to call on my scythe in the void and was fighting them off. I guess this was going on while Lee was shocking away at my body. The Axeman was more accepting of his fate, even threw up a prayer to *Tauros* before they claimed him."

Drogon studied his face, "Why do you look so disturbed by this? You've seen them before - you've even bested one before."

Stein's face was grim, "They spoke to me—it was like a hollow hissing sound. They called out to me by name. They remember me."

"There's a part of me that knows reapers to be the unbiased judges that weigh your deeds and guide you into the afterlife," Drogon explained. "And then, there's a part of me that's betting no mortal has ever killed one of them before for them to understand vengeance."

Stein smirked at him, "Tell me about it."

As Drogon re-equipped Rayne and began to roll up the map, the familiar stomps of Marlow were coming down the stairs. Drogon and Stein turned to meet him.

"Marlow," greeted Stein.

"Stein," said Marlow as he ducked under a rafter to enter the main room. "I'm happy you're standing. Dead doesn't look good on you."

Stein leaned back and ran his hand through the back of his silver hair, "That means a lot to me."

Marlow gave a single nod and faced Drogon, "There are people here for you."

"People?" said Drogon.

"One from the *Splinter*, and two from the castle." Marlow said.

Drogon continued, "Any idea what they want?"

"No."

"Okay, let's do one at a time. May you please send down the man from the *Splinter*?" asked Drogon.

Marlow turned, ducked under the rafter, and stomped back up to the deck of the ship.

"He always did have a way with words," Stein laughed.

A steady pace came down the steps and entered the main room. She was *dragonkin* with tan scales, lightly faded with salt. She wore a flowing light blue robe with heavy combat boots, equipped with a sword and shield on her back. Her eyes were as blue as her robes.

"Thank you for seeing me," she said with a sweet, yet confident tone. "Stein, I am glad you are doing well."

"Thanks. Do I know you?" Stein asked.

"Yes. I served under the Axeman until last night. I was there in that circle and watched your duel; it was incredible," she said, "I was wearing gear assigned from the Axeman, so maybe that's why you don't recognize me?"

"Maybe. Why are you here?" Stein said.

"Firstly, I need to thank you for freeing us. I served the Axeman for five years and never thought someone could fight the way you did. So, thank you, Stein," she said.

Stein showed no expression, "It was nothing."

"I heard this morning that your young friend was able to resurrect you. I claimed my freedom and left as soon as the Axeman hit the ground. It was a dream come true, watching you defeat him. I've been longing for this day for so long and once I was free I wasn't going to waste a second," her lips quivered with a snarl as she spoke. She took a deep breath, "I stole these robes and hid in a warehouse for the night. I thought for the first time in a long time, I would be able to sleep in that warehouse, but I was wrong."

Drogon reassured her, "You're okay, he's not going to hurt anyone anymore."

"I know." She smiled, "He's dead and they made sure of it when they threw his body from the Northern Ridge. I'm not soft and I'm not here for reassurance. Knowing my life is my own wasn't enough for me. Fighting is what I know and I'm not afraid. There was a time when I could be more than a warrior, but I can't remember how to live like that anymore. Drogon, everything that you said last night is true. We aren't animals and we need purpose. *I* need purpose. I want to fight this Donahay dark-magician with you, but I won't spend another second on that ship. I can't do it."

"I understand not wanting to stay somewhere with such dark memories - how can we help?" Drogon asked.

She stood up straight, "Let me travel with you here on the *Yoshi*. I can pull my weight more than most on a ship. I can handle myself in combat. And-" she picked up one of the numerous wooden circlets spread out on the table, "I can fix your **fool's coin** problem."

Drogon's eyes widened, "You're a **sorceress**?"

"I'm a trained **battle-mage**, but sure," she smirked, replying with a lilt in her tone, "what did you think I was?"

Drogon's eyebrows raised, "I saw your sword and shield and took you for a **brawler**."

She chuckled dismissively, "Magic, weapons, I happen to be good with both."

"I've never known a battle-mage - you're an impressive woman."

"I know," she smiled.

Interrupted and stung back to reality, Marlow's stomps echoed and reverberated in Drogon's ears, establishing urgency to wrap up the conversation. Especially in the look Marlow gave him.

"Very well," said Drogon, "you can have the third room on the... right."

Marlow's voice bellowed from the hall, "My room?"

Drogon shrugged, "You hate it down here, anyway."

Marlow snarled, "I will send down the men from the castle."

"Thank you, Marlow," Drogon said as he turned back towards the *dragonkin*, "I never caught your name."

Her robes carried as she started down the hall, calling to him over her shoulder "My name is Maressa. I look forward to saving the world with you," she laughed as she continued towards her new room and entered.

---

"I think you're drooling," Stein said quickly as if he was holding back, "was it because she's a battle-mage, or was it the scales?"

Two sets of boots were thudding down the stairway.

"If she can fix our coin problem, she's already quite valuable," Drogon argued, feeling flush beneath his scales. He ignored it and continued, "The fact that she is attractive is irrelevant."

"So, you think she's attractive? Sounds relevant," Stein smirked.

Drogon turned to face the stairway, "No, it isn't."

"You're blushing."

Drogon touched his face and rolled his eyes. He smirked, "You know; I was cheering for the Axeman."

Stein's mouth hung open in feigned disbelief.

"Too soon?" Drogon asked sarcastically.

A *dragonkin* entered first, clad in heavy armor and displaying a Vian insignia on his shoulder with a long cape. The woman with him was shrouded in a hooded robe bearing a shield on her back and was unidentifiable. As they entered the room, she continued towards them and gestured to the other guard dismissively. He nodded and went back up to the deck.

When he was halfway up the stairs, she lowered her hood. The one who stood before them was none other than Queen Sana. She was much tidier than when they had seen her last night. Her red scales were neatly polished, and her wounds had already been healed by, the best clerics of Vian.

Drogon bowed nervously, "Queen Sana."

Stein remained leaning back against the table with his arms folded in front of him. "I'm surprised they let you out of the castle the day after your kidnapping."

"I have no need for permission," she replied.

"My apologies." Stein nodded.

"Though I could assure you, he does certainly wish to show his gratitude, as do I." She bowed. "That being said, Vian will send her forces to Luray to await your return with reinforcements for the fight against Donahay. I understand King Connero had shown some reservation in the interest of protecting the mainland."

"He promised only three ships when we met," Drogon said. "While the Vian naval fleet is superior, we will be met by hundreds. Donahay's influence grows stronger each day; we may be up against the entire force of the Radiant Empire by then."

"You should receive word soon that Vian will retain three ships here at the mainland and send the entire fleet."

"That's incredible!" Drogon shouted. "The greatest fleet to sail the seas will give us a fighting chance. Thank you, Queen Sana."

"Thank you," said Stein.

"It is I who needs to thank you. You saved my life. Perhaps, by the end of this dark chapter in history, it will be the world that needs to thank you, as well. There are not many who would sail the world in a single vessel to stand against an empire, as you are. I wish you great victory," she bowed. "May the Maker guide you."

As she started towards the stairs, Drogon felt the moment slipping away from him. The breath he'd been holding was slowly loosening as he reached out to her, "Wait.."

She turned to face him, "Yes?"

Drogon took a deep breath, "Last night, one of the crew from the *Splinter* told me that General Krain and-"

Queen Sana held up a hand and smiled. She took a moment to admire him, "I was uncertain if I should say anything... I knew who you were from the moment you ascended the ridge. Your eyes—*his* eyes, I knew it was you." Now it was her turn to release a long breath. "My son, grown to be a heroic **paladin**, like his father. Throwing caution to the wind, like his mother." She raised her hood and wiped her eyes in the shadow. "My son, I hope you'll forgive me. I had to convince myself that you and Krain were dead, so that my heartache would cease. Though it seems I have failed," her head hung low until she was moved by Drogon's embrace. "I fear no one can know who you truly are, Drogon. Connero -will- forgo the battle against Donahay on principle alone. He will commission the entire army to have you killed."

"I understand," said Drogon.

Sana released their embrace and looked up at him, "Whatever became of Krain?"

Drogon shook his head, "I don't know. I was raised by a **dwarf** family in Rayton. I don't remember anything of him."

"Maker praise their hearts for looking after you when I could not," she praised. "I must go before I am noticed. At last, there is another reason I came here. I wanted to give you this," Sana took the shield off her back and handed it to Drogon. "I had hidden it in the king's armory for what seems like a lifetime. This is Krain's shield, the only thing left of his. I have never wielded it and I do not know its name, but I hoped his leaving it behind meant you would find your way home to claim it - if you still lived."

Drogon reached out to tenderly accept it. It was a light, kite-shaped shield of fine craftsmanship. He stared at his reflection in the mirrored finish and ran his fingers over the edge. Aside from the inch-wide golden border, it was lacking detail. There were no scratches or evidence of combat. It could pass for a decorative piece if not for the weight behind it. On the inside, the mounting was clearly of dwarven design from its angular handles of adjustable size.

"Thank you," Drogon said, "I feel terrible taking this from you, especially if it is all you have of him."

She smiled warmly, "I have his memory and I always will. Neither Connero nor time itself could take that away from me. Seeing your eyes instills his presence in me yet again. Trust me, I have plenty; but that shield was meant for *you*."

Queen Sana turned away quickly as a tear rolled over her cheek. Her footsteps paced up the stairs, met with the heavy boots of her guard and faded off into the distance.

"Well," Stein started, "what an interesting start to the day."

"Mhm," Marlow agreed.

"All good things," said Drogon. "We need to keep this momentum and press on; we are really coming together now. Still not quite ready, but I feel great about what we're building here."

Stein laughed, "Oh really? You, Garf—still comatose, by the way. Lee, Marlow, this Maressa, and myself. Are you also counting the crew of the *Splinter;* which I am going to refer to as refugees?"

Drogon rolled his eyes, as though the answer were obvious, "Gwynn."

Stein's silence was chilling. His eye twitched as he glared at Drogon, "Why would we still have Gwynn?"

"She is skilled, has no place to go, and is looking to fight for our cause," Drogon listed. "Is that not enough?"

Stein's lips thinned as his face took on shades of red.

Drogon crossed his arms over his chest, "I would normally be the first person to come to your defense and back you up, but you're just being stubborn because you *felt* something for her. And it's because you felt something for her that you take this *so personally*," he explained. "At least you have someone to make you feel that way - it's a good thing." His eyes traced towards the door where Maressa had disappeared. He could almost sense Stein's attempt to interject, however, Drogon continued, "Maybe you did, or maybe you didn't feel anything for her…."

Stein stepped forward, "I don't think it's ever good to be manipulated. Besides, I would fight my own battles."

Drogon matched his advance, "Then you would be dead, Stein; and whatever you were fighting for would be lost without you."

They were both silent.

Drogon put a hand on Stein's shoulder, "Without working together, we wouldn't be here - we wouldn't have come this far. If you didn't fight for her; Gwynn, Porbella or both of them would be dead or worse. If none of this happened, we wouldn't have the *Splinter*, Connero's army, and I would never have known where I came from. This wasn't pretty, and it surely wasn't easy, but don't you think that—maybe—this all worked out for the best?"

Stein nodded his head, "I suppose it did."

"We have enough fights ahead of us, we'll need every sword, scythe, and bow we can find," Drogon said, "let's keep the momentum going here—let's set sail for Fornesio."

Stein smiled, "Fine. Don't we need to wait for Gwynn?"

"She's sailing with the *Splinter*, unless you'd rather she sail with us?" Drogon asked.

"No, I'd prefer she be as far away from me as possible for now."

"I understand."

Stein reflected on their conversation, "Drogon, what did you mean by that whole *at least you have someone to make you feel that way* thing? You're not lonely are you?"

"Stein, Marlow - we have bled together and I hold you both as true as my own brother," Drogon started.

Stein couldn't help but interrupt, "Oh no, you are lonely..."

Drogon sighed, "While you are always difficult, I would live and die for you."

"I'm only *sometimes* difficult," Stein added.

"So I will entrust this with you... I always wanted more from my life than being a warrior and seeing the world." His eyes stared off, "I wanted to teach my son how to hold a sword and use magic. My daughters, too. I wanted to know what it felt like to be loved like the stories of the goddess **Luna**."

"Love battle and you will never be lonely," said Marlow.

Drogon rubbed his head, "Thanks, Marlow."

"You're welcome."

Stein leaned back against the wall, "What's stopping you?"

Drogon laughed, "More than likely, before this is over - we'll be dead."

"You're dark - aren't paladins supposed to be uplifting?" asked Stein.

Drogon shook his head, "We are only ever supposed to be honest."

Marlow made way to the deck, his stomps carrying up the stairs. He yelled back, "Setting sail."

Stein entered into his room. He stood with the door in his grasp and faced Drogon, "Don't you go rushing into things."

Drogon rolled his eyes, "There is no time for that. Literally, the fate of the world is at stake. I am not open to anything for the foreseeable future."

"Glad to hear it." Stein shut his door.

Drogon turned back towards the table and placed Krain's shield down, covering the map. He drew Rayne from her sheath and held it in one hand while holding his other over the shield. A golden glow of energy chased up his sword arm, through his chest, and down his other arm. It illuminated over the shield with warm waves that emitted a low humming sound. "Talk to me, Krain. I feel some kind of magic here." He focused, closed his eyes, and pushed the ripple of light to flow quicker.

Suddenly, Drogon heard a voice. It was not so much spoken, as it was a thought in his mind, but it was carried in a masculine tone with a soft accent. "Enough of that, Son of Krain, it isn't necessary."

"I knew it." Drogon smiled, "I knew there was something to awaken in this shield."

"It was me," the shield said bluntly, "You have awoken *me*."

"Yes, well... did you not want to awaken? From my understanding, a magical item such as yourself would want to be aware, to experience the world. Am I wrong? I apologize if I was mistaken."

"No apology is necessary, either. I have slumbered long enough, and it is time for me to witness prophecy untold."

"What do you mean by that?" Drogon asked.

The shield vibrated with a soft chuckle, "That is what *untold* would mean."

"I see. Maybe there is something you could tell me, then? About my father? I never met him, but I recently learned of him, and how his relationship with my mother caused him to have to flee." Drogon tested.

The shield spoke with conviction, as if reading the words from an ancient tome, "General Krain Osmodan of the **Architects**. Son of Barthold Osmodan and Geraldine Figh. His soul is entangled with a royal figure, present Queen of Vian named Sana, and no length of time will soothe their grieving for one another."

Drogon was speechless.

"You wish to know if he still lives?"

Drogon struggled, but eventually found the word, "Yes."

"Yes."

Drogon leaned over the table taking slow, deep breaths. "Thank you."

"You're welcome."

"Where is he?" Drogon asked.

The shield began to speak before Drogon even finished his question, "I can't tell you."

"Can't or won't?"

"Can't *and* won't."

Drogon lifted the shield and held it out in front of him, "What do you mean? Then, why even tell me that he lives?"

"I can't and won't tell you *where* he is; because, you are not meant to know at the present time. I told you that he lives, because it is important for you to know. Now, when your paths finally cross, you will believe it is truly him. That is destiny."

"Destiny?" Drogon placed the shield back on the table, and a fake wooden coin slid onto the floor with a spin. "I am a paladin. I believe in the divine, I practice magic, and I have seen the dead rise back to life. Destiny, however, is another matter entirely."

"Your belief in destiny is irrelevant to its existence."

Drogon leaned over the shield, "That may be true, but there is something to be said of free will. How does that fit into your destiny?"

"Life is a series of journeys, and every chapter of this grand adventure has an end. The choices you make, the paths you take are your own tale to weave. Make no mistake, the destination is always the same."

"So, you can tell me when I am going to die?"

"No."

Drogon glared, contemplated for a moment, and rephrased, "Do you know when I am going to die?"

"Yes."

"But you won't tell me?"

The shield kept the same calm demeanor with every response, "Can't and won't."

There was a moment of silence between them.

"I understand," said Drogon.

"You Osmodan's are always quick to grasp it. Do you have any other questions for me?"

"A few, yes," Drogon replied. "What may I call you? And is there anything you can tell me about our journey? Donahay, reapers, our chance at success, anything about this battle-mage onboard?"

"You may call me Prophet. All of those concerns are valid, but only—one—of them is relevant to your destiny. Yours is not as Drogon the paladin, the architect, or the drifting monster-hunter; but in love and creating a legacy that continues to carry the greatness of the Osmodan bloodline to nurture the seas and soil of the land itself.

"I have a feeling most of my questions to you will only leave me with more questions. In what way does me finding love weigh within our chance of saving the world?"

"Is a world without love worth saving?" The shield spoke and the tone carried a smile.

"So, you're a romantic." Drogon laughed as he picked up the shield and equipped it onto his back.

"Isn't everyone a romantic? In their own way."

"I've never really thought about love - not really. This really isn't the time. Donahay threatens the world. I believe in love, sure, but I have work to do. This conversation feels familiar, maybe you should talk to Stein about my love-life," Drogon joked. "Actually, please never speak to Stein about my love-life."

Prophet spoke with confidence, "It's not something you think about, Son of Krain. And it's not something that waits for you to take the time. It happens exactly when it is meant to happen. But you are right; there is much work to do at the present."

Drogon continued to plot a course and organize all the maps and logs scattered about the table. He felt something shift inside him. An awareness that didn't exist before his conversation with Prophet. Maybe it was an understanding of things; be it time or the cosmic flow to the magic of the universe. Whatever it was, perhaps with this clarification, the journey became much more enjoyable.

As the morning shifted into early afternoon, the coast of Vian fell off the horizon and Fornesio could be seen. The skyline carried a dense and fast-moving fog that floated over the sea like a ghost, bringing their clear skies to an end within a few hours of making port.

Marlow was minding the helm, staring off into the abyss of cloud. He let go of the wheel, slid down the handrail, and moved to partially raise the sails and slow their speed. He spun the rope along the pulley with an experienced tug, raising the sail exactly where he meant it to be. Marlow started his way back to the helm when a shadow in the fog caught his eye. He squinted to make it out but couldn't see what it was until the small ship had rammed into the *Yoshi*. He went tumbling down the stairs, splitting several in half, and landed back on the main deck. With his back still flat on the deck, Marlow could see the smaller ship turning to sail alongside them. Matching their speed, he could see the center mast of crimson sail with gold etched trim edging closer and closer again.

His eyes widened and he roared, "**The Red Five**!"

# VI

### The Red Five

*"There is a cannon sounding for you, my precious foe. You will feel it soon enough."*
*The Flail of Korthus - A Tribute to Korthus*

Marlow was back on his feet in a flash. He peered over the now splintered rail to confirm his fears. The small ship indeed had crimson sails and golden trim, flying the *Crimson V* of The Red Five. The reddened wood hull and spiked bow, rebounding from the impact, and turning back in towards the *Yoshi*. Marlow sprinted up the stairs, leaping over those that now lay broken. He reached the helm and spun wildly away from their ship, twisting the ship with violence that tossed cargo and crew below deck.

The figures aboard the deck of the *Crimson V* were shrouded in the fog and their shouting was incoherent, however no fog or splashing of the surf could deafen the boom of cannon fire and the eruption of shrapnel that followed. A slow volley continued as the ship drew nearer. Marlow kept at the helm to guide them away. He reached down to pick up a chunk of wood from the rail and with great finesse, threw it down to the main deck, knocking a reel free and lowering the main sail completely. Their pace quickened, but they didn't gain distance from The Red Five.

Maressa and Drogon stumbled up onto the deck as the ship rocked fiercely. They grabbed a hold of the center mast for balance.

"Marlow!" Drogon shouted, "Are you okay?"

Marlow peered down to them, "The Red Five."

"By *the Maker*, no..." Drogon replied.

There was a moment of silence between them, broken by another cannon booming.

"We have to do something - Drogon, come with me," Maressa beckoned.

"Where are the others?" asked Marlow.

"Stein and Lee are dealing with some water below deck," she said.

Drogon and Maressa approached the ships only cannon. It was more a collectible than a weapon and was questionable if it was ever fired before. It was positioned on a swivel at the stern of the ship.

"A dwarven trading ship isn't known for weaponry, I'm betting this was more for show than anything else," said Drogon.

"Maybe," Maressa said, "but if it can shoot something, it's functional enough for me. Let's load it up. There's a shot right here."

Maressa loaded the cannon while Drogon lined up a shot. She stepped beside him as he aimed down the barrel. He squinted his eyes at first, but opened wide as he heard the boom and could even see the splitting and churning of fog through the air as the sound of hurling air rushed closer. Maressa had seen it as well and in an instant; she thrust both hands out before her. As the cannonball broke through the fog in front of them, aimed right at Drogon and the cannon, it met the glinting of a blue ethereal barrier and deflected off into the water.

Drogon's open mouth shifted into a smile, "A battle-mage can stop a cannonball?"

"Deflect," she said, "I can *deflect* a cannonball, but let's not test my reflexes too often, okay?"

He laughed, "I hope not to."

Drogon settled back behind the cannon and fired. The cannonball sailed through the air, parting the fog into spirals along its path, and settled with a splash beyond the enemy.

"They're small and fast," he said, "maybe we can do this together?"

"What are you thinking?"

"What is the range of your barrier? If I miss, can you deflect it into the mast?" He said.

"Why not take out the crew? There's only five of them, right?" She probed.

"No, their mast," said Drogon, "they only have the one since their ship is so small, we'll be able to sail away without any issue if we can take that out. Shooting them would be near impossible. "

Maressa peered through the fog, "This will be the furthest I've ever tried to cast it - let's do it!"

They began to reload the cannon, but as they prepped their shot, the *Crimson V* made some rapid maneuvers and came up quickly behind them. Their bow was now a mere thirty feet from the stern of the *Yoshi*. Drogon began to line up the shot to align with their center mast.

As he peered down the barrel, his eyes caught a most frightening sight. A **dark-elf** woman stood at the bow with grayed skin, white hair, and gleaming red eyes. She was dressed in the crimson armor with golden trim and held a long sword that was elegantly decorated with multicolored jewels and covered in a thin rippling flame. But it was not her dress, weapon, or even that she was a member of The Red Five that made her frightening, no - it was her face.

Her eyes were fixed onto Drogon's as she broke through the fog and her eyes were filled with bloodlust. They widened into a wild, eager, cynical stare. Her lips were curled into the most sinister grin, partially agape to show filed, stained, fang-like teeth. As she grew nearer, an excited cackle could be heard growing louder and louder.

Drogon shook her gaze, focused onto the mast, and fired again. Another miss. Without hesitation, he began to reload the shot.

The dark-elf leapt off the bow with a strong pounce through the air and this incredible stride landed her on a knee at the stern of the *Yoshi*. She stood slowly, keeping her head down and eyes hidden beneath her hair. Her fangs could be seen twisting into a smile.

Maressa drew her sword and shield, and rushed to cover Drogon, who was still reloading the cannon. She brought her sword down from overhead at the dark-elf; who shifted back to dodge. Maressa made a jab with her hilt that was met with a block and followed up with a bash of her shield.

The dark-elf held fast against the shield bash, not yielding an inch. She reached over with her free hand to grab the top of the shield and, with a twist, spun both it and Maressa mid-air with force. Maressa tumbled; the shield was torn from her grip. The dark-elf held it loosely for a moment and dangled it teasingly with a pouting face before tossing it to the lower deck with a chuckle.

"Well, isn't this cute?" The dark-elf said. "The *dragonkin* couple get to die together. I do so love a love story."

Maressa stood up, "We won't be the ones dying today, Iris."

"Oh?" Iris titled her head with an unblinking stare. "You know who I am, and yet you still want to fight me?"

"We didn't start firing cannons at you and jump onto your ship, so no - we're not looking for a fight, but we can damn well handle one." Maressa said.

Drogon was still loading the cannon, "Do you need a hand?"

"No," said Maressa quickly and turned back to Iris, "this is your last chance to leave, mercenary."

Her head was still tilted in the same position and she was staring off in a trance. Iris finally spoke, "Give me Stein and the happy-healer, and I promise I won't filet you for the next few days and use your meat for bait."

Maressa felt a lump in her throat from the thought, "What do you want with them?"

"Our contract is for Stein. But you see, he killed a friend of ours some time ago. We want to repay the favor using his cleric-friend and a cage of hungry rats!" she said with excitement.

Maressa held out her sword and ran her shield hand above the length of the blade. Jagged shards of ice formed along the steel with waves of smoke coming off of it.

"What are you going to do with that? Chill some drinks for me and the guys?" Iris smiled.

"**Everfrost**. It will freeze your flesh from the smallest cut. Even if I only nick you, over time it will be fatal, unless you know some rare-magical treatment." She looked Iris up and down, "You don't look the brainy type."

"Oh?" Iris glared and ran her hand along the length of her sword, the rippling flame becoming a thick and molten ooze that gleamed with intensity. "How about **Everburn**? It will sear and scorch at your meat until you're nice and crispy." She licked her lips, "Well done. Just how I like it!"

Drogon stepped away from the cannon and equipped his sword and shield.

"I don't need help with her," Maressa snarled.

"Stop, we're in this together." Drogon took a stance beside her, "Besides, she's feral and needs to be put down quick."

She sighed, "You're frustrating."

"I can skewer you both like a kabob, this should be fun!" Iris rushed in with a wide slash that let out a two quick thuds against their shields. She spun again, twirling her blade with ferocious swings that Drogon and Maressa were able to nimbly step away from. They capitalized on the wild attacks and split up to flank her. Iris smiled and dashed towards Drogon with her molten blade. They locked swords.

Drogon could feel her slowly overpowering him and pushed in with all his might. He lifted his shield to support his sword arm. The blades pivoted and tussled around one another until he watched as a single drop of magma fell off of her sword onto a piece of his armor. It scorched for a moment and melted away at the plate in a perfect drop shaped hole that continued to fall and sear at the deck. He felt the magic in *Rayne* would protect it from the *Everburn*. However, while he learned the name of his father's shield by conversing with it in private, he was unsure of its abilities to resist such a powerful effect. He dropped it to the deck and kicked it away to grip Rayne with both hands.

Maressa seized this opportunity and jabbed forward, but Iris was light on her feet and kicked herself off of Drogon to evade, staggering him back. Maressa continued her advance, and with every clash and parry of their swords, the ice and magma neutralized one another to expose more of the bare blade.

"Well, that's no fun," Iris said with a frown. "I wanted to sear the meat off your bones."

"You're sick." Maressa muttered.

"And you're meat!" Iris screamed as she ran forward, tossing her sword around wildly as the ice and magma dissipated into smoke with every clash. Her movements blurred with every swing and all Maressa could do was struggle to defend herself.

Drogon leapt into the fray, heaving Rayne with all his might to break up the attack. Iris reeled back, but only for a moment. She regained her footing and began slashing with fury, switching off between bringing her blade down at Drogon and quick swipes at Maressa, but; she was slowing down. Both of them kept up with her together, stepping in circles around her to keep the pressure on. They matched steps naturally, completely out of rhythm and yet perfectly timed to remain on opposite sides of their foe.

But in an instant, Iris was reinvigorated by pure rage and unleashed a whirlwind of attacks against them. Maressa was knocked back while Drogon, caught off guard, felt her blade glance at his side. She laughed manically as he felt the warmth run between the scales of his armor. She moved in towards Maressa again with a leaping kick that sent her stumbling back, crashing through the banister, dropping her sword, and tumbling towards the main deck.

"Maressa!" Drogon shouted as he stood.

Iris was wide-eyed and unblinking. Her eyes fixed onto Drogon and her mouth still hung open as the cackle trailed off, "I want *you,* first."

Iris wasted no time; she pounced towards Drogon and pinned him to the ground. He could feel the wound on his side tearing with the force and his sword fell away. The two were locked in a grip and begun to roll over the deck. Each of them had one hand clutched at the others wrist. Iris twisted her arm ferociously with a blade at Drogon's face and throat. Drogon threw up his knee to toss the dark-elf aside, but Iris held strong and pulled him along. Then, Iris bent back her leg with incredible flexibility and heaved forward with a powerful kick to the gut. Drogon felt the wind rush from his lungs and struggled to catch his breath. This moment of weakness was all Iris needed; she straddled over him, gripped the hilt with both hands, and rushed the blade down.

A whooshing cut through the air before Iris could claim her kill. A shining, golden sword had pierced through her shoulder. It pulsed with radiant magic and buried itself to the hilt, protruding out in front of her with blood and bits of flesh falling over Drogon. Iris touched at the blade curiously and looked over her shoulder to see Maressa standing a distance away with her arm still outstretched from the throw.

She jumped to her feet, more feral than ever before, and charged at Maressa screeching like a banshee. Her sword flailing overhead, Rayne swaying proudly from her shoulder, and every powerful step imitated the sound of thunder across the deck. Maressa reached down and quickly equipped Drogon's shield. She tucked her body behind it and as she steadied her grip, she felt a warmth rush through her body and heard a voice.

The words were not so much a whisper as they were a thought. Strangely, however, the sound was not in her own voice, but with a soft accent. It spoke in a calm and soothing, masculine tone, "Ah, so you are the one? Wonderful. No time for introductions, I see. Speak my name, with your mind or your tongue, and I shall share with you a history."

Suddenly, the mirror-like finish within the center of the shield gleamed a blinding light. Iris squinted and turned her head away without breaking her charge. As the flash dimmed, the once reflective surface became the vision of a battleground. From within the image, a volley of arrows soared towards her and fired out from the shield in a rapid succession of whistles.

*Thunk, thunk, thunk-thunk* and numerous more piercing *thunks*. A dozen arrows dug deep into Iris, from her thigh to her neck, even one tore through her ear. She stood, paralyzed, her eye twitching, and rivers of blood streamed from each wooden shaft into her armor.

*The Crimson V* drew nearer and was now a mere ten feet from their stern. Two figures stood at the bow with weapons drawn. A **goliath** and an **elf**. As their silhouettes broke through the fog, Drogon raced to the cannon and readied to fire again at the mast.

The dark-elf jerked her head to scowl at Drogon. She could see where the cannon was still aimed, and in an instant, threw herself in front of the rushing cannonball. She was carried through the air, beyond the entire ship, and fell with a distant splash into the sea. *The Crimson V,* near enough to have witnessed her point of action, spun hard to starboard and towards the splash.

Maressa stared in disbelief, "What did she..."

"I have no idea what just happened." Drogon shrugged. He gestured towards his shield in her hands, "How did you make him do that?"

"He told me his name," she replied, blinking rapidly a few times before looking at the shield, "it's Prophet." She seemed unsure, but sure at the same time. "I feel so alive. Awake?" She looked at Drogon. "Like I've been asleep for so long, and that right now, in this moment," she began as she stepped towards him, "I'm exactly where I am meant to be." She said this slowly, "Like there is something so incredibly obvious that I have been meant to find."

Drogon's eyes followed her, "I think I know what you mean. I spoke with him this morning. One thing he didn't tell me was that he could fire a volley of arrows from some ancient battlefield!" He huffed. "We spoke about life, and... some other things."

Maressa swallowed before continuing, "I really didn't know what to expect. He said, *so you are the one, speak my name and I will share you a history,* or something like that. Then, it fired arrows. I don't know." She closed the gap between them. "There was something else. Not what he said. No. Just a feeling. A feeling like something inside of me...in my heart had been unlocked for the first time in my life."

Maressa stood before him; her stare fixed onto his yellow eyes as her hands reached out and met his. She dropped the shield to the deck, her hands sliding up his arms to meet each of his

**cheeps**. As they leaned forward, their lips met, and it became known to each of them; they are exactly where they are meant to be.

Drogon's mind repeated his conversation with Prophet from earlier this morning. His eyes widened as he recalled certain words fitting into this exact moment, "He said you were the one?"

"Yes, does that mean something to you?" she asked, keeping her eyes closed and leaning her forehead against his.

"Yes," he pulled her tight against him, the tension of battle fading to a warm, wide-eyed look on his face, "it means everything."

# VII

## The Senate of Fornesio - Part 1

*"It is raw unaltered power that dominates and sways an empire, not its coin, its kings or its laws. You need only place a god on the most impoverished land and its riches will grow beyond measure. It is the weak that plague the mighty and it is self-evident that they must be cleansed."*
*The Black Book - A Tribute to Amon*

The *Yoshi* skipped across the wake like the edge of a knife; parting the water with a crisp splashing sound that slowed as it neared the docks. As the crew aboard steadied its ropes to the bulkhead, the echoes of slicing water faded to a soft lapping against the hull. Lazily, it rocked back and forth, finally at rest in *Fornesio*.

A single plank fell away with a splash.

Drogon stood on deck, with Rayne at his hip and Prophet on his back. He looked out over the port, which was quiet at this early hour of the morning. Small kiosk stands were beginning to open shop and shopkeepers were greeting one another with a hearty, "good morning." Many of them were of exotic cheeses, wines, and almost all had some sort of pastries. There was a sweet smell of fresh baked goods alive in the air that reminded Drogon of all the delicacies that Fornesio is known for.

"What is that incredible smell?" Lee asked with excitement.

Drogon smiled, "I was sure that Marlow would've picked up the aroma first."

From below deck, the quick heavy stomps could be felt climbing the stairs. "What is that?" said Marlow.

Drogon laughed, "There he is. Good morning, Marlow. That is **croissout**, it is a delicacy throughout the world that originated from Fornesio—the sophistication capital of the world. While it is famous, it is rare to come by. Maybe more popular in the circles of nobles and royalty. It's apparently incredibly difficult to prepare properly and shy of perfection it is inedible if you've ever had it done right. But here, you can buy it on the street."

"How much can we buy?" Lee looked out over the port.

"All of it," Marlow added.

"We'll pick some up once Maressa has finished crafting some more fool's coin - until then, we are nearly bankrupt," Drogon said.

Stein had silently joined them on deck, "Are you talking about croissout? Growing up, my family had a chef that would prepare it each Monday morning for us. It's not bad."

"Drogon just told us it's a rare delicacy, and you say *not bad*?" Lee questioned.

"Is it a rare delicacy?" asked Stein.

Drogon sighed, "Oh, the life of a prince. I bet you think all eating utensils are made of silver."

"No," Stein laughed, "but silver *does* make the food taste better."

"I can't." Drogon turned away with a smile and went to greet a pair of port guards approaching the ramp.

"But how?" Lee asked.

"I'm joking," said Stein. "Speaking of being able to joke or even breathe for that matter, I wanted to say thank you. I know this is hardly the life you imagined you'd have, and yet here we are, sailing the world and fighting for our lives in every land. This can't be easy for you and still, *you* were ready and able to save *me* when I needed it."

Lee rubbed at the back of his head, "It was nothing, you saved me tons of times."

"It's not nothing, Lee. I am not someone who normally needs to be saved. In fact, there's not many people who would if they could," Stein said. "As for me saving you, that was a promise I made to you that I plan to keep."

"Thank you, Stein." Lee jumped up and hugged him. He squeezed him for a moment and stepped back. "The only life I *hoped* I would have is a happy one and I think I have that. Might not be how I pictured it to be, but I'm happy."

"Me too." Stein smiled. "And you are becoming braver by the day. It wasn't long ago that you were going against a vetala and fighting alongside Garf. While that shook you - you did it. And when you crafted a **seed of life** by yourself—impressive. Or, how you learned to manipulate a healing spell from Drogon. Even your input to the party is assertive, and I think I speak for all of us when I say you're appreciated."

"Really?" Lee blushed, "I thought I was being irritating for a little while."

"Not to me. You have a strong moral compass; it points in the direction of *good*. If someone found you irritating, they would probably be someone like Tholden."

"Whatever happened to him?"

"I don't care."

Lee was surprised, "Wasn't he your friend?"

Stein shrugged, "He was necessary... and for a brief while, he was committed to our cause of hunting monsters and demons that terrorize my people. That changed the *second* he saw the power of Donahay."

"You think he was afraid?"

"Not exactly."

Lee looked up at him, "Then why would he leave?"

"He's looked death in the eye on many occasions, no, this was him as a sorcerer - as a son of the Moonstorm family. Always on a quest for knowledge and power. It doesn't matter how dark or evil it is; power is power to him."

"It is though, isn't it?"

Stein was staring at Lee, reading his face, "What do you mean? I would think you would be the last person to believe an ends justifying a means."

"Magic isn't good or evil, right? I mean, magic is... magic. What we do with it is everything. *We* make it good or evil - at least, I think so," said Lee.

"That sounds idealistic," Stein started, "Take my deathscythe for example. Forged in the fires of the void to be wielded by a reaper to claim the souls of the dead. It's made to literally scorch away mortal flesh and reap souls... how is that good?"

"But you use it to slay monsters and protect people, so, how is that bad?"

Stein nod showed an appreciation for Lee's sentiment, "Don't lose that voice, Lee. You have a lot of good to offer the world - don't ever be silent."

A smile warmed Lee's face, "Thank you, Stein."

Drogon was a distance away and waved other guards over to him. They gathered around in conversation. After a few minutes, he shook their hands and they went back to their duties. He walked up the ramp and rejoined the party on deck. "I was trying to find out exactly who makes decisions here and it seems the people and the guard are just as confused as I am. I was able to get a bit of information about the government here, though."

"Fornesio is run by a duke isn't it?" Stein asked.

"Yes and no," Drogon replied. "Apparently there are two government entities here. There is the Duke, who controls the military and local law enforcement. Then there is the Senate; they write the laws and dictate how to budget taxes and such."

"So, who do we need to approach for help against Donahay?" said Stein.

"Unfortunately, it seems as if we will have to get the entire Senate *and* the Duke in order for Fornesio to declare war. That's what would be needed for the Duke to mobilize their entire army and be funded. Otherwise, he would only be able to send a small amount for foreign aid and we need more than that," Drogon said. "The guard captain was here at the docks; he is relaying a message to the Duke to see when he could grant us an audience. I was told the Senate holds open house meetings each morning, so we can go there now."

Stein looked blankly at him.

"Diplomacy is your favorite thing, right?" Drogon asked sarcastically.

Stein rolled his eyes, "I wasn't expecting to have to do this so early in the day. Let's get on with it." He started down the ramp with his hands buried in his pockets.

Drogon trailed behind him, "Marlow, may you please look after the ship and check in on Maressa if she needs anything?"

"Do it yourself," Marlow snarled.

"Thank you, Marlow." he shouted back.

Lee went running down the ramp after, but turned back to add, "I'm going to bring you back some croissout, don't worry!"

"Better not forget," said Marlow.

They started through the port, taking in the smells and greetings from all the friendly shop owners. It didn't take long for the party to gather that Fornesio is almost entirely populated by a prestigious dwarven and elven community. Likewise, it didn't take the business-savvy minds of these shop owners long to realize that the group simply didn't have any coin. The friendly greetings became less and less frequent until they seemed to have stopped altogether by the time they arrived at the **Senate House**.

The **Senate House of Fornesio** was a large white building that was similar to a small stadium where you enter from the top. The center stone floor was surround by tiered seating that faced a mid-level row of nine desks. This allowed for the nine-senate members to hear local disputes or propositions while in the eyes of local citizens. The strangest appeal to this structure was that everything was white: the floor, the walls, the seats and decks, and even the torches burning on the wall.

The building's entrance brought the group to a high-level seating area. From there, they made their way down towards the floor. The seating area offered several tiers of benches, and there were nearly a hundred locals scattered throughout and pocketed into small groups. A waist high marble wall surrounded the open floor where some onlookers gathered in a standing area. At a narrow opening with a single-rope barrier, there stood a guard holding a clipboard. He was taking names of anyone who wished to proposition the senate. Drogon added their names to the list and took place in line. After a short while of observing some property fencing and noise complaints, they were gestured beyond the rope.

Drogon, Stein and Lee entered out onto the open floor. There was a lonely echo of boots as they approached the desks. Lee could feel himself growing more nervous as these unfamiliar figures looked down on them with scowling faces. Their eyes eventually fixed on Stein and seemed to recognize him, except for one.

"You are not from around here, who are you traveler?" Asked a *dwarf* with a brown braided beard, peering through thick-but-undersized spectacles. A plaque in front of him displayed *Morvis Greystone - Senate Seat #2.*

"My name is Drogon; I am a paladin of the Mcleod house from Rayton. This is the young master *cleric*, Lee Cheng of **Tristian**. We are here with Prince Stein of the *Radiant Empire*."

Morvis adjusted his spectacles and squinted at Stein, "Why yes, it *is* the prince himself. How have you been, Prince Stein? It has been some time."

"I'm fine," Stein replied. "I see you still haven't gone for new glasses."

"These work well enough," Morvis said as he took them off his face to rub at the lens. "I'll cut to it to save some unpleasantness," he spoke slowly and left a long pause as if choosing his words, "the last time you were in this chamber, you were with Victus. You two had come to negotiate *Vian's* unconditional surrender. I hope you are here under lighter circumstances?"

"I wish that was the case," said Stein "but as luck would have it, it is much worse." He stared down the line of officials as he studied their faces.

The senate members looked back at him with intensity until an elegant elven woman with short, spiky blonde hair began to speak with confidence. In front of her stood her plaque, *Leia Flyleaf - Senate Seat #1*. "You have us all in suspense, Prince Stein, may you please continue?"

Drogon approached, "The Radiant Empire is no longer under the rule of the royal family. The demigod, Donahay, has taken control of their minds and has dominated most of the country. We have information that his intention is to unify *all* nations under his magic. Through sheer luck, we escaped with our lives, and the only reason we fled was to strike back to fight for their free will."

"This is, most interesting," said Morvis. "Are you asking us to aid your group here in a war against your empire? It would seem to me that this is some kind of plot to usurp the throne. Is it?"

Stein's face flushed red, "I am trying to free the minds of my people you old fool! If you think I wanted to come asking for your help, you're wrong. This is bigger than me or any single nation. Vian and *Luray* have already promised their help to stop him and what I can promise *you* is that he is coming."

"Stein," Leia started, "Morvis is simply asking a sensitive question in an insensitive way, please don't be offended by him. We have not heard anything of a shifting of power in the Radiant Empire, so you will have to enlighten us on the situation."

"Of course," said Stein with a coldness in his tone. A foreboding chill deepening in his eyes. "Let me enlighten you-"

Drogon interrupted, "Our apologies my esteemed senate council. This is a sensitive discussion all around. The devastation behind it and the intimate relationships that are, even presently, impacted by it. Imagine an entire kingdom—the most vast, wealthy, and powerful in the known world. Then imagine every man, woman, and child to be commanded by the magic of a demigod. Marching and killing, without question. Fighting and dying, without fear or hesitation. Now imagine those citizens, working tirelessly to ready an unstoppable war machine. This is no longer a figment of our imaginations; this is the current reality."

"You said his name was Donahay?" asked the red-haired *elf* with the plaque, *Sho Mane - Senate Seat #8*.

"Yes," Stein said shortly.

"What interest would he have with the Radiant Empire?" said Sho.

"His interest is with controlling the entire world," said Stein. "I think he picked a great place to start, since now it'll take an alliance of every other nation to stop him."

"It does seem unusual that a demigod would happen to dominate the lands most formidable nation, allow a last-in-line prince to escape, and then you find your way to our floor," Sho explained. "We have not received word from Vian or Luray to confirm what you are telling us."

Stein's jaw clenched with frustration.

Drogon gave a thankful nod, "I can assure you that there is nothing *usual* about this. There is no precedent of an individual dominating more than a few minds at a time. There is also no precedent of a demigod invading a mortal nation to take control. And as I mentioned earlier, our narrow escape was largely a matter of luck." Drogon turned towards Stein, "Didn't Francesco say he would send word?"

"Maybe he only sent word to the duke?" said Stein.

Morvis became agitated by this, "The duke cannot declare war without the consent of the senate and our armies will not march without our say-so."

"I see no facts to support your claim presently," Sho said.

"Prime Minister Francesco may have sent word to the duke of our plight," Drogon said, "but we knew to first come here to address the will of the people. If you are looking for physical evidence, Sho, I can only offer you our survival and the fact that we are here in this chamber requesting your help. Beyond that, I may not be able to give you proof until it's at your gates."

"That sounds like the fear-mongering tactics I might expect from a group of manipulators looking to overthrow the throne," said Morvis.

"Let us not add insult, Morvis," Leia beckoned. "We can discuss this matter more with Francesco and King Connero to shed some light on the nature of this demigod."

"I do not think this is a good use of our resources. They are clearly usurpers as far as I am concerned," Morvis argued.

"We all understand your reservations, Morvis, but we must leave the past in the past and treat any threat as a serious one," said Leia.

"The Radiant Empire has been commanding the nations of the world with their bully-tactics for long enough. I say, if this threat is true, it sounds like they have had a taste of their own medicine - good riddance," Morvis mocked.

"Good riddance, to my people?" Stein shouted, staring him down. "Good riddance!?" He slid his right foot back and held his hands out in front of him.

Lee ran forward and stood in front of Stein. He faced the senate members. "We came here for your help. People are dying, and more people will die if you don't help us."

Sho dismissed him, "You are a boy, you don't understand the politics at play here. There is a lot to understand before going to war."

"It sounds like *you* don't understand, Mr. Mane. I told you people are dying and more people will die without your help, and what did you want to talk about? Not about how to help them or how to save them, no, you wanted to talk about politics," Lee said. "Drogon told you that we came here to hear the will of the people. I don't think you are one of the people Mr. Mane, I think you are a politician."

Lee walked behind Stein and faced the tiers of seating and standing area. The same hundred or so people were scattered about, focused on the intensifying discussion on the floor.

Drogon whispered as he passed him, "What are you doing?"

Lee looked back with wide eyes as he shrugged nervously.

Stein and Drogon turned and stood behind him as Lee faced the people. He took a deep breath, and projected his voice - more boldly than he ever thought himself able, "If you were in trouble, wouldn't you want someone to help you?"

There was some murmuring between people, they didn't know what to say, and seemed unsure how to react.

"Hey, I'm talking to you!" Lee shouted. "You are the people. We are people, too, and we need to know. I'm a *cleric*, if you were hurt and bleeding, would you want me to heal you? If you were dying, would you want me to help you? Would you want *anyone* to help you?"

It was as if the dull chamber was being shaken awake for the first time in decades. There was faint nodding and mumbled sounds, of "*yes, of course, who wouldn't,*" and, "*why is he asking us?*"

"If an evil demigod took control of your mind and body, took you away from your family and made you fight a war for him, would you want someone to set you free?" Lee asked.

All eyes were fixed on Lee and the people were seemingly in agreement saying,

"*I hope someone would help me,*"

"*Maker please not here,*"

*"That's a terrifying thought,"*

*"Is that really happening?"*

And, *"Is that even possible?"*

"This is happening right now in my home, and if we don't stop it then it could find its way here." His voice was still shaking, and he felt a comforting hand on each shoulder. He continued, "would you want help?"

"Yes," They answered.

"Will you help us?" He asked.

"Yes!" They shouted.

There was cheering, and a lot of mumbled discussions from the citizens could be heard,

*"I hope we send the army,"*

*"Please don't let it find its way here,"*

And, *"Maker help that boy and his friends*

The senate stared; partially inspired, but mostly frightened at what they had just witnessed. Stein, Drogon, and Lee turned back to face them as the crowd rallied behind them from the observation areas. After an exchange of glances, Morvis nodded to the guards, and they began to move through the aisles.

"Clear the spectators," Morvis ordered.

Numerous guards and undercover soldiers from the crowd began guiding the citizens out through the exits. Meanwhile, they made sure to keep a perimeter around the floor and the group.

"Oh no, did I get us in trouble?" Lee asked his friends.

"No," Drogon answered, "I am impressed. You nearly started a riot! Stein couldn't even do that until he was at least eighteen."

Stein laughed, "Seventeen."

"You two seem unusually calm about this. They're leading everyone else out and surrounding us. Doesn't that scare you?" Lee said.

"You've just rallied a hundred people, trust me; these politicians will have nightmares of you tonight," said Stein.

As the chamber doors closed behind the last of the spectators, the guards took formation behind the senate and encircled the floor area.

"I apologize for this, but I think we need to have a more private discussion after a scene like that," Leia said calmly.

Stein smiled, "Is there a better way to learn the will of the people than asking the people themselves?"

Morvis quickly responded, "We are the ones who speak the will of the people."

"So, then you will help us?" Drogon asked. He left a moment of silence as he slowly approached the bench. He stopped himself as he noticed the guards showing nerves. "Surely if the people can see reason, you can understand how serious this is?"

"The rabble do not control our military, Drogon. We are a nation of freedoms and not a nation of warmongers. You don't have the right to come before this Senate and rile up our people in fear of being enslaved!" Morvis yelled.

"They are rabble because they want to help?" said Lee.

"You were out of place, *cleric*," said Sho. "If we had any mind to help you, you have certainly ruined it. What you have done here is create unrest and instill fear in our people. We have it in mind to have you jailed!"

"I..." Lee mumbled.

Leia shot a look to Sho, "Surely you do not speak on behalf of the entire Senate, do you Sho?"

Sho's face flushed with embarrassment, "Certainly not, I am simply remarking on what this boy has done here before his misplaced pride consumes him."

"I'm proud of him," Stein added.

"I'm sure you are, Prince of Peril," Morvis mocked.

Stein smirked a most sinister smirk, "It has been a while since someone called me that."

"You must hide your intentions well, as did **Amon**," Morvis replied.

Leia outstretched her arms and hushed the room, "I think we have crossed a purpose from productive to personal. Let us speak to the matter at hand."

"You aren't seriously entertaining this farce, are you?" said Morvis.

Leia peered at the senators, "No one of us speaks on behalf of the entire Senate. That is the folly of the Duke of Fornesio. No one of us speaks for all of the people of Fornesio, which is why we are each elected. With a matter as serious as this, both politically as well as for our national security, we should deliberate to form a just decision. I would like to propose we suspend city meeting for the remainder of the day and reconvene with the prince and his council at sundown with this delicate decision. All in favor say aye."

The chamber echoed with *aye*.

"All opposed, say nay." said Leia.

A single *nay* fell flat before Morvis.

Leia peered down from the bench, "We will see you gentlemen back here at sundown and I insist on your attendance." She nodded towards Lee with approval, "Master Cheng."

M.C. Grimm

# VIII

## The Senate of Fornesio - Part 2

*"In times of great darkness, we must ally with the shadows themselves; for even they live off the light."*

*A Shimmering Mind - A Tribute to Rishara*

Lee, Drogon, and Stein left the building to grab some *croissout.* While Drogon did not want to go far in case the Senators needed them back inside, Lee reminded them of the promise they had made to their minotaur companion back at the ship. They waited until they were in port to ensure it would still be fresh, picked up three dozen pastries with the last of their coin, and dropped them off for Marlow at the *Yoshi.*

As they walked across town, their conversation centered on how Lee riled up the spectators for help. Stein and Drogon boasted how proud they were in his confidence and how he was able to make their situation relatable. Lee couldn't remember the last time he felt so appreciated - or even so happy. Thoughts of his mother filled his mind.

They immediately returned to the Senate House of Fornesio and waited outside on the steps. The sky was swimming in hues of purple and orange by the time a guard appeared to lead them inside.

They began down the stairs with an echo of boot stomps and the clanging of Drogon's heavy armor. Across the chamber, they watched the senators file in and fill their seats as the party continued towards the floor. The guard lifted the velvet rope and gestured them towards the bench. Surprisingly, he was the only guard in the chamber. After leading them in, the guard climbed the stairs and exited the building, leaving the party alone with the nine-senate members.

"Thank you for your punctuality," Leia said.

"Thank you for taking the time to consider our situation," Drogon replied.

Morvis leaned in, "It was your situation until *your cleric* friend went and involved the rabble."

"No," Drogon said, "it was *our* situation well before that. This affects every nation in the world. *Master* Cheng only educated your people when you refused to lead them."

The nameplate before the dwarf with a short black beard and a bun atop his head read, *Brock - Senate Seat #3*. He spoke with a heavy Gashimarian accent. "Morvis," he said, "we spoke of this, and you say you not create problem."

"Yes, fine." Morvis begrudgingly agreed. "We have discussed the matter in great detail and are willing to offer assistance against the threat of Donahay. This assistance is contingent upon a condition. That condition is nonnegotiable. Anything other than acceptance will earn you banishment from Fornesio for the rest of your days."

"You really enjoyed that, didn't you?" Stein asked.

Morvis smirked, "I did insist to deliver that to you, yes."

Stein made quick steps towards the bench, "Shouldn't have sent the guards' home, Morvis."

Drogon and Lee each reached out to loosely grab one of his arms. Drogon spoke, "Let's just hear what they have to say, this is what we came here for."

Morvis narrowed his horror-filled eyes, slid back into his seat, and straightened his glasses. "Yes, thank you."

"Thank you, Morvis." Leia said. "What we are going to ask of you is, in all regard, treasonous. However, I can assure you that without this step being taken, Fornesio will have no part in this war until it has reached our shores. I can also say that our part in asking you for help with this matter is an extension of trust that is risking our lives in a show of good faith towards us to each reach a desirable place for our people."

"We appreciate your trust in us and will not betray it," said Drogon.

"I believe you." She said with confidence. "The government of Fornesio is a delicate balance of political compromises. While the Senate is elected by the people to represent them, after we have collected the opinions and needs of the people, as well as developed a means to satisfy them, the duke undermines us and sabotages our efforts with his thugs. This creates a perception to the people that we are stagnant in our duties and rallies them to trust him when he wishes to consolidate his power and remove the seats of the Senate from government."

"Can he do that?" Stein asked.

"We exist for the will of the people, if they wished to consolidate power under the Duke and waive their opinions, *they can* do that," Sho answered. "It would be more a resignation of freedom than anything. If the people choose to waive their right to a voice and forfeit their freedom from monarchy; they may irrevocably do so."

"The people wouldn't do that, though," Lee added with a tone full of hope.

"They are moving in that direction," Morvis said. "They are convinced that sacrificing their freedom and their voice will give them safety and convenience. The Duke has told them, he has staged events to stricken them with fear, and fear leads to panic and rash decisions. What they fail to realize is that once they have surrendered themselves to this style of government, or any government for that matter, the only way they would be able to have those freedoms again, is through revolution. At that, the duke will remove any threats from the country and plunge us into tyranny."

Stein laughed, "You are aware that Vian, and my own Radiant Empire are a monarchy, right? That I am a prince to the royal family? The vast wealth and success of our nation is driven by the fact that we don't have a *house of petty debate* over every issue. You describe it as tyranny because it costs you a comfortable job with a padded bench and countless benefits. What is so wrong with the Duke having the power to lead Fornesio? Why isn't that a better way than having you deliberate on every issue while being committed to inaction?"

"What a princely response to see the opinions of the people as a waste of time! The lives of anyone other than yourse-" Morvis scoffed.

Leia silenced him with a gesture and directed her gaze towards Stein, "Prince Stein, your family has held a respect of their people and other nations of the world. They have led through fair treatment, sharing equal rights, providing services to the sick and elderly, and countless other great initiatives that have inspired the world to take action. Your family's liberation of the elves allowed my own parents and grandparents to live free. It's inspired other people throughout the world to seek a voice and demand freedom. The Duke does not share the passion and humility of your family's great leaders and as such, people of our land go hungry while he sits in a pampered palace. He is a power-hungry monster, and once he *conquers* this nation, make no mistake, he will widen his gaze. The loss of the Senate would be a step backwards, a devolution of the Vian Kingdoms, and a loss to the people that will be oppressed here."

Stein let out a sigh, which showed he was no longer interested in continuing the conversation. "What is the condition of your help?"

The entire Senate was silent for a moment as they looked towards Leia. She spoke, "Coincidentally, sometime before your arrival, the Duke sent letter to your family requesting an audience. He is looking to make moves towards total rule of Fornesio in the near future and we believe he wanted to absorb some of your family's experience. He received your message from the docks and sent a response, one, which we intercepted. The message invites you and a single companion to the *Duke's Mansion* for dinner this evening, in about one hour, actually. We would like for you to go to the dinner and—using a poison to remain discrete—assassinate the Duke." She passed down the envelope containing the invitation.

"What!?" Lee shouted.

"That turned dark rather quickly," Drogon mumbled as he took the invitation and handed it to Stein.

"Where else did you think she was going with this?" Stein said back.

"You're going to kill him because the people like him more than you? You're crazy! That's not what the Senate is supposed to do," Lee said.

"The Senate is put in place to protect the interests of the people," said Morvis. "Sometimes that means seeing the bigger picture and giving them what they *need* rather than what they *think* they want- especially while they are being manipulated."

"So, can we go back to my original question; what makes you better than the Duke?" Stein asked rhetorically. "He is looking to eradicate your position and have a single party government. Here you are, looking to kill the man, and have a different single party government? You called him a monster. I know about monsters, and one monster is still easier to tame than nine."

All nine members of the Senate were uneasily sitting at the bench. They were staring down, their eyes filled with both anger and surprise.

Drogon pulled Lee and Stein away from the bench, "Please allow us a moment to discuss this."

"Of course," Leia replied to the party as she turned to the other Senate members and began whispering back and forth, as the party moved to the other end of the chamber.

When they were a safe distance out of earshot, Stein began, "What is there to talk about? Why are we going to do the killing of these talking heads?"

"What do you think the Duke is going to talk to us about?" asked Drogon. "If it isn't directly asking us to kill the Senate for him, it will be for advice on how to rule the government after he has killed them, himself."

Stein nodded in agreement, "So? We can at least let him do his own dirty work. We can offer him whatever information or support he needs in exchange for his support in the fight against Donahay."

"And you would want the army of a power-hungry Duke to be in your castle when Donahay is finally taken down? It's the same thing they are asking us to do, both the Senate and the Duke. They are going to want the same thing from us and offer potentially the same reward. We are deciding the future of Fornesio and who we can trust to follow through, but only as far as we need them," Drogon explained.

"We really don't know what the duke wants, yet," Lee said.

"No, we do," Stein added. "I've dealt with him before; this has always been his endgame. More than likely, he would want us to kill the Senate for him to show his commitment. He would probably even expose us so he would be the *champion of his people* and *bring us to justice.* We pretty much need to decide who is less likely to betray us."

Lee hung his head, "This is terrible - did I cause this?"

"No, not at all, Lee," Stein said as he put his hand on Lee's shoulder. "This has been coming for a long time. In politics this is just - the right moment to capture power."

"Stein is right, it's not your fault. You are the only reason that the Senate confided in us with their intentions and plan to preserve the freedoms of the people. I do feel we could trust them to follow through on the promise to help. And if we are comparing their future, freedom with the governing Senate will be better for their nation." Drogon said.

Stein rolled his eyes, "That might not be true. They are pampered diplomats; even they are driven by greed and power. I bet that over time, the nine heads will devour one another, but that isn't our problem. Whatever you want to do, Drogon. I don't care either way."

Drogon looked to Lee, "What do you think?"

"You want *me* to decide?" He asked.

"No one can decide something like this alone. You are a part of our family, and you get to voice your opinion. What do you think?" Said Drogon.

Lee looked down, "I don't want to kill anyone. I made an oath to **Mora** to do no harm. I have been able to put the vetaless out of my mind because I know she was a monster. But the Duke is just a man, maybe there's another way?"

"Listen to me," Drogon said, "we are about to be put in a serious situation. The next thing we say to the Senate is going to matter a great deal. They won't risk telling us their plan, having us reject them, and then walk away freely. We need to choose a side right now, and we need to follow through."

Tears were swimming in Lee's eyes, "I don't want to decide that. I'm sorry if that doesn't help right now, but I can't decide who lives and who dies. I'll help you with whatever you decide, but I won't kill anyone, and I won't pick who gets killed."

"And you don't have to," said Stein.

Drogon turned to the Senate and the party followed up behind him to the bench, "Thank you for allowing us to speak."

"We are eager to hear your thoughts," Leia said calmly.

"We will help," said Drogon. "We are with you for your people and for freedom. We will do as you ask; Stein and I will be there in an hour. Do you have the poison?"

Leia held out her well-manicured hand and levitated down a neatly opened envelope, as well as a small vial filled with an orange liquid into Stein's hand. "That is a **mondook** poison. The clerics in the palace won't be able to resuscitate him with the dose you are holding. It was been designed by a master alchemist with an agent that will take twenty-four hours to activate."

"And you agree that Fornesio will support us against Donahay?" Asked Drogon.

"After liberating us from the Duke, we will owe you at least that, yes," Morvis responded.

"We should go," Stein said.

"When word of his death has reached us, we will assemble the military immediately and send them to Luray, as agreed," Sho stated. "It would be best if you leave Fornesio as soon as possible after the assassination and not return here to us."

"Agreed," Drogon replied.

The party turned and began to head out of the chamber with a purposeful walk.

"Gentlemen?" Leia beckoned, "Obviously, if you are caught, we will have to deny any involvement. That also might make things more difficult to have our people support your cause after murdering their Duke. I trust you will show some discretion?"

Stein turned with a steady pace out of the chamber. He spoke boldly to her over his shoulder, "Do you forget? I used to do this all the time."

# IX

## The Duke of Fornesio

*"If there existed a life that was free from pain, it would simply be called death."*

*Confessions of the Temptress - A Tribute to Eve*

Drogon, Stein, and Lee made their way back to the *Yoshi*. Lee made his way aboard to be greeted by an extremely satisfied minotaur who, moments later, was completely covered in the crumbs of croissout. Lee waved goodbye from atop the ramp and Drogon and Stein started a quick pace towards the Duke's mansion for dinner.

Drogon straightened his armor while he rubbed off some dried blood. He was moving fast, tightening a rivet of his pauldron while adjusting his belt with his other hand. "It's great that we have this whole hour to make ourselves presentable and get across town."

Stein was patting dirt from his robes, "What would we have done with any extra time, anyway? Eat? Sleep? Bathe? It's better this way."

"We're going there for dinner, might have ruined our appetite to eat beforehand," said Drogon.

"Yeah, but a nap would've been nice. Speaking of sleep, how is Marlow feeling about giving away his room?" Stein asked.

"He doesn't care," Drogon replied, "never slept in there anyway. All the rooms below deck are too small for him. I'm surprised there's even a doorway left with all the times he's smashed his horns into it."

"So, you gave his room away because he didn't use it and not because a pretty dragonkin wanted to stay on our ship?" Stein said with a smirk.

Drogon let out a hardy laugh, "I knew you would see that I was attracted to her, know how?"

"Because I know you very well," Stein answered.

"You do, but I must have given her the same look that you gave Gwynn," Drogon said.

"Maybe for one—brief moment—but not anymore."

"You understand why she did what she did, right?" said Drogon.

"She's dishonest and I don't really care why she did it," he said coldly.

"Stein," Drogon started, "I've known you long enough to know that once you make up your mind there's not a lot of convincing you. But you should consider that sometimes someone doing their best with the hand they've been dealt and taking the course of action that they believe in their heart to be right, even though seems impossible and goes against their character. That there *is* honesty in that. There is truth in that intention. There is conviction in their heart that can separate who they *are* from who they *need* to be at that given moment. You are uncompromisingly true to yourself, but not everyone is carrying a **death scythe** and trained to kill fifty men alone. What I want you to know is that everyone, even on the inside, is imperfect; and it's okay to share that with someone."

"I share it with you, don't I?" said Stein, "Isn't that enough?"

Drogon's voice was soft, "In some ways, but not in the ways that I think will make you truly happy. Just…think about it, okay?"

Stein nodded.

They cleared blocks of Fornesio quickly and arrived at the Duke's mansion with a few minutes to spare. Stein helped Drogon tighten the straps of his armor, while Drogon brushed dirt from the back of Stein's robes. While the two were obviously not in formal dress they appeared, at the very least, to be clean.

The mansion was set back into a dense jungle of trees and illuminated by magical lanterns, each floor gleaming a different color. The three-floor structure was arranged with a large, red first floor, a moderate-sized green second floor, and a small blue third floor. It made the building look like a tiered cake. While the festive lighting and elaborate woodcarvings painted a scene of celebration and lighthearted fun, surrounding the mansion was a vast perimeter of tall, iron fencing, accompanied by patrolling guard. It appeared like converting a secluded funhouse into a fort, but still keeping the lightshow.

Up ahead, two dwarven guards in iron armor stood at the front gate, axes on their back. There was a small stone guardhouse on the right where, at the desk sat two more armed dwarven guards. One dwarf stood from his chair and approached the cutout of the structure, "Price Stein, welcome to the Duke's estate, we are overjoyed that you were able to attend."

Stein presented his invitation, "To attend a dinner with the duke is my pleasure. This is my general, Drogon of **Rayton**."

Drogon reached out to shake the guard's hand firmly. "This is a solid perimeter. You gentlemen have some excellent form and leadership, great work."

The dwarf kept a firm shake and raised his other hand up to the back of his head, closing his eyes with a smile, "Thank you sir, we are only doing our duty."

"The Duke is fortunate to have such skilled guard. I'm sure you are well appreciated for your dedication," Drogon remarked.

The dwarf's smile faded, and he tilted his head with a grin, "I suppose. As I said, it is our duty." He made a waving gesture towards the two guards at the gate and they immediately moved to open it. He turned back to Drogon and Stein, "Enjoy your dinner, Prince, General." He bowed.

"Have a good evening," said Drogon.

They walked past the guard and through the tall iron gate. It shut behind them with a squeal and the heavy clang of metal on metal. They began walking up the winding pathway, beyond numerous manicured bushes and water features. It felt as if they walked through a wall of moisture, as the scent of damp woodland greeted their nostrils. Small, lean, brightly colored birds that stood on one leg bathed lazily in the water. Up in a nearby tree, the gentle purring of a large, tame, spotted cat could be heard as its tail swayed at eye level. While perched on a branch, multicolored birds squawked at one another, bobbing up and down.

"You were pretty quick with that general thing, nicely done." Drogon smiled.

"Thank you, *General* Drogon." Stein laughed.

"I can get used to the title. Although I suppose anything beats being a nameless, secret band of monster slayers," said Drogon.

Stein corrected him, "*Elite warriors*."

"Somehow, it doesn't make a difference when you're a *secret*." Drogon stopped and appreciated the lush jungle around them, "The Duke certainly has style in the exotic, where does all of this come from?"

Stein continued their stroll, "Gashimar, mostly. I'm surprised to see a whole ecosystem here, it's beautiful."

"Why are you surprised?" Drogon said, petting one of the multicolored birds on its branch.

"Well," Stein started, "Fornesio is an impoverished country. They regularly plead for food and water from the Radiant Empire and have some of the highest starvation rates in the world."

"So, you're saying that all this," he gestured around him, "is at the expense of people being able to eat?"

"That's what Leia said, so probably," Stein replied, "does it matter?"

"Makes doing this a little bit easier for me," said Drogon.

They approached the mansion and the red glow from the lanterns cascaded over them. As they reached the massive wooden doors, two well-dressed dwarven guards kept their eyes averted and opened the way. Inside, the red faded away behind them and a vibrant white light filled the room. The shine of the wood floor further illuminated around them and highlighted a grand staircase twisting with vines and vibrantly colored flowers. Servants hurried about carrying trays and tidying up each speck of dust as soon as it fell. A slender elf in a white suit greeted them with an expert smile.

"Good evening, gentlemen." His judging eyes looked them over, "the Duke is most pleased you are able to join him for dinner. Might I offer you a dinner jacket or perhaps something more comfortable? We have a tailor on site that could find you something favorable." He waved over another elf that who had a measuring tape hanging over his shoulders.

"That won't be necessary," said Drogon, "A guard and general to the Prince of the Radiant Empire must always be in uniform. Thank you for the thought."

The elf bowed respectfully, "Most assuredly, General Drogon. Is there anything I can offer to make you more comfortable, Prince Stein?"

"No," Stein replied.

"Then please, come with me." He ushered them forward, between the curves of the grand staircase and through a magnificent carved archway of exotic animals and jungle.

Ahead of them was the dining hall with an enormous table in the center. Thirty white, velvet chairs surrounded it and at the head, surrounded by fruits and crackers, sat a plump dwarf. His beard further shaped the roundness in his face and hung down. The bright purple of his tunic hung open in the middle, allowing chest hair to curl out around the trim of his clothing.

His hardy laugh echoed in the hall and he raised up his goblet, "Yes-yes, come-come, I am so happy to see you accept my invitation!"

The elf bowed and stepped aside. Stein and Drogon approached the table, bowed slightly, and sat at the only two settings placed to the right of the duke.

"Thank you for having us," Stein said.

"Nonsense-nonsense, the pleasure is all mine, let me begin by showing my gratitude." He raised both hands and waved over a servant that was positioned by the wall. Each carried a tray of food and drink and served them.

Drogon plucked at some grapes and they burst with juicy flavor. Then, he tried a thin slice of seasoned meat. He continued to eat, "This is delicious. All from here in Fornesio?"

"No-no," the Duke said, "Fornesio isn't a place for the dirt that comes with agriculture and cattle herding. The fruits are imported from Luray, and the meat is from Vian. The very-very best of the best for you, my prestigious guests."

"You're too kind," said Drogon with a forced grin. He was imagining the people of Fornesio starving in the streets, and a representative meeting with these kingdoms to ask for food donations while the duke engorged himself.

Stein sipped at his goblet. His lips met with a familiar, sweet taste. "**Sucrape**? You have outdone yourself, Duke."

The Duke raised his goblet to toast, "To new friends and a prosperous future; for both our kingdoms."

Drogon and Stein met his goblet with their own and they shared a savoring moment of sucrape.

While they savored, the servants collected their plates. The elf in a white suit moved his hand along the table with a scraper to gather any crumbs into his palm and said, "Gentlemen, tonight the duke wished to share with you his favorite meal. Therefore, this evening's entrée features the finest cut steak of *Vian*, accompanied by mashed and seasoned in traditional dwarven fashion potatoes, and a tossed salad."

"Excellent-excellent, you're dismissed, White," said the Duke, "After you bring out another bottle of sucrape."

"Yes, Your Excellence." White bowed.

"Excuse me, White," Drogon said, catching the elf's eye before he started away. "Might it be possible for me to have a tour of your kitchen? I'm not sure what magic is at work back there, but I would love to share it with the kitchen back home."

"Most certainly, general." White bowed again.

Drogon placed his napkin on his seat and stood, "Excuse me, gentlemen."

Drogon and White walked away from the table. By the time they cleared the dining hall, Drogon already had an arm around the elf's shoulder and they were laughing to themselves about how fancy food comes in such small portions. Stein guessed that Drogon had a plan to get the mondook in front of the duke.

"Well-well, Stein," Duke began, "I'm sure your general won't mind missing a small part of our conversation."

"Not at all, politics bores him," Stein said, "If it's not an enemy or a monster to slay; it's not worth his time."

The Duke's laugh was boisterous, "A man of passion and power—I love it, I love it!" His laugh quickly subsided, and he leaned towards Stein. "That's something I can relate to. You see, I am a man who is passionate about power. I am someone who can take Fornesio from this small, fragile kingdom, and take it to great new heights. Something worthy of a true partnership, no-no, *alliance* with your empire."

"You have a grand vision for the country, I suppose?" asked Stein.

"Yes, yes. I want to unify Fornesio under my rule and expand to create the **Fornesian Isles**. That's all I want; to stretch from sea to shining sea. I would lead to establish a country of trade between the greatness of the Radiant Empire, and the wild resources of Gashimar." Duke professed with a smirk of confidence. "Create peace and prosperity while maintaining order and civility."

"Sounds like a great vision; a goal truly worth pursuing. But what is your plan to get there?" asked Stein.

"Excellent question, Stein, excellent. My first challenge is to focus the people here in Fornesio. The senate has clouded their minds with delusions of equality and democracy, when truly they seek power only for themselves," Duke replied.

"Is your vision not the same?"

"Similar perhaps. But I'm sure you could agree that nine minds will never agree on how to run a country to reach a vision as grand as mine. No-no, nine members of the senate will create a country of inaction and foster a *parasitic* population of entitled fools that therefore feeds off the rest of the world. Would your own empire be as great were it not for a single authority, enacting his vision? What are we as civilized men without a unified cause?" He closed his eyes, "Let me tell you the answer. We become a country lost unto time like a ship lost at sea. With a crew that is capable and well-bodied, but rowing in circles. Each following their own direction on misguided *freedom* that is, in all aspects, servitude to a corrupted senate."

"The senate claims to represent the people. Don't they meet with citizens throughout the day and try to come up with policies to help them?" Stein asked.

"Oh, come now, Stein, I meet with *people,* too. Carpenters, traders, diplomats, business owners and the like! But the rabble? Must we solve problems for those unwilling to solve problems for themselves? We are a country of power and ambition. We need to run like a business, not a charity. Don't you agree?"

Stein did in fact agree, but he was uncomfortable. He twisted in his chair with a nod and retreated for a moment into his thoughts. He was torn—is killing the Duke the right thing to do?

Would a senate be any better at running the country, at fighting Donahay? Who are they to decide? As these thoughts raced through his mind, he found himself thinking of Lee and how he was the only one of them with sense to walk away.

The kitchen door opened and Drogon came out with an elaborate bottle cradled in his arm. He moved across the room towards the dining table and stood next to Stein. "Duke, you have the most wonderful kitchen and your staff is second to none." Drogon removed the cork with a silent ease and poured Sucrape into the duke's goblet,

"Yes, yes, they're some of the best in the world. Many of them were raised from childhood to be the culinary masters they are today. Stein and I were just speaking of the greatness that can come from being led by men with a vision, and they are my vision in practice," Duke replied as he turned to Stein, "Imagine that vision, *my* vision, to the scale of an entire country."

The doors to the lobby opened, and White, who was dismissed some time ago entered the dining hall. He led in two additional guests to the chairs at the left side of the duke and across from Stein and Drogon.

Drogon placed the goblet down with an unblinking stare.

Stein's eyes widened and he stood quickly.

The broad human had a shiny scalp and rosy cheeks. He wore the royal blue uniform of a Radiant Empire general that was decorated with an impressive display of medals. He was turned towards the duke and wore a face without expression. They recognized his broad physique and baldhead in an instant—it was General Dart.

Prince Victus was beside him, facing the duke without expression. He stood as pale, tall, and lean as Stein with similar but distinguished tribal markings on his face and neck. His long blonde hair was flat and falling straight down to the middle of his back. He wore no uniform, but instead ornate leather armor reinforced with chromed plating and trim.

"Wonderful, wonderful! I am so pleased that the Radiant Empire would send such a party to share my vision," the duke boasted as he sipped his fresh goblet of sucrape. "Prince Victus, General Dart, please sit."

They both took a seat and looked to Drogon and Stein with a purple hue in their eyes.

"It is good to see you, Prince Stein," said Victus.

"Likewise, Prince Victus," Stein replied.

"The Radiant Empire is a whole different level, isn't it?" Duke started, "Sophisticated and poised—I mean; your kingdom is the height that I aspire to elevate Fornesio!"

"Your words speak too kindly," said Victus, "as we are but humble princes. To be burdened by the weight of leadership is our birthright."

"No, no, I cannot speak kindly enough of your family." The Duke smiled. "But what you say is true; the burden of leadership is a heavy weight to carry. And yet, we are the only ones who can save the people from destroying themselves."

"Most assuredly." Victus agreed.

The Duke leaned back in his grand chair, "I was speaking with Stein of some business before you arrived – I would have waited, but I wasn't aware you were coming."

Victus looked across the table towards Stein, "I don't believe the prince was aware I received the message you sent to the **Crystal Palace**. You see, he has been traveling."

The duke glanced back and forth at them, "This must be a pleasant surprise then? Stein, Drogon, please sit."

Slowly, Drogon and Stein pulled out their chairs and sat.

The Duke leaned forward, his eyes focused and moving about the table, "As I was saying, Stein and I were having a conversation about the nature of government and the importance of vision. You see, I have grand ambitions to reshape Fornesio in the image of your great empire."

Victus kept his eyes fixed onto Stein, "Fascinating, do go on."

The Duke continued, "I wish to remove the senate from their seats of misdirection and unite Fornesio under a single vision. Then, I would move to unite the **Vian Kingdom** to form the Fornesian Isles and build an alliance worthy of the Radiant Empire. Together, we can sway tides of the oceans!"

"What a vision to have," said Victus. "We have a similar vision, but much grander."

"Please, please, do tell," the Duke beckoned.

Stein pressed, "Please do."

"To unify the world under *our* vision," Victus smiled, "and have every man, woman, and child see the world through the eyes of the king himself, so that they may cherish the opportunity to be their best selves to better serve him."

"To serve *him*?" Drogon's eyes narrowed in anger.

"Of course." The Duke coughed and sipped again at his sucrape. He cleared his throat, "Only then could they carry themselves and lighten the weight burdened onto us, their leaders."

Victus turned his gaze to the duke, "Precisely." he paused in thought for a moment. "Duke, I find your cause to be worthy, and the Radiant Empire would like to aid you on this quest in the interest of our joint prosperity."

"Excellent, most excellent!" The Duke cheered. "There is so much to be done, but first is the matter of the senate."

Victus had not yet blinked since arriving in the dining hall, "Dart can see to that before the sun greets your window."

Dart nodded with a grunt, the muscles on his neck tensing down his shoulder in a formidable show of strength for such a simple gesture.

"We would ask," Victus continued, "that after you have full control over Fornesio and her army that you would honor our new alliance with a demonstration of commitment."

The Duke was rather pale, "Anything you need will be done."

"Command your fleet to Luray and…"

The Duke coughed loudly, blood spraying over the table as his eyes streamed with thick crimson tears. One hand grabbed at his throat as he gagged. The other swung wildly, knocking his goblet onto the floor and shattering the entire bottle of sucrape next to it. He squirmed about his seat, writhing in anguish before he finally slumped forward onto the table with an unblinking stare. The light faded from his eyes.

Stein stood, pointed back and forth between Dart and Victus, and shouted, "They've killed the Duke!"

M.C. Grimm

# X

## Brotherhood

*"I, Stein, third prince of the Radiant Empire, hereby vow upon my eternal soul; to protect the first prince with my life. I will die in his service. Should I die defending his person or cause, may my death be prolonged; so, I may give every part of my spirit for him. May I break every bone, be torn of my flesh, as I fight in his name - I make this oath to the Maker."*
*Stein's original royal oath and induction as a Gallant.*

The servants ran from the room in a panic, dropping platters and knocking into one another in the doorways. At last, Stein, Drogon, Victus, and Dart were alone. They knew their privacy likely wouldn't last long. The corpse of the Duke had his face planted firmly into his plate of food. Blood was spilling from his mouth, filled the dish, and began to overflow onto the table. The tense silence was broken as a stream of his red essence began to drip onto the floor.

Drogon spoke first, *"Command your fleet to Luray.* What are you doing, Donahay?"

Victus tossed his hair back over his shoulder, "You will know soon enough. I am still Prince Victus, dragonkin. Donahay is seeing to matters back at our empire."

"*Our?*" Stein's voice quivered with rage as he shouted, "Donahay has no right to our kingdom!"

Victus was completely unmoved by Stein, "Why would you use that word again—*our*? You became an exile and a fugitive the moment you fled the laboratory. *You* have no right, Stein."

"I was being tortured for our father's sick experiments."

"*Break every bone and be torn of my flesh,*" Victus said. "Sound familiar? Your oath as a boy was quite specific. Were those just words to you? If the will of the royal family is to use your life for the greater good, is that not then part of your oath?"

"The greater good?" Drogon mocked.

Stein stood from his seat, "Then consider my oath fulfilled! I was torn open, mutilated inside and out. I was infected and dissected, over—and over—again. After *our* father was done with me, I was killed. I gave my life for *our* royal family, and now my life is my own."

Victus was in thought for a moment. "You are right. Your oath is fulfilled." He stood from his seat, the purple glaze over his eyes grew darker as he spoke, "And yet, you still live. And now that you know the smallest part of our plan, I can't very well let you leave here." The chrome from his leather armor began to shift as small links that emanated a faint orange glow. The movement was accompanied by a faint sound of metal on metal clangs, like a chain being quickly dragged across a hardedge. It traced down his arm and into his hand to form an elongated shape, which then molded into a thin blade.

Dart rose with his fists up, keeping his elbows tight, and faced Drogon with a bounce in his step. A frost formed over his fingers and covered up into his forearm. Then, it grew thick spikes from the ice over his knuckles with menacing sharp points.

Drogon equipped Rayne from her sheath and Prophet from his back. He locked his stare onto Dart and took a defensive stance.

"You are one of the few people in this world that I hesitate to kill, Victus," Stein said, his eyes softening. "Once I've killed Donahay, your mind will be your own and this can be done with. My fight isn't with you. Don't make me do this."

"Your sentiment is wasted, Stein," said Victus coldly. "This won't be like our old sparring days. Donahay has given me power, and I am guaranteed victory."

"So be it." Stein slid back his right foot and held his hands out before him. The light itself between his palms twisted the air in a flash of darkness. He held the obsidian shaft with the long, crooked blade of his scythe reaching out before him. It ignited in time to burn away a tear from his cheek, "I will free you, Victus."

Stein's scythe easily cleared the width of the table with his first two swings. He cleaved back and forth with a blur of flame that rained down embers over Dart and Victus as they ducked beneath it. Drogon and Dart made their way towards the far end of the table to face off, as Stein focused on his brother.

While his side-to-side slashes were quick, he was trying to keep Victus on the defensive. Stein brought the scythe straight down, blade first beyond the table. He twisted it as the shaft hit the surface and cleaved it back towards him; a narrow miss of catching

Victus in the back. In another movement, he swung into the air, just to shower Victus with cinder. There was a faint smell of burning hair as the blonde flowing locks were speckled with ash. Stein had the advantage of reach and continued his attacks with tireless ferocity. He wanted to keep his distance as he knew Victus was nimble and skilled with a long sword.

Victus ducked under the blade again, "You're as erratic as ever, but you're not fast enough."

More chrome from his armor began to move as links to his other hand. It formed a small throwing dagger, which he quickly tossed over the table with precision. Stein spun the shaft and it deflected the knife with a high-pitched *tink*. Another cut across the room, *tink*. Then another, *tink*. Stein was spinning and twirling, never losing momentum, as dagger after dagger was knocked from the air. *Tink, tink, tink.* He hated being on the defensive, but it was satisfying to know he could keep up with his brother's renowned dexterity. Finally, the only remaining chrome was the elongated blade in his hand.

The purple in his eyes was intense as Victus leapt up onto the table. Plates shook wildly and crashed onto the floor, shattering into pieces. Victus brought his blade down at Stein and it was met with the crooked length of his scythe. Then, he spoke with the same lack of emotion, "I have the high ground, Stein." He brought the blade down a second time, and then a third.

Stein could feel the strength behind each of his brother's attacks; Victus was stronger than ever. He also didn't notice, while blocking the third swing, that Victus raised his empty, left hand. In an instant, a rippling, purple energy surged outward from his palm and threw Stein back. He soared through the air, against the wall on the far side of the dining room and collapsed as if dazed. Victus walked along the table and turned his attention to Drogon.

Drogon charged at Dart with a bash of his shield but missed. The large man was surprisingly evasive for his size and broadness. He bounced with each step and stood only on the tips of his toes with ice-spiked fists hovering just under his chin. Drogon spun on his heel with an arc of his sword, another miss. With this, Dart took a quick step forward and launched into Drogon. Spikes of ice were blown apart against his platemail with a jab into his chest. His left jab followed up with a smash against Drogon's well-placed shield. The ice broke away but reformed nearly as quick. Dart was on the assault with another right thrust into Drogon's abdomen. A dust-like frost exploded into the air as the spikes shattered, but one spike had pierced between the armored plates. Drogon felt a pain shoot through him. In an instant, he assessed the non-fatal wound, and countered by driving his blade forward. He felt relief as the blade found resistance in the tense muscle of Dart's upper thigh. It might not kill him, but it would at least slow him down.

Dart moved in with a limp, and Drogon saw a reflection in his purple eyes gleaming. He saw Victus approaching along the table behind him. He turned and met the elongated blade with an overhead block of his shield. At the same time, Drogon slashed towards Dart, who leapt back clumsily, slipped on a platter, and tumbled to the floor. Drogon focused on Victus and heaved upwards, bringing up his sword and locking blades. The height difference helped Victus push all his weight down, bringing Drogon to a knee. Victus raised his left hand outward and surged a purple energy towards him.

Drogon narrowly managed to shift his shield over in time to block and, surprisingly, felt no impact from the burst of energy whatsoever. Instead, the polished surface of the shield rippled.

Victus held the lock firmly, "What a fascinating shield, where did you get that?"

"It's a family heirloom," said Drogon.

The shield was aimed towards Victus. In the immaculate, polished center, looking back was a reflection of himself that was puzzling. The image didn't quite copy his motion. His sword was locked at a slightly different angle and his hand was outstretched; just as it was a moment ago. Suddenly, that same purple wave of energy erupted from the mirrored-surface and threw Victus up into the air and plummeting down at the center of this enormous table. He was laid out and coughing for air, but only for a moment. His chin pointed towards the ceiling as his eyes met Stein's. He gasped.

Stein was standing on the floor at the far end, wearing a maniacal grin on his face. In one smooth motion, he swiped his scythe from left to right, severing the legs from the table. It crashed to the floor before him and created a slide of plates, glasses, and foods. Sliding towards him, headfirst and flat on his back, Victus was emotionless. Stein hoisted his scythe over his shoulder, cutting through the air with a trailing arc of flame and drove it through Victus' chest, impaling him to the table.

The purple glow faded from his eyes. He coughed forcefully, and blood erupted to shower over his face. "Stein?"

"Victus." Stein dissipated his scythe and knelt down to catch him. He sat on the floor and held his brother in his arms.

"What... have I done?" Victus mumbled, his voice shook with remorse.

"It wasn't you," said Stein, "It was Donahay. It was *all* him, and he'll die for it!"

The blood saturated their clothes and began staining the marble around them. Victus looked up at him, "I saw myself doing it—*all of it*."

"It wasn't you!" Stein tensed his grip, not realizing until he felt Victus wince in pain. "I'm...sorry."

Victus shook his head slowly, "No, don't be. You did what had to be done. I would have done the same thing." He coughed again, "Don't get me wrong, I certainly would've been quicker about it. Maybe made it look more impressive; you know—for the ladies?"

A single tear streamed down Stein's cheek as he scoffed softly, "More impressive than a death scythe?"

His voice became a whisper, "Just let me have this one."

"Alright... Just this once." Stein held him close and looked away.

"Stein?"

Stein felt himself flinch at the weakness leaking from his brother's voice, "Yeah?"

With a feeble reach, Victus set his hand to Stein's cheek, "I...am so grateful to have lived by your side." Stein could feel the gasp in his brother as he struggled to breathe, "My life…has been…honor…."

Victus felt heavier in his arms as Stein hugged him tight. His warmth dissipated as quickly as it had from his scythe. Stein's stare became rigid. Fixated on no particular point in front of him as he stewed in the thoughts of grisly murder painting the halls of the **Crystal Palace** with Donahay's blood and mutilating the severed head. It may have been out of revenge or rage, perhaps it was pure madness; Stein no longer cared which. His thoughts only focused when he heard a heavy thud meet the floor a ways behind him. The thud of a muscled, hulking, unarmored man having suffered a fatal blow.

Drogon approached from behind him, sheathing his sword and resting a hand on Stein's shoulder. "I am sorry, Stein. He is with the Maker now." He reminded him, "This is not your fault."

"Of course it is, Drogon." Stein was monotone and continued to stare off into the distance. "I drove my scythe through his chest. I aimed for his heart to kill him quickly, but I missed and gave him the opportunity to relive everything Donahay made him do."

Drogon came around and knelt down on the floor with him, "You had to-"

"Stop," Stein interrupted. "I don't need to hear one of your speeches. I know it had to be done, so—I killed him. And now, we need to move on so I can pay Donahay back by peeling the meat from his bones."

Drogon looked on silently, wearing a supportive look of concern.

The doors swung open behind them as Fornesian guards rushed in. A few of the servants from dinner trailed behind, pointing towards Dart and Victus and chanting, "*Murderers.*" Drogon stood with his hands raised, approached to meet them, and offer a favorable explanation. It was, of course, one that implicated Victus and Dart as the killers and traitors to the empire. With Drogon's natural diplomacy, it was easy to convince them. Still, for Stein, the details were irrelevant. He killed his brother. Next, he would kill Donahay, with or without an army besides him.

The walk back to the *Yoshi* was silent. Drogon respected the space he knew Stein needed and allowed himself to fall behind. Stein received many stares from commoners and guards alike as he was covered in blood. While the black of his **deathrobes** hid much of it, the splatter on his neck and trailing fingertip-streaks down his cheek painted a clear picture to match the scent of death radiating from him. They arrived back at the ship to a brooding Marlow, a smiling Maressa, and Lee.

Lee skipped towards the ramp, "Welcome back!"

Stein said nothing, pressed past them, and headed below deck.

The party knew not to follow him.

As Drogon ascended to the deck, he hugged Maressa; giving her a gentle squeeze before finally letting her go and turning towards Lee. Lee looked away with a scornful frown on his face.

Drogon knelt down, "It's not you, Lee. Stein is going through some trying times right now. It's probably best to give him some space."

Lee's confusion showed in his eyes, "But aren't trying times exactly when you need your friends most?"

"For some, yes. For Stein, I don't believe so."

"Okay," said Lee, "I understand."

"Did everything go over smoothly?" Maressa asked.

"I'm not sure *smoothly* is the right way to describe it." Drogon searched for the right words, "I can say that Fornesio will be sending their fleet to help against Donahay. The senate will be satisfied."

Maressa squinted curiously, "So why is Stein upset?"

"Victus and Dart were here."

"Why do those names sound familiar?" she asked.

Lee gasped, "Prince Victus?!"

"Yes," said Drogon. "Victus was Stein's oldest brother and the one who swore him in as a Gallant. He was the heir to the Radiant Empire. Dart was the general of the Radiant Empire forces."

Lee studied Drogon's face, "What do you mean *was*?"

"I won't ever lie to you, Lee. He was here to negotiate with the duke to attack the army we're amassing in Luray."

"How could they have known?" asked Maressa.

"The Duke sent a message to meet with the royal family to talk about eliminating the senate so he could take over Fornesio. Apparently, they both had the same plan to get rid of one another. Donahay intercepted the message and sent Victus to gather an ally against us."

Maressa leaned back on the rail, "Smart plan on his part. We wouldn't have stood a chance with the empire at our front and Fornesio at our back."

"Only, we got here first, and now the senate is with us. Lucky timing, really. I wonder if we'll meet some of his messengers in Vishnin, or Gashimar."

"We should assume we will," said Maressa. "Clearly he knows what we're up to. At the very least, we know he'll be ready for us. We should be prepared to encounter The Red Five, or some other of Donahay's servants at every port."

"Agreed," Drogon replied.

"Wait-" Lee heard his voice grow louder, "So you killed them? You killed the Duke and Victus?"

"We had no other choice, Lee. It was us or them."

Lee was silent for a moment. Suddenly, his eyes widened, and he ran towards the stairs below deck, "Oh no, Stein!"

Lee ran so quickly that he tumbled down the last of the stairs, without losing his momentum. He crashed into the wall with a bounce, jumped up, and kept running. Then, he cleared the central room and charged through Stein's door.

"Stein - I'm so sorry, but I..." Lee stopped.

Stein was standing over his bed with an opened pack, exposing ropes, rations, and other items for travel and torture. He didn't turn his head or stop cramming into the pack, "I'm leaving."

# XI

## <u>Splitting the Party</u>

*"... I promise to kill for you," Stein said coldly. "Anything that threatens you or that needs to die; I will kill it. I think it's a good thing that this is so hard on you, but it can't keep you down forever. I don't have the same problem. Killing is easy for me - always has been. We can play off each other's strengths; it will be good for both of us." Stein's promise to Lee.*

Lee's mouth hung open in disbelief, "Where... are you going?"

"To kill Donahay," Stein said with conviction.

"Aren't we going there together?"

"No, I'm going alone."

"Why?"

"Alone, I will be able to slip in *without* an army. I know the Crystal Palace better than anyone. Alone, I can leave now and have my hands around his throat within a week," Stein said while reaching past Lee for a belt of potions.

Lee stepped aside, "That's it?"

Stein kept packing.

"That's it?!" Lee shouted.

Stein was still packing.

"So, you're going to try to take on a demigod alone? The whole plan to gather allies and take back our home wasn't happening fast enough for you?"

Stein kept his calmed tone and hands grabbing items around the room, "You wouldn't understand. This is something I can do; I can stop this—*now*."

"So, this is you running *towards* Donahay, and not running *away* from Victus?"

Stein's eyes drifted across the room and fell upon him with the weight of an anchor. There was a chill in his stare that felt as if it dropped the very temperature in room.

Lee took a breath, expecting frost to be carried in his exhale, and continued, "We have a plan and it's working. Maybe not exactly as we hoped. But we have Luray, Vian, Fornesio; that's all of the Vian Kingdoms to help us stop him."

"Not. Enough." Stein annunciated each word, "Every day that we wait more people fall to him. They are either slaves of his mind-control or killed; buried and paved into the foundation of *his* new world."

"We are going to Vishnin and Gashimar, maybe **Ferece** and **Chun**, too. We'll get more people to join us."

Stein stepped towards him, his voice booming, "How long would you have us wait, Lee? Do you need to wait until there is *no one* left in the Radiant Empire to save? What good is stopping Donahay if we have to kill every dominated man, woman, and child to get to him? We don't need to drag this on, I can stop this, now."

Lee swallowed hard and stepped towards him, "If you really believed that, you would've done it already. You would've gone off on your own before we even made it to Luray. And you know what? I would have us wait until we are ready. All you'll be doing by going there to get yourself killed is making us weaker. Stein, you are the strongest of us - we need you here."

Stein hesitated, "Drogon is the strongest of us. He can join the nations together in case I don't get to Donahay."

"*I* need you here!" Lee yelled.

Stein's eyes softened.

"You said you'd look out for me, keep me safe, and make sure I never had to kill anyone. How can you do that if you're not here? How can you do that if you're dead?" Lee fought back the tears in his eyes. "I'm sorry about Victus, but you can't throw your life away because of it." Lee annunciated, "You. Promised!"

A raspy voice came from the hallway carried by a hard accent, "*We* need you both, Scrap."

They both looked to the door in suspense and after a few dragged steps, a green-skinned man appeared in the doorway. He stood wrapped in bandages. His lean build comparable to a partially starved human, with the jaw and teeth of an orc. The **half-breed**; Garf.

He nearly collapsed in the doorway before Stein caught him and they both sat on the floor.

Lee slid over on his knees and hugged him, "Garf, you're awake!"

"Not so tight," Garf said weakly, "It was hard to sleep with all this yelling."

"I'm sorry," said Lee.

"I was joking," he replied. "Scrap, do you mind grabbing me some food? I'm starving."

"Of course!" Lee stood and ran from the room, his feet racing away towards the galley.

Garf leaned back against the doorframe, breathing heavily, "How long was I out?"

Stein thought for a moment, repositioning himself across from Garf, "Almost a month. We were starting to wonder if you'd ever wake up."

"Me too." Garf smirked. "Heard you and Lee going at it. What did I miss?"

Stein sighed, "You should probably try to rest before taking on some stress."

"I've done nothing but rest for a month. I want to get outside my own head for a bit. Been trapped in my thoughts for a month - ya know?"

"Well," Stein started, "The short version is that I killed Victus, and now I'm packing to go after Donahay by myself."

"Victus was the long blonde-haired guy? Had some people shoot and stab me? The **kai** that tried to kill us?"

"Yes."

Garf scoffed, "Good riddance - to the void with him."

Stein stared at him, remembering how dense he could be, "Victus was my brother, Garf."

His face twisted as he sat silent for a moment before mumbling, "Sorry for your loss."

Stein leaned back and tilted his head up to the ceiling, "Lee doesn't understand that I *need* to do this."

"Do what now?" questioned Garf.

"Go after Donahay alone, and end all of this before there has to be some great war. Killing is what I do best, so I should try. The politics is better left to Drogon, anyway, even if it's just as a backup plan."

"Maybe," Garf replied.

"That's all you have for me?" Stein laughed.

Garf threw his hands in the air jokingly, but found himself wincing in pain from the quick movement, "What do I know? I've been out of it for a month! You know what you need and if you think you need to go—go. I'll look after the kid."

Stein stood, grabbed his pack, and stood in the doorway. He turned back towards Garf, "I will end this."

"You're not gonna say goodbye?"

"It'll be easier this way."

Garf nodded, "Anything you want me to tell the kid?"

He moved quickly and silently towards the stairs, "Just that I'm going to keep my promise."

"I don't know what that means, Stein."

"He will."

Stein avoided every creaking step and ascended into the salty spring air. He made his way across the deck silently, observing Maressa untying a rope from a cleat down on the dock and Marlow adjusting the rigging, readying to sail.

As Stein met the top of the ramp, Drogon's voice carried from behind and reached his ear with a softly spoken, "Be careful."

Stein turned to face him.

"You're not going to try to stop me?" Stein said.

Drogon smiled, "I know that once your mind is set on something, you have to see it through. Just know that while you lost a brother today; you will always have family here." Drogon reached out his hand.

"I know." Stein shook it firmly, "We'll see each other again once this is all over."

He turned and descended the ramp. Maressa and a few dockhands were helping to get the *Yoshi* out to sea. He walked past them before stopping in place. Thoughts were racing on how he would get back to the Radiant Empire, but that wasn't all that was on his mind. While he didn't know Maressa well, he still felt there was something left to say to her.

Stein approached Maressa, "Drogon is the best man I know. Take care of him."

"I intend to," she smiled. "You should really head back on the ship, we're just about to raise the **gangway**."

"I have some business to take care of, but I will meet up with you in the Radiant Empire."

Maressa wore a look of confusion, "Okay, sure. Safe travels, Stein. I look forward to seeing you again."

The sun began to set, painting the port in different shades of orange and red. Stein walked into the crowd of merchants and navigated through the kiosks, eager to sell the last of their pastries before closing up for the day. He picked some up to snack on and loaded up his pack. Stein sat to eat them and watched as the *Yoshi* sailed towards the horizon. While he had no doubts, he suddenly lost his appetite. He packed up the rest of his pastries, completely reckless about the amount of crumbs that would be covering his torture devices. *Like Donahay would complain,* he smiled to himself.

Stein spotted a few small vessels that he would be able to captain alone. While it would cost him extra time, it would be within his ability. He kept searching as he wanted to keep his options open and planned to wait until nightfall anyway. Of course, there was always the option to hire a crew, but once they arrived in the Radiant Empire, they would be killed, or worse - and Stein only wanted a demigod's blood on his hands.

After another hour of surveillance, darkness fell over the docks. The sweet smell of croissout was carried away with the ocean breeze and the shops were silent; save for a few that were rushing to finish closing. Stein made his way to a small sailboat he spotted earlier that would fit his needs and stepped aboard. It was silent. Whoever owned this ship was either away or quietly waiting inside. His eyes searched the docks for any passersby when he noticed something familiar. There was a shadow of a larger ship at the far end of the port. If his eye hadn't seen it before, he would've dismissed it for a distant, black cloud. Once he made it out, the details came to the surface; dual masts and double-axe shaped anchors. The *Splinter* was in Fornesio.

Stein vaulted from the sailboat and headed towards the far end of the port. It didn't take long for him to arrive at the base of the ramp where was he was met by a familiar dwarf - the new captain of the *Splinter*. He wore fitted brown and black leather armor that complimented his ponytail and long braided beard.

"Edgar," said Stein.

Edgar met him with a handshake, "Aye, if it be Stein. I thought you were aboard the *Yoshi* and heading towards Vishnin? We were to set sail at dawn to meet with you. You see, we had an issue with some rats that slowed us down."

"That's a bit of a story. My question to you is what is the captain of a ship doing guarding the ramp?"

"Old habits I guess, eh?" Edgar shrugged, "And once my scout told me you were heading over here, I thought it'd be best to great you me-self."

"You knew I was here?"

"Aye. Don't know why, though."

"I'm looking for passage," said Stein.

"Then why leave your ship?" Edgar laughed.

Stein paused a moment, "Drogon is leading the way to unite kingdoms against the Donahay and the Radiant Empire. I am going to get into the Crystal Palace, myself - I'll kill him before that battle becomes necessary."

"Sounds crazy." Edgar replied, "I like it!"

Stein smiled, "I had a feeling you would."

Edgar turned and started up the ramp with Stein, "Now when you say, 'get into the Crystal Palace by yourself', do you mean that we would get to storm the castle with ya?"

"That would undoubtedly be suicide," said Stein.

"That's what we thought about you facing the Axeman."

"Yes, but I did *technically* die."

Edgar stopped and planted fists into his hips, "I'm not saying we go charging in headfirst and blow your cover, but there's got to be something that needs doing aside from dropping you off?"

"There will be, I can promise you that," he replied.

Edgar scurried up quickly and smacked Stein on the back, "That's all you had to say! Crew, drinks down and sails up, we leave for the Radiant Empire in ten!"

Stein's presence alone foretold bloodshed and the crew could smell it. There was a cheering from the deck as the restless dualists sprung into motion. Resting was not the life they were accustomed to and they were overjoyed to see Stein and Edgar approaching the helm.

In ten minutes, the sails were full, and the *Splinter* was skipping across the waves. With one moon new and the other waning crescent, the blackness of the ocean blurred with that of the sky. It appeared as if they were sailing straight into the void itself. For Stein, it felt appropriate. He left Edgar at the helm and leaned over the railing.

Stein's mind drifted to thoughts of Lee and the others. He knew they were heading towards Vishnin, a secluded and self-sufficient village of **florens** that cut ties with the rest of the world generations ago. While known to be suspicious and unwelcoming of outsiders, as well as trained and capable warriors, they weren't rumored to be violent, and yet having never been there; he didn't *know*. The uncertainty briefly plagued Stein's thoughts. He was confident knowing Drogon could talk his way out of a hostile situation, Marlow could cleave any threat in two, Maressa could outclass a fighter *or* mage with ease, Lee would keep the party together, and Garf...well he would be stuck on the ship and couldn't cause any trouble for the rest. With this, Stein stared into the darkness, lost in his thoughts.

A sweet female voice met his ear, well pronounced words spoken with tenderness, "It's nice to see you, Stein."

Stein turned to whomever was speaking to him and emerald eyes peered back at him, "Hello, Gwynn," he said.

Her fiery hair swayed in the breeze, "I would've come to see you sooner, but I had to see to the crew first."

"It's fine."

"While I am truly happy, I'm also surprised to see you here. What made this sudden change of plans?"

Stein turned back to face the abyss, "Donahay has somehow learned of our plans. He knew we were gathering forces outside of Luray. We've had to make moves sooner than expected."

"Do you think he's ready to organize an attack like that already?"

"I don't think he is, yet." Stein replied, "He was trying to ally with the duke here in Fornesio. If he's looking for allies, then he isn't ready."

Gwynn leaned over the railing at his side, "We may have arrived a while after you, but my scouts gather information quickly. I heard a bit about what you're talking about. The Duke was assassinated, you know?"

"I know."

"So were his assassins."

Stein faced her, "I know."

She sought to console him. Tentatively extending herself as her eyes measured him before taking the plunge and slipping her arms around him. "I am so sorry, Stein. I can't imagine what you're going through. Victus was a great man, he deserved so much better than this."

"I'm not *going through* anything," he snapped and stepped away from her. "I know what needs to be done, and I'm going to see it through."

"Sure," she said, leaning back over the railing. She quickly realized that her sympathy was unwanted and felt the need to change the subject, "Is Lee back with the *Yoshi*?"

"Yes."

"How does he feel about this plan of yours?"

"What do you think?" Stein scoffed, "He hated it, but it's not his decision to make."

Gwynn stared up at the dim light of the moons, "No, but I imagine he misses his father, and cares enough to be worried about you."

Stein opened his mouth to speak, but no words came out. He remembered a conversation in Luray with Lee and Gwynn. When she mistook Lee for his son and neither of them corrected her. Both of them rather liked the idea and knew it without ever speaking of it.

Gwynn looked back towards the faint glimmer of ocean, "I'm sorry, that was insensitive. I know it wasn't an easy decision for you to make, either."

"It's fine," he said coldly, "Helps me remember why I don't want you with us on the *Yoshi*."

She faced him, "Oh, because I helped the boy be heard? I thought it was because I had to trick you into saving a *child*, my sister?"

He stared back at her, "You being manipulative has something to do with it, yes."

"It took a lot for me to decide to come say *hello* to you, Stein. Half the things you've said to me are threats, the other half are just cold. I was hoping we could put it all behind us; the bad and whatever good we *thought* we might've had. Now, I know that you are just too caught up in your own darkness to let anything good into your life." Gwynn turned to walk away, "I'm done talking to you - goodnight, Stein."

His voice followed after her, "I have plenty of good things in my life; great friends, and son."

"Oh yeah?" She didn't turn around or break stride, "You look awfully alone out here... where are they?"

Stein's eyes swam in the blackness of the tide with both reflection - and anger.

M.C. Grimm

## Fear the Reaper

*"And each seed planted will potentially bloom, in its own time. And all those that bloom shall eventually wilt and die; returning to the soil of the land to provide essence to future life. So is the natural order of living, so the circle of life."*
*Circular Harmony - A Tribute to Hyriel*

Stein had killed in the past for lesser offenses than his confrontation with Gwynn. In that same past, it never would've bothered him. After all, this was a solo mission. For reasons unknown to him, he found himself more upset than enraged. Her words illuminated the clear fact that he was alone. However, while he knew he was doing the right thing, he felt as if his heart was in another place.

All the private rooms below deck were luxurious and assigned to different leadership aboard the *Splinter*. Edgar kept the Axeman's old room, with an ornately decorated door and a plaquae that read the word *Gold*. The chief mate or second in command, whom Stein had not met, was in a room labeled *Silver*. Leaving the third private room to Gwynn as the scout leader; her door written with *Bronze*. The numerous members making up the rest of the crew strung up hammocks in the belly of the ship. Stein preferred his solitude on deck at the bow.

He was nestled with his back against the railing, sitting upright and using his pack as an improvised pillow. He found a comfortable position fairly quickly, after all, it wasn't the first time he'd done this. The ship rocked gently as it cut through the wake, the sound of water spraying off the hull and scent of the mist accompanied each calming bounce. Stein fell asleep, or so he tried.

As his eyes grew heavy and he finally quieted his thoughts of the day, he became aware of an eerie silence around him. The spraying noise faded away and the salty smell was gone. Stein shook himself awake to witness that everything around him was in black and white. It was strangely illuminated by the light of the moons, but the absence of color was unnatural, yet familiar. There was no hint of the warm night wind, but a chill hung in the air. He stood and walked across the deck without a single creaking groan from the boards, or a slap from the rigging sounding around him.

A voice hissed through the void with an unnatural malice. Like a long contemptuous exhale, carrying disgust with a feminine tone, "Steinnn." It held onto that final note.

Stein looked quickly to see a slender, cloaked figure perched up in the crow's nest. He shifted back as she leapt down, the unmistakable black deathrobes were motionless in her fall. She landed a few spaces ahead of him with a bended knee in complete silence.

"Death is not the end, Stein. There is nothing to fear," she said.

"Fear?" He smirked, "Do I look afraid?"

Her face was hidden beneath the cloak, but the red glow of her eyes fixed on him as her head tilted slightly, "No, you look lost. That is because you are not meant to walk this world any longer. It is time you come with us."

Stein started to pace in a circle around her, "You *know* I'm not coming with you."

"It isn't my purpose to force you from here, though I will if I have to. In order to accept your next life, you must accept that this one has come to an end. Otherwise you will remain lost in the void until you cease to exist altogether."

"I don't really believe in all that," he said, "so you're wasting your time."

"Very well then, Stein. Do remember as you stumble through the void that it didn't have to be this way. To be honest, after what you did to one of my kind, I was hoping you would say that." She lifted her arm and stretched out a skeletal hand from her robe. The light blurred and created a blackened flash. There was an audible snap as the blackened shaft of a scythe appeared in her grip. At the head, a smoothly curved blade shined. It was immaculate and the edge gleamed like a razor catching some unknown source of light from this gray place.

"One last thing," Stein started, "I was expecting one of you to find me a lot sooner. What took you so long?"

"We've always known where you were, Stein. We only needed to wait for you to leave **Mora's** chosen."

"Mora?" He paused. "*We?*"

Stein spun on his heel to see a second, hulking, reaper creeping over the rail behind him. In an instant, the figure likewise summoned a scythe to his boney hand. The red glow of his eyes peered out from beneath his hood. His voice was throaty and deep, "It matters not. Mortal affairs are no longer your concern."

A reaper stood on each side of him. Stein's eye drifted back and forth between them. He was still and calm, "*Mora's chosen*; are you talking about Lee?"

"Yes," the female reaper replied, "his abilities had an effect on us."

"What? He's a cleric - he's just a boy," Stein said.

"He is *Mora's chosen*."

"What does that even mean?"

"The boy has..."

"It is irrelevant," the male reaper interrupted, "Tethered to a fate constructed by gods. It is a destiny that is not yours to walk and no longer within your grasp."

"It is completely relevant," Stein protested. "He is my son, and his fate is his own. It doesn't belong to you, or even Mora! And you have no idea what is within *my* grasp." Stein slid back his right foot and held his hands out before him. The emptiness between his palms twisted the air in a similar darkened flash. Appearing in his hands was the obsidian shaft of his scythe, with the long, crooked blade - roaring with flame.

"You defy nature, the very balance of life and death. And further you would defy the will of the Goddess of Mercy?" the woman spoke with conviction.

"For my son, I would defy Death, himself."

The male reaper's eyes glared at him, "You are aware that he is not of your blood? He is not your kin."

Stein sighed, "He's adopted... you must've been an orc in your life, am I right?"

His eye narrowed as he dropped down into an aggressive stance.

"You are hopeless," the woman said, "The void beckons your name, Stein. "

They said simultaneously, "May your nonexistence spark new life through the realm," as they both heaved their weapons and slashed forward.

Stein leapt straight up, feeling, and hearing the air slice beneath his feet. His offhand grabbed part of the rigging with a swing and he kicked off the center mast to nimbly land further towards the bow. Both reapers were now in front of him. He crouched down, holding his scythe at his back, and gesturing with his hand, "Come."

The reapers dashed towards him, weaving between one another as they approached. Their movements were silent, it was as if they were hovering across the deck. The woman reached him first with a flying kick that narrowly missed. With sheer agility, she planted the butt of her scythe onto the deck and raised her body horizontally, lunging forward with a vaulted drop-kick. Even though he was able to get his block up, the force behind her attack staggered Stein back towards the rail.

Before he could regain his footing, the man was towering over him. The first swipe was slow and easy to dodge, but the second was quick and precisely aimed at his neck. Stein leaned backwards over the rail as the reaper's blade whistled past his face, cutting free strands of his white hair.

Stein lifted off the rail and thrust his boots into the man's gut. It shoved him back towards the mast with a stumble. Embers fell in the air as he twirled his scythe in front of him and advanced towards the woman. She bobbed and swayed between the spinning blade until her back met the rail. She dropped under a vicious slash and rolled past him with impressive acrobatics.

The reapers stood side by side again, and begun a synchronized butterfly spin with their scythes, stepping towards him with a quickening pace. The sound of slicing air was only broken by the periodic clang of the two blades glancing off each other in their advance. It was impressive for Stein to witness; these two reapers must work together often. Otherwise, they have similar fighting styles from their life, or maybe their experience as a reaper. If that was the case, they might be more predictable than he originally thought.

Stein stepped back further, avoiding the blur of blades. He spun on his heel, darted towards the rail, and leapt off of it and through the air. He soared over the spinning blades with a twist, and while midair made a single, precise cleave towards the reaper below him. He landed further back, near the center mast on a knee and stood slowly. A grin covered his face and he raised up a large, orc-like skull, impaled, red glow fading from its eye sockets and the torn hood from a deathrobe falling away. The male reaper's headless skeleton fell to the deck. It blew away as dust in the nonexistent wind while emitting a faint sound like steam.

"Korthius," the female reaper muttered as she picked up his scythe, "you shall be avenged."

Stein watched the skull crumble to dust, "Avenged? You came for *me*. You brought me to this place. You thought you could best me, claim me, and reap my soul? Make no mistake, the only vengeance will be mine. Before I allow your *non-existence to spark new life through the realms*, what does it mean that Lee is Mora's chosen?"

"For you—it means nothing."

"He means more to me than you could imagine, reaper. What does it mean?"

"That the goddess has plans for him."

"You said before that I had to be away from him for you to come after me. Why?"

The reaper stared him down, "Remain ignorant, Stein. You are damned. I have wasted enough words with you!"

"I feel the same."

The reaper was holding a scythe in each hand, allowing her hands to slide towards the lowest part of the shaft in order to maximize her reach. She spun and slashed as wild as a tornado. Each of her swings were met with the metal-on-metal clang of

Stein's block. He stood poised and controlled, even he was surprised to be so calculating in a fight. Each of her moves was chaotic and sloppy, not anything like the finesse he faced before slaying the other reaper.

Stein leapt back and ducked under a swing, allowing one of the reaper's weapons to bury into the center mast. The wood cracked and split partially but wedged it in still. She gave it a mighty tug, but it wouldn't break free easily. Stein seized the opening and jabbed her hard across the face. Her hood flew back, exposing the off-white bone of her skeleton. Unlike other reapers Stein encountered, this one still had bits of tightened, decayed flesh still clinging to the bone in some areas. Stein was unmoved and followed up with an upward cleave.

Her scythe wielding, skeletal arm spiraled through the air. It bounced over the rail. The elbow was partially bent, and it was still clutching the death scythe as it dropped through the ocean surface in silence, without so much as a ripple. She leapt back, outstretching her remaining digits with ferocity.

Stein threw his weapon over his shoulder, "You still want to continue this?"

"We are relentless. We are going to reap you. I am here to claim you and there is nothing that can stop me."

Stein's crooked smile curled up his face, "Oh, I can think of one thing." He lowered his blade and started towards her.

There was a flash of blinding light and Stein was forced to cover his face. He felt the salty breeze and the warmth of the sun stinging his skin. The rigging was slapping against the mast with a familiar thud, and the deck was alive with the Splinter's crew stomping around him. He was standing amidst the desk, flames continuing strong on his scythe.

Edgar ran up to him, "Where ye been? We thought ye were lost to the deep!"

Stein squinted, shielding his eyes from the light, "I was on deck all night. Wasn't I?"

"Well if you were, we couldn't find you."

Stein dissipated his scythe, "I'm here now. Where are we?"

"Not far, I'm afraid." Edgar stepped towards the center mast, a recognizable crack and split deep into the wood with a blackened singe near it. "We had some weather in the night. Lightning damaged our main sail. It'll be repairable, but we're relying on the others to carry us a great distance."

"Lightning didn't do that."

"Aye, it did. We heard it below deck. When I came up, it was still burning a bit through the rain."

Stein stared at it, his mind racing with questions. *Could the reapers attack have caused a lightning strike? Coincidence? No, it couldn't be coincidence. Perhaps both realms are more connected than I thought.*

Edgar's voice was a float in the sea of his thoughts, "Alas me boy, we're not much further from Fornesio than last night."

Stein started towards the helm, his eyes now mostly adjusted to the sunlight, "We have a change of course."

"Already? Where to?"

"To Ferece. We're going to make a quick stop and then rejoin the *Yoshi* in Vishnin."

Edgars stern face melted into sorrow, "Why? What about *stopping the war before it starts*?"

"We won't make it there. We were met by two reapers last night. I killed one and the other escaped. They're not done coming after us."

"After you, ya mean?" Edgar interrupted.

Stein pointed to the mast, "After us. As long as we are distanced from Lee, the reapers can come here."

"Lee? What does the boy have to do with anything?"

"I'm not sure, but I think I know someone who can help me find out. She's only a couple of hours out of the way."

"As long as there be blood for the crew; they were reborn when they heard about a battle against the forces of Donahay at your side."

Stein smiled, "There will be plenty of blood where we're heading."

# XIII

## <u>Welcome to the Shire</u>

*"The land gives us our life, water from the streams, food of the
forest and soil. To seek the outside world is to deny the paradise
and bounty we have been blessed with here in our homeland and
introduce it to those who will wish to steal it away from us. Praise
Tiaya and praise the paradise of Vishnin."*
*A Prayer to Tiaya*

The island country of Vishnin was painted with all the red,
orange, and yellow the sunrise could offer. It was massive and
rivaled the size of Fornesio. From a distance, it appeared as a
wilderness of dense forest that traced the entire perimeter and as
far within as the eye could see. Large, brightly colored birds soared
through the air, and the squeaks and snarls of wildlife gave no hint
of civilization within. The *Yoshi* encircled the island and found no
ports or ship landings of any kind. The party dropped anchor and
gathered on deck.

Lee was leaning over the rail, admiring the sound of
foreign creatures. The green and tan of his robes showed fading
from their time in the sun, "This is beautiful!"

Drogon rested a hand on his shoulder, "It is."

"Why are we here?" asked Marlow.

"Simple," Drogon replied, "we're looking to recruit them
against Donahay."

"I've never heard of this place," said Lee.

Marlow nodded with agreement.

"They don't interact with the rest of the world by choice, hence no ports," Drogon explained, "But within that wilderness is a formidable village of florens. They have been self-sustaining for generations off a land as bountiful as you can imagine. It's no paradise, no, it is riddled with dangers. They're survivors. They are led by a champion; his name is Tarkus, Tarkus Milton, if I remember right."

"What are florens?" Asked Lee.

"Don't call them halflings." Maressa leaned over the rail next to Lee.

"Really?" said Lee, "Why?"

"It's offensive to them. Who wants to be called a half-being of any kind?" Maressa said.

"What about Garf, he's a half-breed...or is there another name for that?" Lee asked.

Garf was sitting on the deck, his legs outstretched and sipping on a tankard of what is most certainly ale, "Aye Scrap, I'm a half-breed, alright. There's no soft way to say it."

"Is there another name for your...race?" Lee was unsure if just asking was being rude.

"Believe me, half-breed is the least offensive name to call me."

Drogon approached Garf and reached down his hand. He moved his fingers, beckoning Garf to hand over the tankard. Garf let out a grunt and handed it over. With a sniff, Drogon proceeded to pour its contents over the side and tossed Garf his canteen. He sipped at it with a disgusted look on his face.

Drogon rejoined the group, "It doesn't matter what race you are. I don't know you as a half-breed or son of Simone. I know you as Garf, be the best version of that you can be."

"Aye." Garf held up the canteen with a toast and pressed it to his lips, twisting his face in disgust.

"Drogon, I don't understand," Lee started, "if the florens here in Vishnin are cut off from the rest of the world, why are we here? Why would they even help us? Wouldn't we be better off trying to get the army of Chun and Ferece?"

Drogon joined them at the rail, "They're not known to be open to outsiders, sure - that's why a small party going shore would be best and less intimidating. Tarkus, the Champion here, was trying to change all that. From what Stein mentioned to me back in **Sundale**, Tarkus is looking to open Vishnin to the world. And to be honest, likely sooner than later, Donahay will set his sight on the precious resources here. This is not the introduction to foreign politics I would want them to have, but this is going to reshape the world for all of us. If they were going to help us it would be because they are intelligent enough to see that it is now or never and that they trust in what we tell them enough to act. As for Chun and Ferece; they have been at war with one another for as long as history can remember. It is a *fact* that they will not put aside their differences for anything - not even the end of the world. Stein and I felt this strongly enough to avoid charting the course altogether."

"Whatever started all that with Chun and Ferece?" asked Maressa.

"I have no idea," Drogon laughed, "and I don't think they know, either."

Garf stood up, "Let me get my blades and I'll be ready to go."

Maressa peered at him, "Go where?"

"If only a few are going to shore, I want to be a part of it. I need to move around a bit." Garf replied.

"I think you should relax here at the ship, maybe stretch out, and do some exercises," Lee said.

"Exercises?!" Garf argued, "I'm no lass, Scrap, the only exercise I do is with my blades or my..." he trailed off as he went down the stairs to gather his things.

"Garf, bring a crossbow instead, and please," Drogon yelled towards Garf and then turned to Maressa, "Maybe keeping him at a distance will help. Up for babysitting with me?"

She smiled, "I'd love to."

Lee jumped in place, "I want to come too, I can help."

Drogon thought for a moment, "It may be dangerous—are you sure, Lee?"

"Yes, of course."

"Okay. I have a feeling Garf won't take no for an answer, and the safest place for him is as close to you as possible. So, you can come, but you stay right next to me or Maressa, understood?"

"Yes, yes definitely!" Lee ran downstairs to gather his things.

Marlow stomped away, frustrated to yet again be stuck on the *Yoshi*. He began tending to the rigging and tightening some loosened knots.

"Don't be like that, Marlow. We're going for a *less* intimidating look with Vishnin. We'll get you out there in Gashimar," Drogon shouted to him.

Drogon slanted back on the rail next to Maressa who was still looking out over Vishnin.

"Beautiful place," she said.

"You're beautiful," he replied, a tenderness carried in his tone.

Maressa turned around, pressing her elbows back onto the rail next to him. Her arm and hand grazed against him ever so gently, "Last night," she whispered, "the way you held me was beautiful. It was perfect, actually."

"I couldn't agree more." He leaned in to kiss her, but heard footsteps running up the stairs.

"I'm ready," Lee planted his staff firmly on the deck.

Garf was right behind him, "Aye, can't wait to get some dirt under my boots again."

Drogon, Garf, Maressa, and Lee climbed into a small rowboat off the starboard side. Marlow took to the pulley to lower them down slowly. His strength as a minotaur made working the load of their weight an easy task. As the rowboat met the water, the party saw only Marlow's horns looming over the rail. They detached the rope of the pulley, and Drogon took to rowing towards the shore.

The tide was coming up and did much of the work to bring the rowboat in. Drogon jumped out once the water was knee-deep to pull them up into the sand. He offered each of them his hand to help them out but held tight an extra few seconds to Maressa.

"Now what?" Garf asked bluntly.

Drogon's eyes traced the tree line, "Let me get my bearings and we should be able to move towards Vishnin."

Garf proceeded to stretch out his shoulders and legs with awkward poses making sudden, sharp movements and grunting.

"I'm not sure that's the right stretches," said Lee.

Garf twisted quickly, a painful groan escaped him as his joints cracked, "Oye, I'm just loosening up a bit. Hard to when Drogon won't let me drink."

Drogon was still taking in the surroundings, "You're useless when you're drunk."

"That's ridiculous, I'm *Garf* if I am drinking or not," Garf replied.

Drogon's stare fell upon Garf, "Yes, you most certainly are." He pointed towards the tree line, "Over there it looks like a path. Lightly traveled, but I'd bet it leads to Vishnin."

"It might be patrolled," Maressa added, "We should stay sharp."

The pathway was narrow and kept them moving single file. Drogon led, followed by Maressa and Lee, then Garf at the rear. As they moved through the forest, they observed some of the most sizeable spiders they have ever seen. Perched up on a tree branch was a large, well-nourished bird with shiny, bright blue feathers. They moved past slowly as it watched them, and the bird opened a spread of pearlescent tail feathers that rose several feet and into the canopy of leaves above it. While exotic, this bird had a majestic beauty that the party could only describe as divine as they admired it. They continued along the path for about an hour. Drogon knew they must be almost at the center of this forest.

The woodland creatures became quiet. Drogon held up a fist to signal a stop. A signal that Garf only noticed when he tripped over Lee and met the trunk of a tree with his shoulder, and a loud thud.

Before they could draw their weapons, a faint movement in the brush around them became an eruption of leaves and loose branches. A dozen florens sprung out, instantly surrounding the party. They were camouflaged with paints and foliage attached to their clothing. They stood between four and five feet tall and wore elaborate leather and hide armors that demonstrated a fine craftsmanship. Each had a crossbow aimed or a sword, sharpened and drawn, ready to attack.

The group raised their hands into the air slowly.

"We mean no harm," said Drogon, "We've come to meet with Tarkus. I am Drogon of the Radiant Empire."

As the words of *Radiant Empire* crossed his lips, the florens stepped closer, showing contempt and rage towards the very name of the kingdom.

One of the florens stepped forward with flowing brown hair waving behind her. She lowered the weapons of the man and woman next to her. Her armor was slightly different in that it revealed the smooth, pale skin of her neck and chest. It also consisted of a shortened cape off the shoulder clasps. Her tone carried authority, that of a seasoned veteran, "Stay your weapons for a moment." The other florens took a step back. "I am Ary of Vishnin. What is your business with Tarkus?"

Drogon kept his hands at shoulder height, "He sent word to the Radiant Empire some time ago looking to open conversation. We're not sure what his intentions might have been, but there is a lot going on in the world that I'm sure he'd want to be aware of."

"So, then you're not with them?" Ary asked.

"With whom?" Drogon probed.

She said, "The two men and woman in red."

"A woman? It couldn't be...did she have white hair, red eyes? Crimson armor with golden trim?" said Maressa.

"Yes," Ary replied, "what do you know of them?"

Drogon relaxed his shoulders, "They're called The Red Five. They attacked us out at sea."

Ary scanned them up and down, "And yet, you still live? With what I've witnessed, anyone whom they wished dead would have met **Tiaya**."

"A lucky cannon shot blasted that woman, Iris, clear off our ship. We used the opportunity to get away." Maressa looked to Drogon, "How could she have survived?"

Ary's face was stern, "No one could survive a canon blast. We must be speaking of different people. This woman, a dark-elf, fought like a demon with a goliath and elf in similar armor. They attacked in the night two days ago: murdering two of our scouts and four of our guard. We did not expect such power from three warriors." She hesitated. "I will tell you this, since I don't believe you are with them; Tarkus is dead. It would seem that was their goal because they left soon after. The dark-elf, skipping and singing as she left."

A brief silence.

"Tarkus is dead?" asked Garf, "Is there someone else we can talk to?"

Drogon shot him a silencing look before turning back to Ary, "We are sorry for your loss. The death of a leader is a most difficult time."

"Your kindness is appreciated, yet unnecessary. Those warriors were of the Radiant Empire, so it was *your* people that did this - even if you are unaffiliated with them," she said.

"I understand your hesitation to allow us in, but there is something terrifying going on out in the world and those warriors are only the start of what is to come. We need to speak with your people," Drogon said.

Ary glared at him, "Are you threatening us?"

"No, we're here to help," Lee offered.

"What makes you think we need your help, child?" asked Ary.

"With the dangers that lay across the sea; we need each other's help more than ever.," said Drogon. "And his name is Lee Cheng, the Master Cleric from the Radiant Empire. He can help any of your people who might be wounded from the attack."

Ary looked over the party and took a moment to think of what to do with them. "I am intrigued on what this world threat might be. It's become apparent we are not as informed or isolated as we hoped. I will allow you into Vishnin should you agree to relinquish you weapons from here on. I would also like to ask you, Master Lee Cheng, if you would tend to one of our ill."

"Of course, I will." Lee parted with his staff.

Drogon handed over Rayne, but was left with his shield.

Maressa, likewise, kept her shield.

Garf gave them his crossbow and all but one of the thirteen knives and daggers hidden on his person. The last one, he knew they couldn't find without a most intimate search.

Ary and the other florens of Vishnin kept them surrounded as the group was escorted through the forest. The trail wound through shrubbery and tall trees with brightly colored leaves. The entirety of the walk they heard faint chirping and song of birds and wildlife. The deeper they hiked, the more potent a smell of dampened wood was carried on the wind.

At last, the party broke through the tree line to see a large open field - it was the most vibrant green of rolling grass hills they had ever seen. In the center of this vast field was a cluster a small, reddish, wooden huts and cabins that were nestled near to one another. The structures were partially covered a similar vibrant moss and vines of brightly colored flower tangled up along them.

What disturbed this immaculate bond with nature was the hundred florens that were hurrying around the field rolling boulders and dragging freshly downed trees and lumber. Many were soiled and carried an air of exhaustion about them. Surrounding the village was a partially constructed wall. Presently it was only five feet tall, but the supports looked as if it would stand twenty feet once it was completed. Only a single foundation was laid for a gate to enter.

They walked through the dirt-worn paths of Vishnin. The people distanced themselves from the outsiders, stopping their work to pierce the party with judging stares. Some whispered, others spit on the ground, but all of them wore a look of fear or anger.

"I'm not so sure we're going to get the help we're looking for here," whispered Maressa.

Drogon hurriedly replied, "Without Tarkus, I'm not sure either, but we're already here and we have to try."

They followed the sway of Ary's long brown hair as she led beyond the gathered workers and through the village of small, meticulously landscaped homes. At the center of these houses was an elaborate town square, complete with a center stage and various gazebos, benches, and swings. The decorative gardens surrounding the square were brilliantly colored with blues, yellows, greens, and purples.

Here, there were many florens organizing chairs and tables of foods as if setting up for an event. Atop the stage were several cushioned seats and a podium. On the north side of the square was the largest building in Vishnin yet and set apart from the rest. It was constructed of a blackened, dark wood, seasoned by the sun and weather for an unknown and timeless period. They were led up to the porch and stopped.

Ary turned to face them, "This is the **Champion's Estate**, Tarkus' former home. Vyran is inside, he is the one you'll want to speak to."

"Is Vyran the next Champion?" said Drogon.

Ary was hopeful, "That remains to be seen."

"Is there an election process?" asked Maressa.

"No. It is a spiritual trial. Vyran must complete the **Trials of the Champion** in order to become the leader of Vishnin. Until he or any worthy floren completes the trial, we are in an idle period of focused survival. For the first time since Tiaya blessed us with these lands, we are worried that the world seeks to destroy us.

We're building walls to defend ourselves," Ary explained, "This is not his home, at least not yet. Vyran is grieving, you see. Tarkus was like a father to him. I know he is under a great deal of pressure to step into the role of Champion - it's what the people need of him. But he is a family man, I don't think it was ever the path he wanted."

Drogon nodded, "I understand. May we speak with him?"

"Yes," she answered. "I have told you what we are going through so that you will understand there is much emotion surrounding him and to choose your words carefully."

"We appreciate that," said Maressa.

Ary continued, "May I bring your cleric to check in on Kreia? Our **shaman** has been struggling to relieve her sickness."

"Absolutely. Would it alright if Garf stayed with him?" said Drogon.

"That would be fine."

"You have a shaman? Here?" Lee asked excitedly. "Can I meet him?"

Ary began leading Garf and Lee towards one of the neighboring houses, "*Her*. Our shaman is a woman, and her name is Gala. She is an elder and practiced alchemist.

"Oye, she sounds more like a witch to me," Garf chuckled.

Ary smiled, "She prefers *shaman*."

As Ary, Garf, Lee, and a handful of the floren guard walked down the dirt path; Drogon and Maressa stood at the bottom of the step with the remaining guard loosely positioned around them.

One of the guards spoke, "We'll be out here. Vyran is inside. Come back out this way when you're done."

"I'm curious, why would the escort stop here? You kept a tight leash on us through the entire town so far," said Drogon.

The guard laughed, "The escort was for your own protection. Your Vyran's problem for now."

Drogon responded with a nod and both he and Maressa started up the stairs.

The wood of the stoop was similar to that of the building. Every inch was blackened as if it was scorched by some intense and consuming blaze. Lashing lines ran up the planking, showing where flames once licked up the building like a hungry monster, unable to devour its prey.

Given the smaller stature of the floren people, the size of the door surprised them. The door was eight feet tall and spanned the entire width of the stoop; nearly six feet. It was similarly scorched with an axe-shaped handle protruding out. The blackened wood of the handle was rubbed smooth from use.

The door was massive but to their surprise, it opened smoothly given the enormous weight of it. They stepped into an open kitchen and dining room. A table was centered in the room with books and papers thrown about and at the head sat a floren man. His sandy blonde hair was cut short and matched the scruff that traced along his face and chin. Bloodshot blue eyes were affixed into a journal he clasped in his hands. His voice carried an educated and defined pronunciation, yet cracked with sorrow as he spoke, "What is it that you want from me?"

Drogon and Maressa approached the table but did not sit.

Maressa gripped the back of another chair, "We came to meet with Tarkus and heard about what happened here. We are sorry for your loss."

Vyran didn't move his eyes from the pages, "About two days too late to meet with the Champion. What is it that you want with *me*?"

"We're not sure," Drogon answered. "Tarkus sent word to the Radiant Empire some time ago about opening up communications with us. I assume he meant to open trade. Do you know anything about that?

Vyran inhaled quickly through his nose, "Tarkus always wanted to experience the world outside of the shire. He was trying to sell the people of Vishnin on his vision of learning your cultures and sharing the bounty of Tiaya since I was a child. I was his biggest supporter to send that message out and believe me, there were many objections to sending it out. I never would've supported this if I knew it would get him killed."

Drogon pulled out a chair for Maressa and then for himself. As they sat down, Vyran closed the journal and looked at them.

Maressa leaned in, "We don't know exactly why The Red Five came after Tarkus, but we don't think it's because he wished to open up to the world."

Vyran stared back at her, "They were *your* people, weren't they? How do you not know?"

"We aren't with The Red Five," Drogon assured him, "They tried to kill us out at sea not long ago."

"That's fortunate you did not meet the same fate as our Tarkus," said Vyran.

"The Red Five is a group of mercenaries from all over the world. Right now, we believe they are working for Donahay," Maressa explained.

"Am I supposed to know who that is?" Vyran asked.

Drogon rested one elbow on the table, "Donahay is a demigod. He possesses the power to dominate the minds of others and has taken over most of the Radiant Empire. We think it's possible he wants the resources you have here and looked to assassinate Tarkus to weaken your people."

Vyran pounded his fist on the table, "He's succeeded! Vishnin and the entire world is a lesser place without a man with the character of Tarkus! We have no Champion."

Drogon and Maressa exchanged a glance. They communicated the grief and hopelessness they felt within Vyran.

Drogon started, "Vyran, I know this feels like the worst possible time—because it is."

"There really is no good time for these kinds of things," Maressa continued, "There is no good time to lay our heroes to rest. There is simply the here and now when it happens and how we react to it. How we become more in order to make up for having a world that is even less without men like Tarkus."

"Ary brought us here to speak with you," said Drogon, "Why would she do that?"

Vyran looked to her, "Ary seems to be under the impression that I should attempt to take on the title of Champion, but that is not what I have ever wanted with my life. I only wished to be a husband and father, but even that escapes me. I feel it all being pulled away. And that, no, that is not something a Champion does—a Champion doesn't lose."

"What do you mean?" asked Maressa.

Water welled in his eyes, "My wife, Kreia, is sick. Our shaman hasn't been able to heal her, and so I watch her slip further away as the days pass. And if it wasn't enough to be helpless as my sweet Kreia wrestles death; my son suffers the same illness."

"You think it was The Red Five?" Drogon probed.

"Unlikely. They attacked two nights ago and killed Tarkus. It was clear that was their intention. My Kreia has been sick for weeks and Ryker, a few days," said Vyran.

Drogon's yellow eyes gleamed, "I am so sorry to hear about your family. Ary brought one of ours to check in on them."

"I appreciate that, truly," Vyran's words radiated his sincerity. "So you have shaman among your people, as well?"

Maressa explained, "I feel we're not familiar with what your shaman do, exactly. There are great healer's outside of

Vishnin who we refer to as clerics. A skilled cleric could attach severed limbs or even bring someone back from the dead."

Vyran shifted in his seat, "That sounds like an amazing and terrible power."

"Like any power, it could be used for either end - I suppose," said Drogon.

Vyran tipped his hand in agreement, "Our shaman, Gala, she can create remedies and potions that cure most ailments, but certainly not death. I have never heard of one being resurrected outside the blessings of Tiaya - not by any mortal woman."

Drogon spoke with pride, "Our friend Lee is a Master Cleric. I have seen him resurrect two men with my own eyes."

"I have seen one of those miracles myself," added Maressa.

"This power Lee wields, where does it come from?" asked Vyran.

Maressa turned to Drogon, "Wasn't he born with these abilities?"

Drogon thought for a moment, "You know, I have never asked him that. My apologies, Vyran, I don't know. Most clerics or sorcerers are born with their gifts, so beyond that I am not sure if it is divine, pactful, studied, or something else entirely. His father was also a Master Cleric, but I don't believe he has studied to have his level of skill."

Vyran took a deep breath as if a weight was lifted off his chest, "It doesn't matter, I was only curious. I have great hopes for what he might do for my wife and son. My family's health has been the greatest worry on my mind. Now perhaps, I could focus on some other issues."

"Is there something else on your mind?" Maressa probed.

Vyran studied them a moment as if reading their intentions. He decided to trust them further, "You're too kind... Our shaman tells me that we are to suffer a devastating attack in five days time. She tells me that a small-albeit-powerful band, perhaps these *Red Five*, are waiting in **Hell's Crater** to the north. She tells me how I, and I alone, can take them on - element of surprise or something to that affect. Perhaps Tarkus could have..." he allowed a silence as he reflected on the name, "Tarkus was a father to me, I supported everything he believed in whether it was popular or not. So, if my destiny awaits at Hell's Crater, what choice do I have? Regardless of what I believe to be true or logical, I have to go," answered Vyran.

"I told the village about Gala's prediction but they seem to believe I will meet my death and that The Red Five will come to extract vengeance against them. So I encouraged them to fortify and they decided to build a wall. For all I know, that is what is exactly what is going to happen, so who am I to say otherwise? While I'm not their Champion, for the time being they respect me enough as Tarkus' right hand to do just that."

Maressa spoke softly, "This is a lot of faith to put in your shaman. Your people are building a wall and preparing for battle and what if she's wrong? Or what if she's right and you find yourself up the Hell's Crater alone against an army?"

"Walls can be leveled even more easily than they are erected. And I am one floren among thousands; my people will survive without me."

Drogon and Maressa were silent.

Vyran scoffed, "That's all of my woes. You've heard them. I am unfit to be Champion."

"That's a lot to take on all at once. Lee, is one of the greatest clerics in the Radiant Empire. Ary was bringing him to look in on Kreia and your son," said Maressa.

Drogon stood up, "And maybe we can help you with Hell's Crater. Unless you feel you have no other choice than to go alone for this victory."

Vyran thought for a moment.

"And it's not my place to say, but I don't think being a Champion means you always have the answers. I think sometimes it means admitting that you don't know and being open to the possibilities - improvising along the way. All you need to be a leader are followers; they'll inspire the best in you." Drogon added.

"You're too kind...I doubt you traveled across the seas to help me with my family, so I ask again; what was it that you wanted with me?" asked Vyran.

"Let us help you with your wife and son - then grant us some of your time to speak again," replied Drogon.

Vyran rose, "What would you need with something so fleeting as time?"

Maressa stood and pushed in her chair, "To talk about the *woes* of the world."

It was the first time Vyran smiled, "Done. Know that by helping me with my Kreia and Ryker, you will have returned *my world* to me, and I will owe you a debt I can never repay. Let us go, the hour is upon us for Tarkus' memorial, and then I would like to check in on my family."

"Of course. Thank you for speaking with us. And also, for trusting us in your village," said Drogon.

"I don't trust you," Vyran added, "I do trust that you are capable, and that you didn't murder Tarkus. For now - that is enough. To trust you even to that capacity is a decision I don't make lightly in these uncertain times. Don't make me regret my decision."

Maressa assured him, "We have no ill-will for your people."

Vyran crossed the room and opened the door, stepping aside to allow them through and into a beam of spring light, "Oho!" he boasted, "I'm not one who cares on your *intentions*. Should your actions bring harm to my people, willful or not, you will find yourself at the painful end of my axe."

Drogon nodded respectfully, "I understand. And I share those same feelings for the safety of my party while we are here in your village," he smiled, "Only I have a sword, I suppose."

Vyran nodded in response, his eyes glancing down to Drogon's empty sheath, "I understand."

Drogon held out his hand in the open doorway, "Rayne," he said.

The guard carrying their equipment was pulled off from his seated position and tumbled through the dirt. The remaining floren guards stood and readied their weapons, unsure what just happened before their eyes. While their other equipment laid scattered in the pathway, Rayne cut through the air with precision hilt-first to meet Drogon's open hand. He quickly slipped it into his sheath.

Vyran laughed as he led the way out of the Champion's Estate. "Give them their weapons back."

# XIV

## <u>The Cure for Guilt</u>

The blackened structure disappeared in the distance behind them as they made their way back to the town square. Citizens gathered around, huddled tightly on benches, and lining the dirt streets. It became evident to the party just how vast the population that resided here was as the mass grew, filling the standing room, and sparing only the decorative gardens.

There were three chairs atop the stage and two were occupied. In the first, closest to the podium, sat an older floren woman with braided, gray hair that fell to the middle of her back. Her skin revealed her years of life that eroded to permanent wrinkles of a smile, though now strained to that of heartache. In the second was an ancient, corpselike floren. His skin was wrapped tightly over his skeleton with his eyes sunken into the blackened sockets of his skull. The loose robes draped over him were faded and soiled in a way that no amount of washing could ever truly clean. Behind the chairs and podium was a blackened casket, the lid closed, and both surrounded and covered with ornately arranged flowers, the sweet scent of which was carried on the breeze.

The woman stood and the crowd went immediately silent. She approached the podium, but when she reached it, she stood over it, hiding her eyes behind the thin strands of hair. "My friends and family - thank you for coming out. Today I give my best friend, husband, and Champion—Tarkus, back to Vishnin. This is the hardest thing I've ever had to do...stand here like I wasn't completely broken and alone and tell you how things are going to be okay. I know they will be, in my heart of hearts; I know *we* will be okay. I just don't feel okay myself right now. I don't know if I will ever again."

The old man pushed to his feet and slowly moved over to her side. He rested a hand on her shoulder.

The woman continued, "These are uncertain times. Uncertain, unprecedented, and perilous times. We need our Champion now more than ever. It is the duty of our strongest to embrace the role and be the pillar of strength we need so desperately right now. I have my feelings on who should attempt the trials, but I will put no pressure on anyone to take on this lifetime obligation. Any worthy floren will be able to complete the Trials of the Champion. Please, decide quickly. Thank you." She sobbed softly and stepped off to the side of the stage.

The crowd was silent for a moment before some soft words of encouragement found their way to her.

"We're with you, Jayde," said one of the florens.

"It *will* be okay!" Yelled another.

The old man stepped up to the podium and the square fell silent again.

"I know we have some outsiders in the crowd, so I'll introduce myself." The man started, shaking in place as he spoke, "My name is Gampy. I am the eldest floren to call Vishnin home and have been blessed by Tiaya to work these lands my hundred and thirty-four years. Yesterday, I buried a great man. One of the greatest men I done ever known."

A man's voice erupted from the crowd, "For Tarkus!"

"My man!" Gampy pointed to the spectator and continued, "Building his tomb was hard for me; harder than any tomb I have ever constructed. *Why?* You might ask. As I dug for our beloved Tarkus, I had to reflect on our previous Champions, Taid, and his predecessor, Amwer. A line of great heroes whom I have been commissioned to create their final resting place. There's no good time to lose a loved one - no good time to lose a hero. But sometimes, oh sometimes, it happens when we are least prepared for it. And here we are now asking *what do we do now?* And I told you, I have seen many great men and women move on to the graces of Tiaya, but there is always a need for another to step up and fill those shoes. That's right. Where there is a will, there is most certainly a way. And there is only one man I know fit to be our Champion. He is that man right there." He pointed out with a shaking hand, "Vyran. Vyran, we need you to take on the trials and lead us."

Jayde came back to the podium and stood beside Gampy, "Vyran, it must be you. Tarkus always knew it would be you. He believed in you and I think I speak for all of us when I say, we believe in you too."

Vyran marched steadfast to the stage and the crowd parted for him as he moved. Ascending the stairs, he hugged Tarkus' wife and shook Gampy's hand before taking the center. He hung his head for a moment in a silent meditation. The gathered florens waited with anticipation. He cleared his throat, and stood tall, "These indeed are large shoes to fill and I scarcely feel I'm the person to fill them. These people took away our Champion and there's nothing more that I want then for this village, this great village, to survive. I look back at all of our hardships, of all the things we've gone through... and I know that we can endure *together*. Everyone has been trained and everyone knows what needs to be done. If you have any doubts, we can hash this out, but now, we need to prepare for what's to come in the next five days. Day in and day out, we need to fortify this area. We need to rekindle the lessons of our military training and do everything we need to do so that when these invaders arrive, they know the people of Vishnin were *never* the folk to cross."

Cheering and shouting echoed in the town square. The gathered florens showed their patriotism with fists in the air and confident boasting.

"We'll beat them down!" One shouted.

"Grind them to bits!" Added another.

Another floren laughed, "They'll regret ever stepping foot in Vishnin."

Gampy stepped out next to Vyran, holding his hands in front of him and waving downward at the mass of people, "Easy now, y'all," he started, "Vyran, we know you are a leader - there's no doubt about that. But will you do it? Will you clear the Trials of the Champion?"

Vyran looked out over the crowd, his blue eyes reflecting the intensity of the sun. The long silence of his stare made the hesitation clear - he was conflicted. A lifetime commitment of dedication to the role of Champion. His own needs and that of his family would become second to the needs of the people; this was as much a sacrifice as it was an honor. A heavy weight burdened his heart and mind. He took a deep breath, "Yes."

While the citizens of Vishnin roared with excitement, Vyran's face was flush with remorse. It felt to him as if he attended the funeral of both Tarkus, and of his way of life. He descended from the stage and started a slow walk down the dirt streets of residences, rubbing at the blonde scruff of his beard. Drogon and Maressa followed quickly after him.

The fading voice of Gampy sharing stories of Tarkus and great things he did for the community throughout his life. As tales faded in the distance, Maressa and Drogon shared a look of concern for the potential future Champion.

Vyran moped onward, aware of their judging looks, "I'm fine - really. It's just a lot to process at once."

"It would be overwhelming for anyone to manage what you're going through," Maressa said. "Is there anything we can do to help?"

Vyran nodded, "With luck, you already have. I am taking you to my home. I pray to Tiaya that your cleric has been able to make sense out of this sickness my wife and son are suffering from."

"You mentioned your shaman already tried to treat them," Drogon started, "Did she have any idea what made them sick?"

"No," Vyran replied, "She spoke with the spirits and blended some disgusting brew together that she said would buy her more time to diagnose them. It's been long enough that I have been helplessly watching my Kreia..." he stopped, staring down at the first porch step.

They arrived in front of a cabin constructed of the familiar reddish lumber. Vyran's family home stuck out from the others around it, not because of the structure or size, but from the garden and moose-themed decoration. The garden itself was as meticulously kept as the others were but featured a particular variety of color. Many tall plants surrounded the porch with thin, long leaves that grew off of a tall stalk. The top portion of the stalk was covered in quarter-sized, pink flowers that smelled of berries and citrus.

Vyran stepped up, opened the door, and led them inside.

They entered into a living, dining, and kitchen area with two doors on the far side that entered into adjacent rooms. Lee was sitting at the kitchen table lazily sipping tea with his hand planted firmly into his cheek. Garf was eating from a bag of dehydrated fruits and laying out on the sofa with a muscular black dog. Upon seeing Vyran, Drogon, and Maressa in the doorway, the two of them stood up quickly.

"Hi!" Lee approached them, offering his hand to Vyran, "I'm Lee; it's nice to meet you."

Vyran shook his hand, "Yes, you too."

"I hope you don't mind, I helped myself to some tea while we waited for you all. And Garf was feeling hungry."

"Oye!" Garf protested, "You immediately rat me out like that?"

"You're holding the bag," Lee said.

"Maybe, Scrap, but they hadn't seen it yet," Garf replied.

"They definitely saw it," Lee joked.

Garf pulled the bag that was now hidden behind his back, "No, they didn't."

"We did," said Vyran.

"Certainly did," Maressa added.

"I didn't even know you were *trying* to hide it." Drogon shrugged.

Garf placed the now empty bag on the table and sat down, "Aye." The dog came up beside him, licking at his fingers.

Vyran pulled out a chair for Maressa but did not join the two at the table. "It's fine, make yourselves at home. And half-breed, please stop feeding my Lily, you'll spoil her further," he laughed, "Lee, did you already check in on Kreia and Ryker?"

"Yes, and I have something to show you." Lee quickly led Vyran into one of the bedrooms.

This bedroom was hot with fever and small enough that the few items of furniture appeared cluttered. It was clearly the room of a twelve-year-old boy with a quality wooden sword and metal puzzles scattered about. Books were piled on the floor next to a child-sized bed including: *Ode to Tiaya, Swordsmanship v.1, Lord of the Jewel, Hallowed Death by H. Potter,* and others. The bed was slightly outgrown by its occupant and centered in the floor with a dresser and chest to either side. A floren boy was laying still, a cloth on his forehead.

Vyran squeezed himself to sit on the edge of the bed, "He's not burning to the touch and he has color in his face—*amazing*. What did you do?"

Lee shushed him, gesturing that the boy was in need of rest, and ushered him out of the room and into the next.

The master bedroom was only slightly larger than Ryker's. Centered on the far wall was a double bed with a nightstand on either side. A floren woman lay to one side of the bed, covered with a sheet up to her breasts and breathing softly. Chestnut hair bunched atop her head in a thick bun that, if undone, would easily flow to her hip. Smooth, pale skin ran with beads of sweat to trace her features as her hands rested on her stomach. To say she was beautiful would depreciate the true radiance of her loveliness.

Vyran sat on the edge of the bed and rested his hand over hers on her front. He leaned down to kiss her head.

She groaned softly, "Vyran?" her voice was hoarse.

He jumped, "Kreia? My love, you're awake!"

"I feel…" she slowly leaned over the side of the bed and heaved onto the floor.

Vyran rubbed her back and helped her back to the flat of her back, "It's fine, don't worry, I'll take care of that. When did you eat something?"

"Earlier today," she said weakly, "After...medicine."

Lee handed Vyran a readied glass of water and began cleaning the floor, "Right after I gave her a treatment, she woke up. I wanted her to try eating something right away and she kept it in for a good while. That's a good thing! Next time she eats, she should be able to keep it down."

Vyran leveraged Kreia up and helped her sip at the water. She took the glass from him with both hands, finished it, and laid back down.

Kreia handed Lee the glass, "Thank you, precious. I am just going to rest."

"That's a great idea. We'll be just outside if you need us and I'll check in on you in a bit," Lee said with a bow.

Her eyes closed with a groan and she quickly fell asleep. Vyran kissed her forehead and both he and Lee left the room, closing the door silently behind them.

Drogon, Maressa, and Garf joined Vyran and Lee in the kitchen area.

Vyran refilled the glass of water and began drinking, trying to slow his racing thoughts. He stared out of the window as he spoke, "I am grateful for everything you've done for my family. In a way I could never repay, I am indebted to you." His eyes swelled, "You've saved them from the clutches of death - given me my world back."

"You don't owe us anything," said Lee, "Mora gives me the ability to heal, and I use it."

Vyran crossed the room towards Lee and embraced him, "Thank you."

Lee was muffled in his grip, "'Er 'elcom."

"I need to ask," Vyran started, "How did you do it? Gala has been caring for my Kreia for weeks and I've witnessed her health steadily declining. You're here for a few hours and - she's awake and eating! How is that possible?"

Lee's eyes darted around the room and found Garf who was nervously fidgeting at the dog's head.

"What's wrong?" Vyran asked.

"I'm not sure how to say this," Lee mumbled.

Vyran stared at him, "Then just say it, you've done nothing wrong."

"Okay. Just know that this is a tricky situation to be in," Lee raised his hands.

Vyran was confused, "What situation?"

Lee took a deep breath, "**Barcenic root** would grow perfect in this climate, probably somewhere in the woods surrounding your village. Kreia was further along with... the condition. That helped me figure it out in order to treat them both. It was a bit of a stretch at first, but once I tasted this," he lifted a wooden cup and pitcher from the counter, "it all made sense."

"Gala's brew? What's wrong with it?" asked Vyran.

"Barcenic root is used to make poison," Lee explained, "The bitter taste, and even the smell, is from some other herbs mixed in to mask that this is just plain poison."

Vyran's look of relief faded away, "That's impossible. Gala isn't capable of murdering one of our own."

Lee lifted an olive-green vial from within his robes, "The medicine I gave them was just an **antidote**."

"You're *sure* it was a poison in that pitcher? You know how serious this is, Lee," Drogon asked.

Lee nodded, "Yes, there's no doubt about it. I wasn't sure how to tell you, that's why I wanted to show you how much better they're doing now after only an antidote."

Vyran sat at the table, silent, staring into void of his thoughts.

Drogon took a seat beside him, "Do you have any idea why someone would want to do this?"

Vyran shook his head.

"You mean why Gala would?" Lee asked, "It was her medicine."

"There's always a chance someone poisoned her medicine, right?" Maressa said.

Vyran kept his gaze on the surface of the table, "Gala was the only one coming in here to tend to them." He stood and began pacing. "She was the only person encouraging me *not* to attempt the trials. She insisted I focus on my family and reminded me how they'd be lost if I was pulled away by the responsibility of leading the village. What if her visions are revealing to her that I shouldn't be Champion? Maybe... I shouldn't be."

Maressa rested a hand on his shoulder, "You have been through so much so soon. You don't need to decide your entire life in this moment."

"But I do," said Vyran. "Every day without a Champion is a day we are unprepared for whatever is to come. Where we cease to progress and stagnate in a mindset driven solely by survival. It is a way of thinking where cultures go to die."

"And that might be true, but that doesn't all fall on you. That doesn't mean you have to take this all on while dealing with the loss of a leader, a family illness, and what seems like the betrayal of a town figure." she added. "You're allowed some time to grieve..."

"You're right." Vyran said as he walked towards his bedroom. "I need a few minutes." He closed the door behind him.

Maressa looked towards the now-closed door, "I suppose some people only need a few minutes to process all that."

"He's going to be okay," Lee said. "Kreia and Ryker are on a quick road to recovery and I'm sure that will help clear his mind."

Garf nodded, "I don't really see what all the fuss is about."

Maressa glared at him, "He buried a father figure, has been watching his wife and son suffer for weeks, pressured to be Champion, and just found out the village shaman tried to kill his family... you don't see the *fuss*?"

"Oye, you don't have to list things like I'm some kind of fodder," Garf said with a wounded tone, "I'm just sayin', people die all the time. People try to kill *us* every day. Imagine if we set up camp anytime someone shot an arrow in our direction?"

"That's insensitive," Maressa sighed.

Drogon's tone was gentle, "Garf, imagine if it was Lee and I that were sick—what would you do to Gala?"

Garf grabbed the hilt of his sword, "I'd gather Stein and we'd slit her throat!"

"Okay," Drogon continued, "Now imagine you and Gala are both public figures and can't just commit murder openly."

"We'd slit her throat while she slept," he replied.

"Let's then imagine that days before all of this, Stein was killed by the Red Five," Drogon added.

Garf was silent.

Drogon's eye feel softly on Garf, "Vyran just lost his Champion, those closest to him are ill, and the one who caused it is a trusted village elder. We'll give him all the time he needs."

Garf sat down on the couch, petting Lily behind her ears, "Aye."

The front door opened abruptly and a floren woman walked in carrying a pitcher, one that matched the one on the counter. She wore shoulder length green and brown robes of leaves and bark. They covered her wrinkled, leather-like skin. Messy, gray hair stuck out in all directions, as if she had flown through the village to get here. It did not appear she noticed them until the door closed behind her. When her eyes looked them over, there was pure shock on her face.

"You!" She yelled. Her voice was as coarse as the bark on her robes, "Who...who are you and what are you doing here?"

"I am Drogon. This is Maressa, Garf, and Lee," they each gestured respectfully, "and you are?"

Her hands were shaking, "I haven't seen you before. You... you shouldn't be here."

"We're friends of Vyran, he knows we're here," said Maressa.

"No, no, no!" She shouted. "You shouldn't be here!"

The bedroom door opened and Vyran stepped out. He slowly shut it behind him. As the latch clicked closed, he spoke. Although he said a single word, his voice carried a fierce intensity at the volume of a whisper, "Gala."

Gala's face flushed to a shade of red, "Hello, V-Vyran, I came by to..."

Vyran's head tilted, "To what, Gala?"

"To-to...to."

"To administer more of you *medicine*? You have been poisoning my wife and son." Vyran began a slow walk towards her as the party moved aside. "I demand to know why."

"Vyran, I don't know what..." Gala was interrupted.

"Enough of your lies, Gala!" Vyran's voice shook the pitcher free from her hand with a crash. "Speak the truth at once, or I will cut that lying tongue from your mouth."

Gala pleaded, "Who are these people? What have they filled your head with?"

"What have *you* filled the blood of my family with - speak while you are still able, witch," he threatened.

Gala took a deep breath and recomposed herself. The warm fear in her face smoothing over to a cold calmness. "You cannot be Champion, Vyran."

"Because *my family needs me*, is that right? To protect them from deceitful witches?" Vyran mocked.

She shook her head, "You will lead Vishnin to ruin."

"Oh, is that so?" he glared, "How?"

"Outsiders," Gala explained, "They will come and go from our beloved Vishnin as they please - claiming it as their own. Our paradise will become as troubled as their own foreign lands. These people bring their problems, wars, and diseases to our doorstep. You, just like Tarkus before you, would welcome them with open arms. You, like Tarkus, would see only the benefit of their goods and curiosity in their cultures and falsely believe that is something worth exposing ourselves for."

"There was a vision of this?" asked Vyran.

"Any *worthy* floren could see this if they would open their eyes. You are blinded by loyalty to Tarkus. Must we make the same mistake with another Champion?"

Vyran moved closer still and was now within arms grasp, "Spell it out for me, Gala. Why did you poison my family?"

She was stepping further and further away until she knocked into the wooden door, pinning it closed, "To save our people from the fate that your leadership would subject them to." Vyran was near enough that she could feel the heat radiating off his face, "I wouldn't have killed them. I'm not without love for you and your family. I simply wanted to direct your focus towards your home life and discourage you from attempting the trials. I knew I couldn't reason with you."

Vyran was overcome with emotion and the muscles in his face began to twitch. His hands were shaking, tightly balled as fists at his sides.

Drogon and Maressa exchanged glances.

"There is something with all that which doesn't make sense," Maressa said as she moved next to them. "Maybe there's more to your ways than I understand, but the timeline doesn't line up. Kreia has been sick for weeks and Ryker for a few days. Yet, Tarkus was killed two nights ago. If all of this was to keep Vyran *focused on his home life*, how could you have possibly known something would happen to Tarkus?"

Gala glanced between Maressa and Vyran, her pupils flickering anxiously, "How could I know something would happen? To Tarkus? I don't know wh..."

Vyran lunged forward, pinning Gala against the door with his elbow in her chest. The impact shook loose a painting to the floor with a flop. He leaned into her while drawing his axe, "Speak the truth this instant, or know that these words will be your last."

"Panic filled Gala's eyes, "A vision!" She proclaimed. "Yes! A-a vision."

"Awfully convenient," Vyran muttered, raising his axe to her face, "Kept secret until now?"

Gala groaned and wrestled for a moment in vain before finally surrendering, "Go on then, Vyran - kill me. Take my life as you feel a *Champion* would. An old woman, unarmed, and defenseless."

"You are no simple old woman, you vile witch. You'd put on a show for our guests? The same guests who exposed you as a traitor? You're repulsive," said Vyran.

"I simply did what I felt would protect our way of life...from you and your intentions. From Tarkus' legacy." Gala was limp, being held up only by the force of Vyran's grip. "Do what you will with me, I have no regrets."

Vyran could feel her bones bending beneath the pressure of his arm. His axe shook with anticipation as it grazed the side of her neck. The blue of his eyes could see only shades of red as thoughts of his ill wife and son passed blinding him. He pressed firmly, the razor-sharp edge piercing a shallow wound in her neck. Several thick beads of crimson ran along the edge and dripped over his hand.

"Vyran, wait." Drogon reached out, "This is your place and your decision, but are you sure this is the right thing to do? If you are to be Champion, what would your people think if they saw you like this?"

Vyran's fierce hold on Gala remained. He witnessed a glimmer of hope in her eye, a look that enraged him further. He snarled, "I'm not going to kill her, not yet. Being a commoner, that would mean exile of my entire family. However, as Champion, I would construct a most appropriate form of justice for you, Gala."

"But you *can't* be Champion - you'll ruin everything!" she argued.

Vyran grabbed her by the neck and flung her out of the way of the door. Dragging her in his grasp, he led the party out and down the street. The people of Vishnin looked on, murmuring and speculating with whispers back and forth. He dragged her to the town square towards Ary and two other floren guards.

Vyran tossed Gala to the ground at their feet, "Gala has confessed to the attempted murder of my wife and son. Lock her up in the stocks until I return."

"You can't do this, Vyran!" Gala weakly rested on her knees. "You are not the Champion and have no more authority than I to sentence someone to the stocks."

Ary lifted Gala to her feet and turned to Vyran, "Are you going to clear the trials?"

Vyran spun on his heel, "I'm going right now."

"You can't!" Gala cried out, "We must stop him!"

Ary and another guard carried Gala towards the stock and pressed her down into the structure. She struggled and pleaded as they latched her in place and stood watch, ignoring her cries.

Garf, Maressa, Drogon and Lee followed Vyran through the dirt streets again. Florens gathered, mumbling as they passed.

The familiar voice of Gampy rang out, "What's going on, Vyran?"

Vyran did not break pace nor turn to face anyone as he spoke. His voice carried authority, "Gala attempted to kill my wife and son. She is now in the stocks to protect us all from her witchcraft. I am going to **Tomb Thirty-Eight** and will be back soon."

Numerous voices carried through the streets.

"He's going to attempt the Trials?" said one.

"Think he can do it?" One asked.

"Of course, that's Vyran ya know!" Answered another.

But none were louder than Gampy's, "You can do it, Vyran!"

They continued past the crowds, through an elaborate agricultural area, up a hill, and crossed a bridge over a small stream until they arrive on the outskirts of Vishnin in a cemetery. Nearby, the sounds of florens laboring could be heard as they constructed the vast wall around the village.

The iron gate complained with a loud squeak as they entered. Mausoleums and plots surrounded a manicured landscape of flowers and colorful shrubbery that decorated the entire area. Vyran was focused. He found his way towards a modest mausoleum, a structure of charred black stone similar to that of the Champion's Estate. Over the door was a heading, written in a language the party had never seen.

Vyran turned to face them, "I am indebted to you in more ways than I could ever repay."

"No thanks are necessary; it's the job of a cleric." Lee smiled.

"Not only did you save my wife and son, but you exposed the truth behind Gala and her treachery." Vyran reached out to Drogon, Lee, and Maressa and hugged them. "Thank you. From the bottom of my heart, thank you."

They embraced, appreciating the sincerity and tenderness in the moment.

"Oye, it was nothing," said Garf nonchalantly.

Vyran blinked the pools away, his eyes falling on Garf seemingly unimpressed, "Yes, yes, I'm sure it was." He relaxed his embrace, "From here, I go on alone. This is my trial and whatever awaits is my destiny to face."

Drogon nodded, "We'll go see what we can do to help around the village and await your return."

"Make yourself at home and if anyone gives you a hard time, tell them you're a friend of *ours* and that the Champion will soon return." Vyran moved towards the massive stone door of the mausoleum. With a glow of yellow light, it slid open, revealing an abyss of moving shadows. He stepped inside.

In this same moment, a voice was heard in the distance. Shouting in their direction and carried on the wind. It was Ary's voice and she was yelling out, "Intruders!"

Vyran retreated, but the stone door hurled itself shut with a *thoom* that echoed between the other structures - sealing him inside. He would need to face the Trials of the Champion before he could help his people.

Drogon placed his hand on the door of the tomb and spoke loudly in hopes Vyran could hear him, "We will take care of things out here - go do what you have to."

## <u>Reunion</u>

*"Know the currents of the wind and sea, tame the soil, and conquer the mountainous peaks and abysmal lows of the land – then, and only then, will you know true godliness."*
*Claiming the Heavens - A Tribute to Hosridon*

Drogon, Maressa, Garf, and Lee turned to face Ary. Her face was red, and her forehead ran with beads of sweat. It was clear she had sprinted through the entire city to get here. She keeled over for a moment, a disappointed look over her face upon taking notice that they were outside *Tomb Thirty-Eight* and Vyran was not among them.

Ary caught her breath, "I was hoping to get to Vyran before he started the trails."

"Is there any way we can just - open the door?" asked Garf.

Ary shook her head, "Once the trails have begun, those doors will not open until he is dead or Champion."

"Then we won't see him until he is Champion," said Lee.

Ary smiled, "That right. Alas, that means we are further unprepared. Invaders have anchored off the west coast and made land. They are in the forest and now we must face them without Vyran."

"Vyran wasn't with you when you came for us," Drogon said.

"He was the one who told us to bring you alive. Otherwise..." Ary trailed off.

"I understand," Drogon replied, "We're here to help, let us come with you."

Garf yelled, "Oye! You were going to try and kill us!?"

"Do we need to discuss it?" Ary said, turning to head back towards the village. "Vyran recommended we allow you an opportunity to demonstrate you character - and so we did."

Drogon, Maressa, and Lee followed after her.

Garf stood in place, unsure whether to be insulted or relieved, "And you're all fine with that?"

"You said so yourself, Garf," Maressa was walking with the party and shouting back towards Garf, "people are always trying to kill us."

Garf caught up to the party and they quickly made their way through town. There were no florens working on the only partially constructed walls, and many of the people were sitting around enjoying foods and having merry conversations. They raised tankards towards Ary as she passed. There were even a few raised towards the group.

They kept an accelerated pace as Maressa commented, "This is the first time I've seen the people relax since we've been here."

"You must remember—we've never had outsiders here in the village until the red people," Ary started.

"Red people?" asked Garf.

"The Red Five," Lee whispered.

"Why didn't she say that?" he whispered back.

Ary continued, "In many ways, our people haven't lived such a hard life, or one that is so filled with fear since the days of **Tarasque** and **Vishnin the Strong**. We have been able to enjoy a pleasure of existence with Tiaya. Normally, outside of studies and training, we have one work hour each day. Vyran has been pushing over six hours of work each day and it has taken a toll on us."

"Over six hours? He's brutal." Garf laughed.

Ary faced him and spoke with a calmed grace, "I feel sorry for you, Garf. You, who have never known an easy, blissful life and feel it makes you stronger or better than others. Your hard existence has not yet allowed you to learn the pleasures of appreciating what it feels to truly live. We as a people sometimes take for granted how Tiaya has blessed us. Perhaps once life has returned to normal; you will experience our ways and learn that six hours of work *is* brutal. Life is meant to be lived, not worked." She began her quick walk again, "For now, we should hurry."

They cleared the village and Ary recruited several soldiers along the way with the summoning wave of her hand. As they entered into the western woods, they crossed the area where the party first encountered Ary and the other floren guard. The dense trees kept them tight together and walking in single file. Light fiultered down in various hues of orange and yellow and bathed the canopy in a wash of color. The forest was quiet.

As they rounded a ridge of stone, the sounds of combat could be heard. The slicing of a weapon and whistle of arrows was muffled by the bark and rocks around them. A most sinister snarl echoed. It could be faintly heard coming from the south and caused the party to stop in their tracks.

"The intruders?" Drogon asked.

Ary shrugged, "If it is, then the **Yokai** will make short work of them. That snarling is no ordinary beast, it is a forest demon."

"You mean there's demons out here with us?" Garf looked around nervously.

"Just the one. He normally awakens around sundown. It lives in the southern part of this forest so don't worry, we will be safe." Ary explained, "We are near the coast, we can check on your vessel and see theirs as well."

"Let's go." Drogon said.

After a very brief walk, their boots met the soft, yet supportive cushion of sand. The white grains were painted the orange of the sunset and left a sloppy trail of footprints behind them. Ahead, at the edge of the sea, a lone dwarf was sifting through items in his dingy.

Ary drew her sword but kept a distance between them. "What's your business in Vishnin?"

The dwarf didn't look up from the boat, unsure what was aimed upon his back. The fitted brown and black leather armor he wore matched the ponytail and long braided beard, "Aye lass, we're looking for some traveling companions that were aboard that there ship," he slowly pointed at the *Yoshi*. "Have you seen 'em?"

Maressa peered around his back, "Edgar?"

He turned deliberately, "Maressa?"

She ran in to greet him with a hug, "We couldn't really make out the *Splinter* with the sails down. I thought you were heading for Luray?"

"Aye, until Stein came aboard asking we take him to the Radiant Empire." Edgar sighed.

"You made it there and back already?" asked Drogon.

"We were attacked," he scratched his head, "err that's what Stein said, anyway."

"How do you not know?" said Maressa.

"It's funny. Stein was attacked, the rest of us were just fine. He made it a mission get back to you as fast as the wind could carry us. He made sure to stop and pick up a **shifter** though."

"A shifter from where? Why?" Drogon questioned.

Edgar shrugged. "Something about requesting help against Donahay from Gashimar. Apparently, this woman has a direct line to the **Padrino**. I can't tell you much."

"Her name's Jua," said Drogon. "That's perfect, Stein really made it all come together."

Ary kept her sword ready, "How many of your people are going to come to our land? We have been open to you, but you ask too much of our hospitality. I ask your friends stay back."

"I apologize, Ary," Drogon started, "Edgar can wait here with the others." He turned to Edgar, "Where is Stein and Jua?"

"The three of them went into the woods, looking for you and the fabled Vishnin."

Ary sheathed her sword, "They are likely already dead."

Drogon's eyes widened, "You think it could be... they were fighting the **Yokai**?"

"We have to help them!" Lee shouted as he started kicking up sand towards the woods.

The party took off at a sprint into the forest, dodging branches and leaping over downed limbs. They navigated back to where they heard the sounds of combat earlier and started south. In a small clearing, they bore witness to the battlefield. Blood was sprayed about and collected in pools on the ground. Faint embers still burned at the trees with wide slashing cuts deep into their trunk. A broken arrow laid nearby, floating in a puddle of blood. They kept still to listen. Silence met their ear along with the earliest noises of the creatures of night.

Lee cried out, "Stein!"

They scanned the shadows around them.

"The Yokai has haunted these woods for a century," Ary said, "We should leave before it returns. There is no hope for your friends."

"No, we have to find them!" Lee argued.

"Your friends are dead," Ary said bluntly.

Lee shook his head, his face twisting to a look of both desperation and disgust, "You don't know them at all. You have no idea."

"You may look for their bodies if you'd like, but I have no intention of dying here." Ary turned to Drogon, "I recommend you carry the boy and leave this place at once.

The snap of a twig drew their attention as they turned with weapons drawn to face the source.

Stein, Gwynn, and another female figure stepped out from the shadows.

"Writing me off, already?" Stein smirked.

Lee ran in with a hug, "I'm glad you're alright."

"Good to see you, Lee. I have quite the story for you later," Stein said while balancing a large, swinging sack on his back.

Ary looked them up and down, and glanced over the carnage that surrounded them, "How is it you still live?"

Stein dropped the sack in front of him and loosened the drawstrings. He slid the wrapping down to reveal an enormous severed head. It rested on the ground to the height of his hip. The creature had blue skin and several horns broken off from atop the crown. Its mouth was partially agape, allowing thick fangs to protrude, and blood to dribble out from its lip. Its yellow eyes were bloodshot and frozen open with a look of fear, or was it rage?

Stein was unmoved, "I killed it before it killed me."

"You had help," Gwynn added.

"Did I?" Stein joked, "I see a lot of arrows in the trees and not as many in the **oni**."

Gwynn glared at him, "The arrows pierced through it. I did not miss a shot. They're covered in its blue flesh," she pointed towards an arrow.

"Just saying, didn't feel like I had a lot of *help*," Stein shrugged.

Gwynn copied his stance mockingly, "You wouldn't have reached its heart if it wasn't riddled with holes."

The mysterious woman seemed to be enjoying the conversation. Her eyes followed whoever was speaking, and she wore a satisfied look on an otherwise plain face that concealed her age entirely. What was most apparent was the shimmer of her skin in the twilight - similar to that of a metallic texture. Her voice was soothing and carried an excited tone, "These two have been quite exciting to travel with. Luckily, I know something about oni."

"You're the shifter Edgar mentioned," Garf stated.

Drogon moved towards her, "Jua, it is a pleasure to finally meet you. I am Drogon."

Jua's eyes narrowed with her smile, "Drogon Mcleod? Brother of Duncan?"

"Yes," said Drogon, "It's a pleasure to finally meet you."

She reached out to shake his hand, "The pleasure is all mine. How is your brother?"

"Still back in Rayton, so I am unsure - but I am hopeful."

She nodded assuredly, "As am I. Stein asked me to send message to the Padrino on behalf of your company. I sent it before leaving Ferece and received a response once we arrived here. The letter I received asked me to read it to you and Stein at once when you were together."

"She wouldn't let me read it until we caught up with you," Stein added.

"The Padrino has his ways. What were you doing in Ferece?" asked Drogon.

"What - you expect me to spend every day back at the clan in Gashimar? Even I need fresh air. And a break from the politics certainly helps," she joked.

Jua reached an empty hand up into the air. With that, a squawk from a nearby tree darted quickly through the air and a crow landed upon her shoulder. The movement was obscured in the settling darkness of twilight that they didn't see when the bird planted a scroll of parchment in her hand. The crow remained poised and silent, save for the metal *ting* of a choker around its neck that read *Giza*.

She broke the wax seal, unrolled it, and began reading, "To Sir Drogon, Prince Stein, and their adventuring companions. I received your message asking for help in an upcoming battle against Donahay. Unfortunately, at this time..." Jua became saddened, "Gashimar will be allocating its military might towards an alliance with Donahay. This provides us an interest in maintaining our agreed independent free will as well as the territories of the Vian Kingdoms. I look out for my own first, I'm sure you understand. Best regards, Padrino."

The group stood silent in the forest as the insects of the night came to life around them. Ary cracked a **star-rod** to illuminate the clearing in dim light.

The excitement faded from Jua's voice, "I am sorry to have to deliver this to you. The **Nyota clan** knows your cause is just, but not even we could go against the Padrino."

Stein was blunt, "Well, that's garbage."

"Complete trash!" Garf shouted.

"Surely he must know that Donahay will not just give him land and freedom? He is a dark-sorcerer, his ambition is greater than that," said Maressa.

Drogon rubbed his chin, "He's leveraging, maybe even waiting to see what damage *we* can do against Donahay and then move in afterwards to take out whoever is left standing."

"He'd let everyone die just for more land?" Lee mumbled.

Jua shook her head, "He is the Padrino, it is always more complicated than one might think."

Lee was staring down at the ground, "Seems pretty simple to me..."

"I cannot defy the Padrino," said Jua, "The Nyota clan wouldn't dare do that. However, perhaps I can lend you some help from my messengers." Giza squawked with satisfaction as Jua rubbed her neck, "Before I head back, would you like me to relay anything to your allies? I have numerous trained crows at my disposal. They are beyond fast, and always find their target."

Drogon nodded, "Yes. I will prepare some letters for your messengers tonight. Thank you, Jua."

"You're quite welcome. I wish I could do more, trust me; I know how much rides on the success of your quest," said Jua.

"Not to appear ungrateful, but is that the reason you're helping us?" Maressa asked, "Just seems like it might go against the Padrino who seems to want us all dead or dominated."

"He said we can't send our forces, so I won't, but it said nothing about crows. And there was not even a rumor throughout Gashimar before this letter that we were going to war with anyone; Donahay or your allies. Alas, it is not my place to *understand* the Padrino's intentions, but these are my birds. If I'm being honest, it is also because of my relationship with Duncan." Jua looked to Drogon, "Be sure to check in on him for me, okay?"

Drogon peered at her, "A *relationship*?"

She giggled, "Less formal, I suppose."

"I..." Drogon looked around.

Jua's voice grew sterner, "I'll also tell you that I know Donahay's forces are already assembling in the port of the Radiant City. Whatever your plan is - you're running out of time."

Stein was blunt, "How could you possibly know that?"

"My crows were the ones relaying the communications between Donahay and the Padrino. Donahay thinks they're allies," she replied.

"We should head back to the village," said Ary, "Drogon, do you mind addressing what we spoke of back at the beach?"

"Yes, right. Stein, Gwynn, the Vishnin people would prefer less outsiders in their home. Mind hanging out at the ship?" asked Drogon.

"Actually," Ary interjected, "anyone capable of slaying the Yokai would be celebrated among my people. I would like for you to come."

Stein nodded in agreement.

"I'd be honored to see your village, Vishnin is rumored to be such a paradise," said Gwynn.

"I would like to wait back at the *Splinter*," said Jua, "Bring your letters when you are ready for me to send them."

Drogon turned to Garf, "Mind waiting back on the *Yoshi*?"

"Why me?" he protested.

"I'm sure Marlow would appreciate your company. It's been a while since he was able to talk with you," said Drogon.

Garf frowned, "Alright, fine."

"And that Yokai-head is mine, don't forget," said Jua. "Half-breed, do you mind helping me back to the *Splinter* with it?"

"Carry it yourself," Garf replied.

"Actually Garf, it's a favor for me," Stein urged, "I lost a bet and owe her carrying it back to the ship."

Lee was curious, "What kind of bet?"

Stein laughed, "I thought cutting off its head would kill it. Turns out we had to destroy its heart."

"I was right about that, wasn't I?" Jua chuckled.

Stein rolled his eyes, "Yes, you were."

"Fine, I'll carry it for you," Garf said reluctantly.

"You should take this," Ary offered as she pulled another star-rod from her pack.

Jua held up her open palm, "That won't be necessary. I am quite accustomed to the darkness - comes with the job."

"And I see just fine," Garf replied.

Jua smiled and stood aside, watching Garf heave the massive severed head over his shoulder and start towards the beach. The rustling of leaves beneath their feet faded as they disappeared in the veil of darkness.

"Are they going to be okay in the woods now?" Lee asked.

"Yes. With the Yokai dead, there's nothing else to fear in this part of the forest," Ary answered.

Ary, Gwynn, Lee, Drogon, Maressa, and Stein hiked through the crowded forest in silence. They appreciated the beauty of **glowvine,** creating a dim, blue light from the branches overhead and illuminating the canopy of leaves above. A faint peeping and chirping of frogs and crickets accompanied their footsteps that was occasionally silenced by the snapping of a thick branch.

They arrived back at Vishnin just as the two moons crested overhead. Construction of the wall was no further along from when they left earlier. The party navigated through the now familiar streets until they arrived at the town square.

"We don't have outsiders often here in Vishnin, so there is no guesthouse in our village. However, we have room at the barracks if you don't mind bunking up with some recruits," Ary offered.

"That will do just fine," said Drogon, "Before we settle in, how long do the trials normally take?"

"Depends on the Champion, really. I couldn't say. Pleasant dreams," she dismissively gestured two fingers from her forehead and walked away.

"They'll never have visitors at this rate," joked Maressa.

"It's nice of them to let us stay, though," Lee said.

Stein scoffed, "If she wasn't going to, she should've told us when we were close to the ship. I also wouldn't have minded sleeping on the beach."

"The beach would've been nice," Maressa added, "especially on a night like tonight."

"Are you kidding - this is beautiful! You know how many foreigners have walked these streets before us? Probably zero," said Gwynn, "This is an amazing experience. We should really take it in; we may never come back here. I mean, after Stein, they may never allow outsiders again."

Stein scowled at her.

Gwynn shrugged, "You're kind of rude."

"Only to people who deserve it," he replied.

Suddenly, a soundless eruption of light filled the night sky. Rays of green, gold, purple, and blue streaked across the sky as if beaming from the ground itself; seemingly from somewhere nearby. The party sprinted through the streets, chasing the light to its source, and found themselves standing outside the Champion's Estate. Light and waves of energy were pulsing out of the structure as colors painted the glass. With a singular, quiet sound of *thuum*, the light retreated back into the building until at last, only a faint teal glow escaped the windows. They ran up the stairs and threw the door open.

The grand table and chairs had been moved with care and the area rug was folded neatly and tucked aside. Inscribed on the floor, beneath where the rug once covered, was a large circular **glyph** that was still humming with magic. Vyran was standing in the center of the room, his hair windblown as if he had been carried in the clutches of a winged beast for the past hours. His pants were torn from the knee down off his right leg; which was streaming with blood and tattered flesh, gnawed by something with massive fangs. The look on his face was one of both pride and fatigue. He was peering down at what he held in his hands, a **great axe**—unlike any, the party had ever seen.

The handle was crudely chiseled from a clear, blue crystal that sparked with magical energies harnessed within it. At the head, the crystal continued, but an array of colors traced around both heads of the axe. The purple, gold, green, and blue energies, created a featherlike flare at the edge of the blades - similar to the feather of a peacock.

Lee pushed past the group, "Vyran, your leg!"

Vyran was shaking in place as his legs wobbled beneath him. He panted as he spoke, "The **Axe**... **of the Champion**." His eyes rolled back as he collapsed to the floor.

# XVI

### <u>The Champion's Law</u>

*"For one, we love; unconditional and unlimited love."*
*Le Plume - A Tribute to Tiaya*

The tender warmth of the mattress seemed familiar, and that smell, that soothing smell of Kreia. Before he opened his eyes, Vyran knew he was back at home. He kept them closed and laid still, hoping to rest for a few more moments.

Lee's voice came from the far side of the room, "Oh good, you're awake."

"No, I'm not," Vyran whispered.

Lee laughed, "Oh come on. How are you feeling?"

"Like I could sleep a while longer," he replied.

"Alright fine, I'll wait outside with the others."

Vyran heard the door open, a faint sound of pleasant conversation reaching his ear before the door was gently tugged closed. He turned to the pillow next to him and was surprised to find it bare. With wide eyes, he threw the sheets off and stepped onto the floor. Another surprise stopped him in place.

A fresh bandage covered his leg from his foot to his knee. There was a subtle pain burning up his leg, much less intense than he remembered and undoubtedly credited to Lee's care. His leg felt strong enough to support him, maybe even stronger than before. While that was intriguing, there was something else that instilled in him a sense of panic. At first, Vyran thought it might be gauze or cushioning, but from the top of the bandage, thick white fur protruded out. He tried to pull it away and felt the tug on his skin. This white, wolf-like fur was attached. While he studied his leg, he noticed his foot slightly more elongated with a shift in the height of his heel. Vyran sat at the edge of the bed, lost in thought a while longer.

In the dining area, Stein leaned against the wall while Kreia, Gwynn, and Lee sat at the round table. There was a blue tea pot in the center with a plate of cookies beside it. Lee was sure to position himself as near to them as possible. He picked one from the plate as he sat down and made short work of it.

"Lee, how is my Vyran?" asked Kreia, her voice still slightly hoarse.

Crumbs fell to the table, "He's healing up nicely, still some things to clear up when he's ready. He wanted to sleep more and I thought it was a good idea. It's good that we gave him a little space, we were in there all night."

"I still feel I should be in with him," said Kreia, looking anxiously towards the door.

Stein was pouring her more tea, "You need to take care of yourself, as well."

She nodded.

Lee finished the cookie, "We probably have time to go catch up with Maressa and Drogon."

Stein shook his head, "No, I think they wanted some alone time."

"They won't have any *alone* time if they're *together*, now will they?" Lee scoffed.

Gwynn giggled, earning a look from Stein. She cleared her throat.

"I mean that they want to be alone, together," Stein explained.

Kreia smiled, "Oh young love, so sweet you could take it for honey."

"What do you mean?" asked Lee, "They aren't in love."

Stein's face was sour, "Come on Lee, you're going on thirteen now, you must notice these things. They've been giving each other the eye since Vian. And they've been way too *mushy* since we encountered The Red Five."

"I did notice a glow about her," said Kreia.

"Like; *I'm so happy and in love* kind of glow, or the other kind of glow?" asked Stein.

Kreia smirked in response.

Lee leapt to his feet with excitement, "She's pregnant?"

Stein's folded arms dropped to his sides as his gaze fell on Lee, "So you don't pick up on the lovey-dovey stuff, but you know what *the glow* means?"

Lee laughed, "Of course I do! I'm a cleric, I've delivered babies before."

"Call it—mother's intuition," said Kreia, "We women can tell these things. Most of you men are pretty slow to pick it up."

"That is true," Stein agreed, "many of the help around the Crystal Palace had their families living in the castle, and I never knew until I saw another baby crawling around."

"That could be tricky if it's true," Lee stated.

Kreia was curious, "Why? Because you're out at sea often?"

"Because when a dragonkin is 'pregnant', that just means they are going to pass fertilized eggs. When I was taking care of a dragonkin back in Tristian, she passed eight! A few months later, the eggs hatched and needed incredible amounts of attention for at least a year. Dragonkin mature very quickly too, about six times faster than humans. So, after that first year, they are really six years old.  That's why they need so much attention; they're growing up and learning everything so quickly. That pretty much lasts until their third year, by then they are full grown and you probably couldn't tell Drogon apart from them because they're adults - mentally and physically," Lee explained.

"That doesn't seem like a problem," said Stein, "just sounds like we'll need to hire a couple of babysitters," he laughed, "You know, I thought you were going to say it was tricky because Donahay may have taken over the world by then."

Kreia's face reflected the shock in her tone, "What do you mean? Who is Donahay?"

The joyous energy in the room twisted into something anxious.

"They didn't..." Gwynn's voice trailed off.

Stein's eyes fell heavy on Lee, "Drogon didn't talk to them about Donahay?"

"Not yet," said Lee.

"Why not?" asked Stein.

Kreia leaned hard against the table, rattling the teacups on their saucers, "What are you talking about?"

Vyran's voice carried from the bedroom doorway, "It's okay, my love."

"Vyran!" Kreia leapt to her feet and embraced him in the doorway, "I'm so happy you're up and about."

"I feel surprisingly...powerful?" Vyran questioned his choice of words, "I wanted to ask you about that, Lee."

Lee smiled from ear to ear, "I used some advanced healing magic along with some *heartbane* and *eel wheat* mixtures, nothing special."

"No, I mean..." Vyran showed them the fur under the bandage and his misshapen, elongated foot.

"Oh, Tiaya," said Kreia.

"Ew," Stein mumbled.

Lee stood and approached him, kneeling down eye-level to his leg, "This wasn't me, but I couldn't miss it when I cleaned your wounds. I was going to ask you about it; thought it might be a floren thing or something that happens to the Champion."

Vyran shook his head, "Absolutely not. It's none of those things."

"Well, what caused those wounds?" asked Lee.

Vyran's mouth hung open in disbelief. The question connecting different thoughts in his mind to make sense of his condition.

"What is it?" Lee grew more concerned.

"The final trial. I was falling from the sky and landed in a strange, dense forest," Vyran started.

"Like the west wood?" asked Kreia.

"No," said Vyran, "like no place I'd ever seen."

"So literally anywhere in the world *except* Vishnin? Got it," Stein joked.

Gwynn whispered a hiss, "Rude."

Vyran continued, "It was unnaturally dark and the forest was alive with all sorts of mystical beasts. I admired them briefly. **Unicorns** and **wisps** lived here; it was a most beautiful sight! But they fled as if hearing something familiar to them - something terrifying. A great white wolf, as massive as this entire house! It found me, spoke to me, and then...hunted me. It was **Fenrist**. He challenged me to a game of cat-and-mouse, one that I lost. I should be dead; consumed and destined to run as his quarry forever. However, fate had other plans for me because it was then the most miraculous thing happened. A peacock freed me from his clutches. While Fenrist fangs bit deep into my leg and tossed me about like a toy, I prayed to her. It was Tiaya who saved me, I know it was; I felt her grace. She gave me this," Vyran drew a plume from within his vest. It shown brilliantly as blue, gold, purple and green began illuminating around it.

"That's beautiful," Lee and Kreia said simultaneously.

Vyran held it before him, the vibrant colors reflecting in his eyes, "It's divine."

"Sounds great," Stein said dismissively, "so you were bit by the Great White Wolf and now your body is changing into what appears to be a **werewolf** in his image."

"No, not a werewolf," Lee added, "maybe more of a **wolftouched**?"

"He does seem to be in control of himself," Stein commented.

Vyran looked back and forth between them, "I *am* in control of myself."

Lee stood up, "That's great to hear! Let me know if you feel any different. We'll just keep an eye on it."

Kreia was at ease, "Your calmness is reassuring."

"If he's is in control than it must only be affecting him physically. That means he'll be okay," Lee explained.

"*Only* physically..." Vyran sighed.

"It's a good thing and certainly beats the alternative," said Stein.

"What was the alternative?" asked Vyran.

Stein leaned back against the wall and crossed his arms, "Well, what do you do with a feral dog?"

Kreia, knowing her husband, held firmly to his shoulder. Vyran stayed where he was, "I don't want to assume you were threatening me. Who are you, anyway? I haven't seen you with the others."

Arching a brow, he simply replied, "I'm Stein."

Vyran's voice, unknowingly, grew louder as he spoke, "Well Stein, I have no idea where you come from, but around here we try not to threaten people we've just met in their own home."

Stein pushed off the wall and started towards the door, "You're right." When he was nearest to Vyran, their eyes locked and he said, "You have no idea where I come from." He continued his walk out of the house and closed the door behind him.

"Lee, you should really look to remove the stick from your friend's-" Vyran was interrupted.

"That's not a kind way to talk to our guest," said Kreia.

"Kreia, he was out of line," Vyran argued.

Kreia's look silenced him, "He's still a guest."

"It's okay, Stein is a really good person. He's just a little impatient sometimes, and he doesn't really sugarcoat anything," Lee explained, "trust me. Give it some time and I'm sure you two will be great friends."

Vyran looked skeptically towards the door, "We'll see about that."

The door opened again. Drogon and Maressa stepped in with beaming smiles. They closed the door behind them and observed the tension in the room, allowing their expressions to settle.

"How are you feeling, Vyran?" asked Maressa.

Vyran sat at the table, "As good as a *wofltouched* could feel, I suppose. Your friend just left."

"We saw him," said Maressa, "he said he was going for a walk."

Vyran leaned back on his chair, "Hopefully a lengthy one."

Kreia swatted at him and turned to the party, "So would you kindly tell us about this *Donahay*?"

"Vyran, when we spoke about that *fleeting time* to talk, this is the conversation we were looking to have," said Drogon.

Vyran rested his arms on the table, "I see no better time than now."

Drogon, Maressa, Gwynn, Vyran, Lee, and Kreia sat at the round dining table. Vyran poured tea for everyone and grabbed a cookie, leaning back and providing Drogon with his undivided attention.

"We were speaking about the woes of the world, and I think there are some troubles that may find their way to your shores; I know they will," said Drogon, "Donahay was a powerful sorcerer who had grand ambitions. He viewed himself as a god and set out to find his way into the heavens. Eventually, he did just that, used a combination of alchemy, sorcery, and engineering to pierce the veil and corrupted part of the heavens, expelling all sorts of creatures to the world as we know it."

"We call it, the **Era of the Beast**. Back when the Tarasque appeared and ruled these lands, terrorizing our early people. At least that's what the stories tell," Vyran explained.

"That was from Donahay, attempting to transcend from a man to a god - and succeeding. He was not a god like **Solihart** or Mora, no, that was impossible since he was born a man. But he became something greater than an ordinary sorcerer, a demi-god. His specialty was mind control, limitless and timeless; Donahay could strip you of your free will by simply looking into your eyes. A lesser man might only take hearing his voice to fall under his spell. And with that; you are his slave eternal."

Vyran leaned forward, "That was a long time ago. Tiaya tells us the bringer of this darkness, your Donahay - he is long dead."

Drogon nodded, "That's what we all believed. But then, *we* encountered him in a village on the eastern coast of the Radiant

Empire. A village called Sundale. He dominated everyone; every man, woman, and child and forced them to work until the exhaustion and dehydration claimed them. When we got there to stop him, a third of the population was already dead."

"So, you've killed him, then?" asked Vyran.

"We fought through his mind-controlled army to get to him, but then he surrendered. General Dart, our commander at the time, ordered us to take him alive. If I knew then what I know now, we'd have taken his head right then and there," said Drogon.

"If I was with you, he'd have an arrow through his skull before he could even wave the white flag," Gwynn added, "I'm surprised Stein let him live."

"Stein wanted to cut off his head and bury it, but I was following Dart and our orders were to bring him in alive," Drogon said, his eyes pinned to the floor, regret filling his mind.

Vyran raised up a hand, "It's not on you Drogon, whatever happened from there on was on your General Dart and his decision."

Drogon's eyes met his, "That may be true, but it feels all the same to me," he continued, "Donahay was taken to the **Magestry**, a prison specialized for magical beings tucked away underground beneath the capital. It's a fate worse than death; so I've been told. After that, we went to Tristian on our next mission."

Lee's eyes widened, "The vetala."

Drogon nodded, "Yes. Tristian is where young Master Lee joined our ranks. By the time we finished off the vetala, Donahay was waiting for us on the outskirts of the city. Not only did he manage to escape the Magestry, but he used his magic to dominate the entire capital, including Stein's brothers and parents; the royal family, and their elite guard."

Vyran twisted in his seat, "So, Stein's whole family is under this mind control? That must be a lot for him to cope with. I had no idea. I was insensitive towards him - Kreia, you were right. I never would've even guessed he was royalty, either."

"Donahay would have taken over most of the Radiant Empire by now and they are the most formidable kingdom in the known world. We have been traveling to unite the nations against him and his forces, but we're running out of time. Vishnin alone is no threat to him and while you won't be the first land he conquers; know that he will *not stop* until he has created an entire world in his image. I know you haven't meddled with worldly affairs, yet somehow rumors of floren might have spread-" Drogon was cut short.

Vyran interrupted, "You have done so much for my family - more than I could ever repay and I am eternally grateful. What you're asking me to do is take my people, who have never left Vishnin, and bring them to fight and die to stop a threat they've ever known. One that might be stopped before finding its way to us."

"You're not the first leader to suggest that our party may not need your help," said Drogon, "but I can assure you that it will take every capable nation, including you, to help us. If we fail on this first attempt... if we are killed or dominated, Donahay will be unstoppable and your people will be promised the same end. So, while your faith in us might be a compliment I would ask this; would you rather your fate be solely in our hands, or your own?"

Vyran smiled, "You're truly convincing Drogon, a talented diplomat, indeed. However, I need very little influence after all you have done for me. My people are another matter. That is surely a problem I must face - and face it I shall. Today, I will have to address them as their new Champion. There are grander issues than that. For one, we don't have any ships to transport or fighters."

Gwynn was quick to offer, "The *Splinter* is sailing at less than a quarter capacity. It's modified to hold many warriors and can handle a few hundred more, easily. Maybe as many as five hundred more, but it would be tight."

"How long is the journey?" asked Vyran.

"To Luray would be a week or two," Drogon answered, "the *Yoshi* is a trading vessel with an empty hull. I think we could make some modifications, as well, and maybe fit a few hundred more. That is, of course, if they don't mind some cramped conditions."

Vyran nodded, "While we are akin to nature, we floren are comforted by being near to one another. Our homes are typically built as these small cabins by choice, trust me; it will be better to be close together - even more so as we venture away from home for the first time."

Drogon stood from the table, "Well then, Vyran, Champion of Vishnin, will you and your people make a stand against Donahay with us?"

Vyran leapt to his feet and clutched Drogon's hand, "We're with you."

The party all stood around the table. They exchanged looks of promise and conviction to the cause. A hopeful swell filled the room as smiles warmed their faces.

"Then we're nearly ready," said Drogon, "We need to only modify the ships and fill them."

"I will gather the crew and start making some plans for the adjustments. We can gather materials from the forest near the beach," said Gwynn.

"I'll take point on the modification to the *Yoshi*, but we'll need more hands to make it happen quickly," Maressa explained.

"I believe I can help with that," said Vyran, "I need to address my people. I can have them help to make whatever changes need be done."

"How does that work? Do you put up fliers or something?" Lee joked.

Vyran smiled, "Come and I'll show you."

Kreia kissed his cheek, "I'll be here with Ryker. Speak loudly so I may hear you from the window, my love."

Vyran nodded and led the way outside with the party trailing behind him. He began at a slow pace and held the Champion's Axe over his head. His voice was filled with both passion and authority that echoed through the streets, "People of Vishnin, your Champion has returned. I have come to greet you in the square—join me!" He continued onward and repeated the statement with the same fervor.

Windows and doors were thrown open to bear witness. Excited mumbling accompanied florens stumbling out of their door while dressing themselves, tying up their boots as they walked. A parade formed behind them, following down the dirt paths and filling into the square. It was only **half past thirty** before nearly every citizen was in attendance.

Vyran took the stage, being sure to project his voice back towards home, "People of Vishnin, your Champion has returned!"

A deafening eruption of cheering filled the square. The excitement lingered in the air like electricity.

Vyran hushed them, "Yet while the joy of this day is uplifting, I must bring your attention to some most pressing matters. Firstly, Gala, our elder shaman. The *witch* of our village has cast a fear through our homes as toxic as the poison she used on my wife and son."

Enraged shouts and boo's responded.

Vyran continued, "Her fate must be decided, and I choose to show her mercy because I feel death is too good for her. I feel the most appropriate sentence is one of exile, to be without the paradise of Tiaya for the rest of her life. What say you?"

"It's too good for her," one shouted.

"A life without Tiaya is death!" yelled another.

A roar of agreement followed.

"So be it," said Vyran, "when these allied ships leave our waters, Gala will be on them never to set foot in Vishnin again!"

A singular horrified protest shrieked from the stockades, but it was quickly drowned out by other sounds of celebration.

Vyran hushed them again, "The next matter is much more dire. A great evil threatens the world and our great paradise here in Vishnin. These outsiders, slayers of the Yokai and our friends, have come to warn us and ask for our help; to stop the threat before it lands on our shores."

Whispers traveled among the florens, "I heard they killed the Yokai."

"What about the attack in four days?" a voice shouted.

"Lies," said Vyran abruptly, "the witch has sewn enough doubt and fear into us to keep us here in Vishnin forever - that was her goal. This threat by the name of Donahay; he will find his way here if we do not help."

"To protect you all from the horrors of the outside world!" Gala cried out.

"I've never left Vishnin," said a dark haired man.

A young woman replied, "Maybe this Donahay won't come here."

"We should stay here where it's safe," said another.

Vyran held up the Champion's Axe, "Silence! Witch, if you speak again you will enter your new world unable to speak. Good people, we are the proud children of Vishnin the Strong. We, who have never left our paradise, are known for our prowess from mere rumor. The outside world is dangerous, but so is refusing to acknowledge it. We *must* take action and face this threat with our allies by our side."

Cheering and praising followed.

"I wish to send three quarters of our trained forces aboard our allied ships to fight by my side and witness the world. Who among you will join me?" asked Vyran.

A silence fell over the crowd.

Gampy spoke out, "It's not that we ain't happy to have a Champion, but you talking about leaving Vishnin to go to war."

"That's right," said Vyran, "because otherwise, the war will come to us, and we won't stand a chance alone."

The dark-haired man raised his hand briefly, "We don't want to go to war." There was a murmuring of agreement around him. "The outsiders are fighting amongst themselves, right? Let them sort it out as they've always done."

Vyran shouted over the noises of the crowd, "No. Without our help there will be no outside world left. This battle will change the world around us; would you rather leave that to chance?"

A woman yelled out, "If that means not leaving our homes and going to war, yes. It's what we've always done."

"You and Tarkus are the *only* ones that wished for us to leave, but why leave paradise?" another argued.

The florens were alive with praise against going to war. Much cheering and shouting, agreeing, and bolstering one another as Vyran stood on stage watching his words fall upon deaf ears.

"I implore you to see reason," Vyran hollered, "This won't go away on its own. You are being called upon by our friends and the allies of freedom and prosperity itself. I, your Champion, will fight the darkness that approaches our land to keep our homes safe. Who will fight with me?

A few florens moved forward, but only a few.

Mumbling from the masses echoed with: *I don't want to go to war,* and, *I don't want to leave Vishnin, who would ever do that?*

Vyran hoisted his axe high in the air and brought it down into the stage, splitting bits of wood to rain out into the crowd. He left the axe impaled into the deck, electrical energy sparking off the handle, "*You asked me* to do this. I wanted to live a quiet, family life. *You asked me* to be your Champion," he opened his arms, "and here I am. You want to live in paradise? Then there must *be* a paradise. This threat requires our involvement, and I wish I could do more to help you see that. Now, you are being called upon by your Champion. I believe in this cause. I believe that without our help, they will fail. Alas, time is not in our favor and I need you to work with me. From this moment, I enact **Champion's Law.**"

There was outrage among the florens.

"On your first day!" yelled one.

"Hogwash," said a second.

Another showed doubt, "This is truly that great a threat?"

"Vishnin is on the map whether we like it or not. Yes, the threat is great - yet, we are greater!" Vyran commanded, "Stand with me, protect our home. We will all do our part, and right now my part is to tell you to act! I want every fighter to see Ary. Ary will decide if you are part of the three quarters that will be setting sail or the remaining quarter; finishing the wall day and night to protect our village from future attacks." The crowd was silently obeying, dragging their feet as they moved, "I know these are hard times, but know that when this is over, we will be able to return to a home no longer in danger."

Vyran stepped down from the stage where Drogon and the party were waiting. Stein had also rejoined them to observe the speech.

"*Champion's Law*?" asked Stein.

Vyran stowed his axe, "It's the be all, end all. Not my ideal move, but time is against us, is it not?"

"It always is," said Drogon.

Maressa turned to Gwynn, "I think it's time for us to go ready the ships for some construction, wouldn't you say?"

"You're right," Gwynn nodded, "We will meet you all at the beach."

"I'll send more hands soon, we should be ready to move tomorrow," said Vyran.

"You got it!" Gwynn waved as they walked away.

"Gwynn? Maressa?" Drogon beckoned, "Do what you can to have us ready to sail in the next few days."

"We'll be ready," Maressa smiled.

Stein was curious, "Do you have to repeal Champion's Law? Can you govern that way indefinitely?"

"A true Champion does need absolute authority to lead his people. I will repeal the Law once this is done. If I had more time to guide them, I never would've enacted it," Vyran explained.

Stein laughed, "Sounds like a *slippery slope,* as they say."

"It wasn't an easy decision to make," said Vyran.

"Commanding obedience? Of course, it was an easy decision," Stein smirked, "and it always will be."

Vyran's face filled with frustration.

Drogon moved between them, "There is much to do, and now isn't the time."

"Right," Vyran agreed, "I'm going to check in with Ary and help prepare the might of Vishnin for their first sail."

"I'll help you," Stein offered, "How are you going to pack enough provisions if you've never sailed yourself?"

Vyran's jaw clenched, "Fine, come with me, then."

Lee and Drogon were all that remained. They stood aside the stage as the party split into their separate directions. With such a grand task at hand, it somehow felt like it was going too smoothly. The personalities of the group complimented one another so well that the battle to come was no longer painted with doom and gloom. For now, it felt more like an adventure with friends to them both.

"So, what can I do to help?" Lee offered.

Drogon sat down on the steps of the stage, "We can relax for a minute, can't we?"

"Sure, is everything okay?" asked Lee.

Drogon spoke to Lee as he always did, with the same genuine tone of respect and a sense of brotherhood, "Everything is fine, I just wanted to talk to you and see how you felt about all this. In as little as a few weeks, we'll be throwing ourselves into a battle, the likes of which the world has never seen. Are you okay being a part of that? There's a lot at stake, but no matter what happens, it will be ugly."

"I've been thinking about that," Lee was kicking at a rock, "after the clinic, I was afraid of what was going to happen to me. I didn't know how I would survive, or what you and the others really wanted with me. I knew I couldn't survive on my own, but there are places I could've gone. I stayed with you and Stein because I wanted to. I am here because I want to be, and I'm not going anywhere. I think that my life has been very exciting, and I've met people that have given me so very much to smile about. I don't want to die, not anytime soon, but if I do; at least it was fighting for something that was worth it. And to be honest, it makes me a little feel better knowing I will be with people I love. Does that make sense?"

"That makes the most sense, Lee," Drogon nodded.

"Do you think we'll win?"

Drogon looked up to watch a platinum-brimmed cloud bellow overheard. He smiled, "I think we will."

Lee was unmoved, "Even if we win though, what if Stein...you..." his voice trailed off.

"You can't think like that," said Drogon, "that's a heavy weight to carry. Every one of us knows what we're getting into. We are ready to do what we must to stop Donahay. We each are making a choice. You have to make your own and live by that decision."

"What about you? How can you say that you just *accept* death? That's really what you're saying we have to do," Lee said.

The smile still covered Drogon's face, "When I die, hopefully a long, long time from now; I know I will join Solihart in the heavens. Death is natural, Lee. More importantly, death is inevitable. So at some point, we *must* make peace with that idea. I believe once you do that you can live life as your best self and maybe create a little bit of heaven wherever you are."

"That sounds like you're looking at the bright side of death a bit more than I ever could. I'm just not sure there is one," said Lee.

"There is a bright side to everything. That's where I choose to live. Stein can sometimes be the other side of that coin, but you know what?"

"What?"

"It doesn't really matter much does it?" Drogon smiled, "So live your life as conscious as you would if this was your last adventure. Appreciate every moment, fall in love, take chances to do something heroic when the moment calls for it, and always be true to yourself."

Lee looked up to Drogon, "Thank you, Drogon. I will."

"I know you will," Drogon stood and began walking, "now, let's go help ready the ships. Our next stop is Luray. The forces of Vian and Fornesio will be waiting. From there, we take back the Radiant Empire from Donahay."

Lee followed after him, "Will that be enough? You're sure we shouldn't try Ferece or Chun? Maybe that fort to the south?"

"Ferece and Chun have been at war with one another for as long as *even they* can remember. Trust me; they won't be taking on another fight. As for **Fort Titan**," he sighed, "they're tough, but don't play well with others. Not to mention they're out of the way. Gashimar was our last hope for an ally and Jua filled us in on how they are playing both sides."

Lee's voice echoed his discouraged feelings, "So that's it? Just the Vian kingdoms and Vishnin?"

"And us," Drogon laughed.

"It's not funny."

"You're right, it's frightening. We're outnumbered and overpowered, but this is not impossible. We just have to stop Donahay and then all the minds he's enslaved will be free. He is our target. If we get to him, we can end this," Drogon explained.

"If it's that easy, won't he hide behind his army?" asked Lee.

"His ego is enormous. He will know how valuable he is but won't feel threatened by any of us until we are within sword-range. I have a feeling he is comfortable relaxing at the Radiant Castle - probably sitting on the throne waiting to hear that we've been killed. I think we should be the ones to tell him - we are very much alive."

"Yeah!" Lee threw his fist in the air.

"Let's get to it."

# XVII

## Of One Mind

*Yes, my King.*

A red and yellow radiance emanated from the crystal throne, casting a glow about the wall behind it. Perched atop in a posture of arrogance was the imposter - a man of human descent with purple eyes and jet-black hair. His purple robes were crafted with the most elaborate details of gold, fit for royal blood. On his face rested a sinister grin that spread from ear to ear. Upon his head, the jeweled crown of the king of the Radiant Empire. Dozens of other figures lined the perimeter of the room. All of them stood without expression, a purple glow tinting their eyes.

His accent matched his grin as he spoke in the fluent language of pompous, "Treyalt, another sucrape."

A human man in soiled, royal clothing stepped forward to take the empty chalice, "Yes, my king." The disheveled white braid of his beard swayed as he stepped towards the bar cart. He filled the chalice and marched back towards Donahay, "For you, my king."

A sweet scent tickled his senses. Donahay sipped, his eyelids grew heavy with pleasure, "Delicious."

"Are you satisfied, my king?" asked a kai woman in royal garb.

Donahay scoffed, "Satisfied? I am insatiable!"

"My apologies, my king."

"Yes-yes," he dismissed her back in line with the others, "Treyalt, any word from Dart or Victus?"

Treyalt steeped before Donahay with a bow, "No, my king. They have not yet sent word on an alliance with the Duke of Fornesio."

"I don't really care if they ally with us, so long as they don't ally with the dragonkin and that science experiment of yours," said Donahay. "I suppose it would make little difference if they did with Gashimar at their backs and our legion set out before them. Speaking of which, how are my forces fairing?"

Treyalt took a knee, "My king, the final resistance of **Silvermoon** has been defeated. The survivors are being brought here for assimilation. They are arriving now and will be brought in one by one."

"That is excellent. And what of the construction of my fleet?" asked Donahay.

"Your people are working until they are extinguished, as you commanded. We are removing the dead as quickly as they fall. It will be two weeks until you command the most powerful armada - and rule the seas."

Donahay was tapping his foot, deep in thought. He looked up with a scowl, "You bore me, Treyalt. Go work on my fleet until you perish and be sure my fleet is done within a week," he ordered.

Treyalt stood, "Yes, my king."

As the doors of the chamber opened, Treyalt exited. Two hulking guards clad in chromed armor marched in before they closed. They dragged a man in soiled, bloody, yet elaborate blue and orange robes in a strangling grip under his shoulders. Disheveled blonde hair fell over his eyes as they threw him to the ground before Donahay.

The two guards took a knee next to their prone captive, "My king, this is the organizer of the resistance in Silvermoon."

"You look familiar. Is that...is that you, *Tholden*?" Donahay grinned with excitement, "It is you! You're looking a bit worse for wear, but I suppose that's because you've been beaten down. And now, you're bleeding on my floor - moments away from meeting the void." He stood and circled around Tholden, who was pushing up to his knees, "The suffering your *poor* ego must have endured. You fled to the college of Silvermoon after our meet, then? Rallied up the old alma mater?" He laughed, "How many of them died because of you? I would have rather unified them towards a peaceful singular purpose. The greatest minds in the world all *connected.* "

Tholden sat upright on his knees and wiped blood from his mouth. He spoke weakly, "The singular purpose of building your army? Perhaps a monument in your image?"

"To spread this great collective-mind, I need an army to correct the failures of the age - of those that hold on to dead and corrupting traditions. I seek to free people from the suffering of everyday life and inequality. To liberate people from the burden of choice," Donahay explained as he paced. "And to your other question; what greatness should not be immortalized? Do you not have a statue in Sundale with all your *friends*? How are they, by the way?"

Tholden's eyes were fixed on the floor, "We parted ways in Tristian."

"Oh boo-hoo. *I betrayed my friends and now they won't play with me*," Donahay mocked. "You really can't blame them."

"I don't."

"Hard to imagine anyone being able to trust you," Donahay continued, "it's as if you utilize your freewill, only to mislead others. What a darkening impact you have on the world around you."

Tholden's eyes peered up through his hair, "We can't all be a glowing inspiration - like yourself."

Donahay waved his finger and the soldiers, servants, and royal figures positioned around the room simultaneously cheered with raised fists, "My king!"

Donahay leaned down to be eye level with Tholden, "I bring people together and eliminate war and strife. Imagine, when the whole world shares my vision, the greatness that we will create. No more squabbling over lines on a map or who owns what cattle. No more conquests for glory or prideful lust for legacy. We will think on a global scale of survival and progress."

Tholden chuckled, "You think you know what's best for all of us?"

"*All of us* implies a combination of individuals," Donahay started. "None of you *individuals* know what you want, never mind knowing what is best for you. I know what is best for *all* and to start; there is no *us*."

"That sounds vastly overconfident," said Tholden.

"Please Moonstorm, look around you!" he gestured to the surrounding guards and royalty. "It is within my power."

Tholden nodded, "Yes, I see, but I would expect more from a demigod. Come now, I could do better than your ideology."

Tholden could feel his hot breath on his face as Donahay spoke, "*You* manipulated an orphan, an exiled prince, that infuriating, over trusting paladin, and a bumbling half-breed fool. To *escort you* on your quest for power? Tholden, perhaps it is you who should've had grander dreams."

"My mother always taught me to be realistic," Tholden joked.

"Quite true, your limitations are great. The quest for knowledge is one that can only be walked alone. Sooner or later, there is always a falling out. Call it jealousy, call it growth, but it is the prime rule of power; only one can wield it. You remind me of myself when I was a young, foolish sorcerer," said Donahay. "Eventually you either die or live long enough to become wise."

Tholden thought over Donahay's words. He coughed as he spoke, "You may be wrong for all I know - but you may be right. I suppose only one can wield it."

"Of course I'm right," he boasted. "You don't live as long as I have and not learn these things along the way. Another thing I've learned," Donahay knelt down and tilted Tholden's chin up to meet his stare, "Those without choice can't *choose* to betray you."

Donahay's eyes filled with magical energy that flickered like the candlelight from a purple flame. Tholden felt the warmth of the glow turn to a burning and then numbing sensation in his forehead. A calm, soothing sort of migraine forced his eyelids to flutter and roll. He felt a stillness overtake his body as his mind wandered, and then - it raced. Flashbacks filled his mind.

*Only one can wield it.*

*You're a fool - as are all paladins!*

"I didn't mean that," Tholden mumbled.

*I see you've met my merry band of misfits.*

*Some are just born with this level of greatness.*

"I am," his muscles contracted and contorted leaving his body shaking in place.

"Give in to the one, true power," Donahay urged, "become one with it. Surrender to me."

*Only one can wield it.*

"Tholden Moonstorm!" he shouted.

The purple glow within Tholden's eyes shrunk and then expanded violently. A ripple of energy cut through the room as an explosion, tossed the guards across the floor with a tumble and into the wall. Donahay toppled behind his throne with a roll. Tholden soared through the air; landing in front of the door with a second wind filling his chest as he inhaled.

Donahay was climbing to his feet, slightly dazed, "What remarkable will you have for one who has demonstrated continuous cowardice. No, perhaps it's not will at all. Drogon had will; you - you have your *pride*. Who would think that would save you? Why not join me - be a part of the power and live to see the future? You're weak by yourself, Tholden. All you have accomplished with your decisions is the most epic failures. You've betrayed your friends and killed any allies you had in Silvermoon. You *wanted* to join me once."

Tholden felt a rush of adrenaline and magic pumping through his veins as his heart began to sprint with anticipation. He stood, ignoring the fatigue in his legs and found his footing. The green of his eyes fell upon Donahay and then back towards the door, which was still open from the explosion of energy. He chuckled to himself as he raised a finger from each hand towards the demigod and started through the chamber door, "**Nevermore**."

He leapt through the door and into a wild sprint, throwing the doors closed behind him. They were immediately blasted into splinters that came down over the hall in a rain of purple kindling. A shout echoed from the chamber, "Kill him!"

Chromed guards stepped off every wall and every doorway, their heads turned to track Tholden like a predator fixed on its prey. With fierce purpose, they readied their weapons and started after him. Tholden executed a series of maneuvers he remembered from an old mentor. He dodged, ducked, dipped, and dived

A second before Tholden could clear the main hall, Donahay stood in the chamber doorway. He raised his hand, extending his index and middle finger with a point towards Tholden. He whispered, **"Hoo koo."**

At the tip of Donahay's finger, a small purple ball of light formed and crackled with electricity. It was accompanied by a deep humming sound that quickly grew louder. The small, purple ball then burst and a beam five feet in diameter of burning, purple light pulsed outward - the deep hum becoming a deafening roar of energy. It churned the air in the room into a lashing wind. Every surface was painted violet as the beam shot towards Tholden and any guards in its path. They shrieked with pain as they collapsed, the chrome of their armor becoming red and white with heat as the room filled with the scent of their burning flesh.

Tholden spun around, holding both his open palms out in front him and snapped his fingers. A blue, oval shaped, ethereal barrier formed before him. The beam crashed against it with a thunderous force. Sparks sprayed violently as Tholden was thrown backwards and pinned against the wall - his feet dangled above the floor.

Donahay's power was overwhelming and the hoo koo proved to be a most formidable magic - beyond the abilities for the tattered Tholden to defend. The blue shield formed white hairline cracks throughout and the wall at his back grew hotter from the intensity of the warring magics. Tholden felt the brick itself surrender to the force. He mumbled to himself, "Inconceivable."

The crumbled stone gave way behind him as his barrier shattered like glass. He was launched through the wall with robes alive with violet flame. The orange warmth of a sunset greeted him as he shot a distance from the castle and started his rapid thirty-foot descent. Tholden shielded his eyes from the embers, unsure if he was on falling aflame or meeting his judgment in the fires of hell. The whipping flames sizzled with a *splash* as the swirling water drowned out sounds of the clanging armor. He opened his eyes and found himself underwater, in the moat outside of the castle. With a kick of his feet, he broke the surface of the water and clumsily found his footing. He quickly limped away from the castle and towards a nearby woodland feeling the anchors beneath his legs more evident with each step.

Donahay peered down from his new window; his scowl twisting into a satisfied grin, "You can't escape me, Moonstorm." His pointed fingers followed the staggering sorcerer, "Hoo koo."

*To be continued...*

# The Tome of Insights

The world of **Radiant Heroes** is another realm of fantasy where only the wildest minds dare to wander. Here, many humanoid species, gods, and magic cover the lands. You will find bold words from the story further defined here in this **glossary**. There are also some hints at what is to come in future Radiant Hero works.

**Amon**– A shapeless and primordial evil that predates most other gods, Amon originated from the shadow created by the spark of existence. His essence is said to live on in the void and in acts of malice and wickedness. Though many of his texts have been destroyed over time, the original tomes are known only as *The Black Book.*

**Amorous Day**- A day recognizing the importance of love, passions, and family that is inspired by the cosmic-love of *Luna, the Moon Goddess* and her *Starshine.*

**Antidote Potion** - This green potion can counteract venoms and poisons, both natural and crafted, throughout the land of Radiant Heroes. While a lesser antidote would be ineffective against a more advanced poison, most adventurers find a minor antidote sufficient to handle most poisonings during through their travels. Comes in varying strengths; minor (pale green), major (olive green), and super (dark green).

**Architects -** The elite-paladin force of the Vian Kingdom of old. First guard to the King of Vian and bloodline of ancient dragonkin warriors believed to be descendents of Solihart himself.

**Asra Clan–** An elven clan nestled in the southern wilds of the Radiant Empire. Independent and self-sustaining, the clan has preserved its traditional lifestyle for unknown generations. Gwynn has stated to be from this clan.

**Axe of the Champion**, **The-** The mythical axe to the Champion of Vishnin. Crafted from the crystalline horn of the *Tarasque* that was slain by the first Champion, Vishnin himself. After the axe was forged, the goddess *Tiaya* imbued it with her blessing to enchant it further. It may only be wielded by a true Champion of Tiaya and upon their death, will disappear until another worthy follower has proven themselves.

**Barcenic root-** The barcenic plant is absent of scent and taste. It is considered inedible; so, it is typically avoided by people and creatures alike. It's canopy-like leaves create an area typical for smaller animals to hide and nest. A combination of animal waste and root composition create a moderate poison without scent or taste that contributes to fever, comatose, and with continued exposure—death.

**Bow–** A ranged weapon for shooting arrows that is typically made from a curved wood with a tightly drawn string.

**Cattletail Rose** – A long-stemmed and elegant flower that comes in a variety of colors. It is gifted to show love or affection due to its beauty. The color of the flowers is dependent on region of growth. Therefore, there are some colors of the cattletail that will likely not be seen in other areas of the world due to import costs.

**Champion's Estate** - In Vishnin, the leader or *Champion* is allowed to reside in this otherwise publically owned and maintained structure since he/she Champion of the people. While people may come and go freely, they typically respect the Champions privacy.

**Champion's Law**- A Champion is a servant of the people. Citizens acknowledge and adhere to him/her out of respect but are open to disagree and not follow those wishes as they are free. However, each Champion may enact a time of total authoritarian power during times of great struggle. Every citizen is required to comply with an order from the Champion until such a task/time is complete or risk death or worse - exile. This is known as Champion's Law and has only ever been required a few times in centuries.

**Chun** - Clan of *shifters* to the south-east of the Great Sea. They have been in constant conflict with their rival *Ferece* for as long as could be remembered. Because of this strife, they have never joined the rest of the world as a developing nation. No one remembers where the feud originated.

**Clan Unkle**– An Orc clan that is led by Simone Unkle and makes camp in the southern wilds of the Radiant Empire. Garf has stated to be from this clan.

**Cleric-** An individual who is capable of performing healing magic and rituals.

**Cocoon Silk** – Silk from cocoons of creatures undergoing metamorphosis. It is most often used when dried.

**Common Tongue**– Is universally spoken throughout most of the continents of the known world. Though every sentient being has the physical ability to speak it and at least a basic understanding of the language, some remote and isolated tribes may be the exception to the rule.

**Commons, The** – The southern blocks of Tristian are built for more functional and practical uses and are therefore more affordable. They are inhabited by the working class.

**Cookies** - You needed to look up cookies?

**Cotton Wheat**– A fast growing crop that sprouts buds stuffed with cotton. It is the one of the most popular crops due to the ease of its farming and demand of its harvest. There is a saying among farmers, "When in doubt, plant yourself some cotton wheat." What did you expect? They are simple farmers.

**Crowlastte**– In the days of old, a kai god was driven to madness by the death of his kin and became restless, vengeful, and murderous. His name was Crowlastte and he became an agent of chaos, igniting sparks of conflicts simply to watch turmoil unfold. The supporters of his madness follow a text known as *The Chill of Death*.

**Crystal Palace**– Also known as the Radiant Castle, this elaborate crystal palace is decorated with the most precious gems and metals available. It is residence to the King of the Radiant Empire and his family.

**Dark-Elf**– Also known as a *gray*, a dark-elf is a cousin to the elf. During the earlier years of the elf species, some took to live in caves while other moved into the forests. Those that remained in the caves became known as the grays. They share the abilities of a heightened dexterity and reflex. A dark-elf has skin of a varying gray shade and a keen sight in darkness. They are sensitive to sunlight, but it is not lethal to them.

**Deathrobe**– A mythical robe worn by a reaper that is tattered, torn, and comes only in black. Not much is known of the abilities possessed by the robe.

**Deathscythe**– A scythe that is wielded by a reaper. It is crafted from the magic of the spirit realm and sealed by the cold touch of death (The Grimm or leader of reapers) itself. Every deathscythe possesses frightening abilities and each harnesses a single element. (i.e. Stein controls fire.) A deathscythe will dissipate to ash if its wielder is defeated, therefore it can't be claimed from a reaper. It can however, being a magical entity; change allegiances to another wielder.

**Dinsley Clinic**- Clinic in Tristian where Master Mulag practices the healing arts.

**Djinn**– Also known as a Genie, djinn are magical beings that feed off the essence of other magical beings. Many djinn bind themselves through pacts with powerful sorcerers, completing tasks in exchange for some of their essence. This relationship typically lasts until the djinn have become more powerful than the mage. At which time, they consume the being entirely rather than simply parting ways. Why then might a mage make a pact? Djinn are cunning and loyal for the time in which they are bound – making them a fierce ally. They are also the only known creatures, other than *the maker*, that possess creation magic (a.k.a. the ability to make something from nothing).

**Dragon Tongue–** Also referred to as Draconic. This language was derived from that of dragons and passed down by many races said to descend from them. Though some races are incapable of creating the pitches necessary to speak fluently, one can be trained to understand it. Some creatures (i.e. Dragons) only speak in Dragon Tongue.

**Dragonkin–** Believed to be descended from the bloodline of dragons. Dragonkin are a powerful species in tuned with natural magic. They are taller and broader than the average humanoid with an armored-like scaly hide, the snout of a dragon, and the fangs to match. This species is made up of many colors, but most are red, green, or tan. Though many have long pointed tails like the reptilian, some are born without. Dragonkin are as warm-blooded as the dwarves and though they can survive in any climate, they favor more dry and arid conditions. (i.e. Drogon)

**Dragonling–** This is a name given to two different creatures. The first dragonling is a newborn (recently hatched) dragon that has yet to develop its ability for flight or reach its toddler size. The second is a descendant of the dragon, one that remains a small size its entire life. This dragonling never grows much larger than a hawk and tends to travel in groups for protection. Some adventurers train dragonling for sending messages and scouting. (i.e. Argon)

**Dwarf–** Stout and sturdy, the dwarven peoples are proud and ancient race. Both males and females are short in stature with broad builds that favor heavy weapons due to their natural strength. Dwarves are resistant to colder climates and dislike tropical regions. This is credited to their stocky build and high metabolism resulting in above average body temperature and a consistent need for hydration. Dwarves do not tend to have magical abilities. (i.e. Nor.)

**Eel Wheat**– A fast growing crop that is meant to harvest after the storm season. Eel wheat grows off the light of the sun *and* the static of lightning. After the crop has been charged by a storm, harvest is performed, and the buds can be ground to a charged dust. It is no longer in the form of lightning energy because the plant has metabolized it. The process results in energy charged dust present in a raw and easily manipulated form. *Eel wheat essence* (charged ground dust) is the base ingredient in a majority of potions.

**Elf**– The oldest species to walk the lands is that of the elves. Tall and lean, an elf is naturally agile with a keen insight into magic. Any skill that requires finesse and dexterity comes easily to them. Their above-average life span is nearly five times longer than that of a human. This allows them to dedicate time towards mastering many skills before even reaching adulthood. (i.e. Gwynn)

**Elven Tongue**– One of the oldest languages in the world, Elven is credited as the first language not made by nature or the gods. If one has the physical ability to speak common, they may learn elven.

**Era of the Beast**- This is a time where the people of Vishnin struggled to survive against the wilds of nature on their land-locked continent. Life was hard and every day was a struggle to survive.

**Eve**– The reptilian goddess of deceit, treachery, and gambling. Many of her followers' regard her as 'lady luck' due to the influence of her will over chance. She revels in lust and greed. Those who seek her good fortune and follow her faith have scribed *Confessions of the Temptress* from their personal experiences with the will of the temptress herself.

**Everburn**- A powerful fire enchantment given to weapons. It's effect lasts until an equally powerful counter spell is used or until it runs out of fuel. The enchanted weapon does not require fuel to burn.

**Everfrost**- A powerful ice enchantment given to weapons. It's effect lasts until an equally powerful counter spell is used.

**Fenrist**- God of the hunt, more so known as *The Great White Wolf.* A neutral deity in the battle of good and evil. It is said that Fenrist once tricked the gods in the heavens and demons of hell into scouring their kingdoms for a secret, magical means in which to kill the other. When they were all in their respective places, he used his powers to seal them in place. His intention was not to stop fighting or save the kingdom of man, but rather to be able to enjoy hunting in peace without either side attempting to recruit him. By the time they each broke free, Fenrist was lost to the wilds of the lands.

**Ferece** - Clan of *shifters* to the south-west of the Great Sea. They have been in constant conflict with their rival *Chun* for as long as could be remembered. Because of this strife, they have never joined the rest of the world as a developing nation. No one remembers where the feud originated.

**Florens**- A race residing almost exclusively in *Vishnin* that resembles a mixture of other races. The short stature of a dwarf, lean build and dexterity of an elf, and the complexions, lifespan, and adaptable nature of a human. *Halfling* is a derogatory term. (i.e. Ary, Vyran)

**Fool's Coin**- A spell that allows the caster to create illusionary gold, silver, or copper coins from another material of similar size, shape, and weight.

**Fornesio**– The eastern island of the Vian Kingdoms.

**Fort Titan**- Southernmost continent with an arctic-like climate. An abundance of raw material is available for mining, but the only ones who dare to operate in such conditions are several clans of dwarves. They have constructed a massive fort, under which is an underground tunnel-city. If raw ore and gold alone was currency, Fort Titan and its territory is the wealthiest in the world. Most however, never come or go from here, except for plentiful trading vessels that are always eager to leave.

**Gallant** - The elite military force of the Radiant Empire. Sworn to live, fight, and die in the name of the royal family. It is an exclusive honor to be invited to join and comes with substantial perks and prestige.

**Gangway** - A ramp or stairway used to help load/unload a ship to the dock of passengers or goods.

**Gardener Park**– A well-manicured park and playground located in northern Tristian.

**Gashimar**– The most massive continent of the known world, Gashimar consists mainly of forests and wilds. It is inhabited by the greatest number of wild races and creatures that lurk within the woodlands and swamp covering the land. Gashimar politically is separated into factions and clans. The most powerful 50 citizens are ranked in strength and possess political control over the clans. Only by achieving rank through dueling may one achieve the title of Padrino, the ruler of Gashimar. Upon becoming the ruler, one would relinquish their name until death and take on the title of Padrino. A duel for the title of Padrino must be to the death. Marlow stated to be born here.

**Gaweed**– A hallucinogenic herb that was native to Gashimar but has since been cultivated throughout the known world. Gaweed is outlawed in many areas because it has limited alternative uses.

**Glowvine**- A vine plant that grows only in rich soil. In climbs trees and over branches with small, flat, green leaves. Through absorption of nutrients from this rich soil, the plant metabolizes by night which creates an illuminating affect. The wide spread of these vines through a forest can cause the entire woodland to glow in the dark.

**Goliath**- A humanoid race whose large size and muscular build rivals that of the minotaur and orc. They appear the closest to human origins of these towering builds with their complexion and body hair, however many of the males are incapable of growing hair on their head. It is such a rarity for a goliath male to have hair that they are often treated as royalty.

**Glyph**- A sigil or magical marking. Typically, a combination of different words-of-power in a language to a particular spell that provide a localized and reusable spell source. This could be a magical trap or destination used in teleportation, but the uses are infinite. In order to know the purpose of a glyph, you must speak the language and be familiar with some degree of magic.

**Great Axe**– A double-headed axe that is used as a large and heavy weapon. Specialized training and strength are necessary to use this weapon effectively.

**Half-breed**– Every sentient race is capable of mating with another. When a dissimilar pair conceives—the child is known as a half-breed. In the majority of cases, the offspring takes on the appearance of the mother's species and shows no evidence to the heritage of the father. In other cases, they take on the build of one with traits of another. (i.e. Garf)

**Half past thirty**- A floren reference to a fifteen-minute interval. The story is told that long ago, Vishnin the Strong misspoke while stating the time during a tense conversation. To lighten the mood, someone made a joke that mocked his reference to *half past thirty* and it became a running joke for years to come. Centuries later, in present times, the humor is lost, and most don't even know what ever made it funny. Still, it is used to measure time.

**Harryman's Herb**– Owned and operated by Lester Harryman out of Premiere. Harryman's Herb caters to the finest ingredients of herbs and spices that any food or clerical establishment could have need of.

**Healing Potion** - By combining aged *heartbane, eel wheat essence* and boiled water one can create a healing potion. One of the most consumed and demanded potions, the healing potion has the ability to mend minor wounds and requires to skill to use.

While this potion (also known as a crimson) is always recommended to be ingested (helps fight infections from open wounds), it may also be poured directly onto the injury. Comes in varying strengths based on the charge of the *eel wheat essence*; minor, major, and super (very rare).

**Heartbane** – A durable herb that grows in a wide variety of climates and conditions. It is a base ingredient used in many healing rituals and potions.

**Hell's Crater** - A crater nestled deep into the northern woods on the island-country of Vishnin.

**Hoo koo**- More advanced spell work may require a simultaneous incantation. Hoo koo is a rippling blast of dissembling magical energy. Any damage inflicted from this Donahay-crafted spell will not heal without similarly powerful magical means.

**Hosridon**— The dwarven god of adventure, travel and voyages. Hosridon was one of the first gods created and, for his love of pioneering, was tasked with mapping out all existence within a tome to share with the other gods. When he had finished his work, he set the book aflame and stated that the complete secrets within it belonged only to The Maker. When the other gods attempted to kill him for his disrespect, Hosridon became impervious to their attacks – credited to The Maker's blessing. Those embarking on great journeys and travels often seek the blessing of Hosridon. His followers created *Claiming the Heavens* to share his story.

**Human**– A common species that is found on every continent. Known for being adaptable to every terrain and climate,

humans are regarded as enduring and diverse. Height and weight vary throughout regions based on diet, exercise, and upbringing. Though the human body possesses no true natural advantages over other races, they are able to take on nearly any art.
(i.e. Lavi, Lee, Tholden, and Lester)

**Hydra** - A large, many headed, snake like monster said to possess blood with some of the world's most poisonous tendencies. While hydra are rare to encounter in the wild, they are more commonly summoned under the control of powerful wizards to defend strategic locations.

**Hyriel**– The elven god of life and nature who was first to plant seeds across the barren dirt of the world after its creation. Followers of his faith worship nature in all of its forms and his instructions for a collaboration of living are chronicled in *Circular Harmony*.

**Isorin**– The elven term associated with being a well-rounded warrior. This would describe someone familiar with multiple fighting styles, proficient with many weapons, or studying multiple magical arts.

**Kai** – A cousin to humans, kai are of a similar build and appearance. The only identifying difference is the natural formation of tattoo-like markings on their bodies that is present from birth. It is said by the eldest kai that these natural markings are the written destiny of the kai who bears them – deciphered only by the wearer. Kai have similar adaptability and abilities to human with a greater natural affinity towards the magical arts. (i.e. Stein, Victus, Vulcan)

**Katasha** – Speed and agility exceeding that of even the elves, katasha are regarded as the swiftest species in the world. They possess a humanoid build with the fur, claws, and head, like that of a predatory feline. There are variations of this breed scattered through the land and all are regarded as katasha. They may appear as a leopard, cheetah, panther, lion, or tiger. (i.e. Prime Minister Francesco)

**Ketash**– The language of the katasha. It is difficult, but not impossible, for a non-katasha to speak
due to the subtle purring used to pronounce certain letters of the language. *Mekora* - My love. *Sucrape* - Purple grape.

**Korthus**– The orc god of war and conquest. His tales of glory and savage battle are documented in *The Flail of Korthus*. It is the war cry to orc barbarians everywhere.

**Luna, the Moon Goddess**- Luna, the most captivating celestial body, is a source of healing and nurturing energies. Also known as the *Green-Eyed Moon*, it is said that she was born from the wishes and dreams of a drifting star known as her *Starshine,* who sought true love in the heavens. From this cosmic union of a fulfilled destiny was born two smaller stars. This family orbits one another in a heart-shaped pattern, creating the constellation-worthy happening frequently admired by lovers and dreamers alike on *Amorous Day* (June 6th).

**Luray**– The western island of the Vian Kingdoms, Luray was originally led by a Prime Minister—an elected official. During the times of the great war from the Radiant Empire expansion, the Prime Minister was never removed from power. At the time, it was considered an issue of national security and the transition of power would create too much instability. Upon his death, the title and role were passed down to his son, Francesco. Present-day, Francesco remains as ruler over Luray with the title of Prime Minister, but the authority of a king.

**Luray Capitol Building**– This building is frequently mistaken for a palace due to the additions and renovations that have been added on by the acting Prime Minister. Though he lives within the structure, Francesco reminds his people that this is a Capitol Building, and the lower floor is open to the public for all political concerns.

**Magestry, The**– A specialized and enchanted magical prison designed to indefinitely hold the most capable master sorcerers and wizards. Although these places are only rumored to exist, and known by many different names, it is believed that there is one in almost every nation.

**Magic-Weapons**- Some magic weapons and equipment have names. This is the name given at 'birth' (being forged and imbued with magic) by the enchanter or smith. The name will follow the weapon for as long as it exists and will only be revealed to the ones deemed worthy *by* the weapon to wield it. By learning the weapons name, one may unlock its abilities.

**Maker, The**– The spirit and power by which all gods, worlds, life and existence has come to be. Though none have any true image of its being, the essence of magic and creation is credited to The Maker - both by gods and lesser creatures.

**Minos**- The language of Minotaur. Pronounces with a serious of low growls and snarls to syllables. Words are often drawn out giving each word an emphasized meaning to determine the intent of each word and therefore the sentence. You will notice a Minotaur speaking *common* sounds broken when it is actually direct translations without the emphasis on driving syllables. *Toren*- One who fights because they are broken.

**Minotaur** – Minotaur are large, powerful, and aggressive humanoid creatures possessing the fur, hind hooves, and head of a bull. Most are incredibly territorial and do not communicate with outsiders. The more civilized Minotaur live in isolated villages exclusively with their own kind and attack intruders at will. It is extremely rare to encounter one outside of its community unless it is pillaging or part of a band of mercenaries. (i.e. Marlow)

**Mondook -** An extremely poisonous orange berry that grows on a particular vine in dense, isolated woodland. It is rare in most parts of the world. Mondook berries are utilized in the crafting of the most lethal poisons available throughout the world.

**Mora**– The elf goddess of mercy, selflessness and healing. It is said her image has appeared to those in need and has shown her to have eyes of gold. The followers of her faith teach the text *A Generous Life* which is followed by every practicing cleric throughout the land.

**Nevermore**- Tholden is very well read and sometimes like to reference different literary works. He finds it funny.

**Northern Villas**– The northern blocks of Tristian are well kept and constructed by some of the most brilliant engineers of the time. These estates are afforded only by the wealthiest families in the city.

**Nymph**- Sometimes referred to as a fairy, a nymph is a small, winged, elf-like creature, possessing of natural magic and a sensitivity to people and their true alignment.

**Nyota Clan**- A clan of traders and merchants made up entirely of a *shifter* population. They deal in rare and magical relics. Of course, they are sometimes referred to as 'smugglers' due to the secrecy and the skeptical nature of acquirement in some cases. While they may sometimes lift rarities from tombs and ruins alike, they are second to none on lore and knowledge of these items in the entirety of *Gashimar*. Often, they are hired as intermediary transporters with a trusted reputation to deliver both goods an currency - for a price.

**Oni**- See *Yokai*.

**Orc** – Rivaling the Minotaur for strength but exceeding them in ferocity are the orc. Although they are not as large, they are still above average in size and weight. They are green or tan-skinned with a wide framed muscular build. Orc live in tribes and tend to be very aggressive towards outsiders. Since they typically have violent raider-like and man-eating tendencies, they tend to be able to make home in the less civilized areas of the world.

**Padrino**– The most powerful individual citizen, deemed ruler of Gashimar.

**Path of Rubies**– The most prestigious and sculpted residential street in Tristian.

**Phoenix Dust** – When a phoenix transcends and turns to ash, some ash may be preserved without disturbing the creature's resurrection. This ingredient is required for some of the most masterful rituals and potions. Phoenix dust is the rarest ingredient in alchemy since the phoenix lives throughout a hundred year cycle and typically transcends in isolation. It is, by far, the most expensive magic ingredient.

**Pike–** A long pole topped with a spearhead and with a double-sided axe blade below. This weapon is frequently used by supporting infantry.

**Premiere–** The residents of the Northern Villas demand only the most exotic of goods. Premiere is the market of northern Tristian that satisfies that demand.

**Quiver–** A container or carrier for arrows/bolts. It is frequently fastened to a sling worn on the back, but can be attached to the bow, leg, etc.

**Radiant Capital, The–** Home to the royal family and capital of the Radiant Empire. The center of the capital is the Crystal Palace along with the most exclusive high-end markets and tradesmen.

**Radiant Empire, The–** The largest and most powerful kingdom throughout the land. It is ruled as a monarchy that has sought to unify many parts of the world through military conquest and economic manipulation in the past. Stein was born a prince to this kingdom.

**Rayne–** The long sword carried by Drogon. Its properties include radiant and healing magic. Rayne has displayed its loyalty and faithfulness to Drogon which allows him to tap into its abilities.

**Rayton**– A moderately sized fishing town located off the coast of the continental Radiant Empire. Drogon claimed to have family there.

**Rim of the Clouds**- The second highest mountain range in the world, but with the vastest span. Treacherous conditions are only one of the hazards; wild creatures and ancient magics linger here and prevent many would be heroes from completing their climb.

**Rishara**– The katasha goddess of cleverness and cunning. She is praised for her wisdom of life and tactics in combat. Rishara is given recognition for providing innovation and refined skills to lesser creatures, allowing such industrialization as turning grapes into wine. Those who seek wisdom ultimately seek her favor and follow her teachings in *A Shimmering Mind.*

**Reaper** - Equipped with a deathscythe and deathrobes, a reaper is an entity who serves to collect the dead and escort them into the beyond. It is rumored that the reapers were once mortal beings whose abilities and compassion qualified them to be offered to sacrifice their eternal rest to fulfill the duties of a reaper. There are numerous reapers throughout the land to serve this purpose. They are organized by something/someone referred to as a Grimm, or simply—*Death.*

**Reptilian** – A common race in the wilder parts of the world, reptilian are also known as lizard-men and scalers. There are many breeds and colors depending on the region of origin, but all are of average height and are covered with a scaled hide. Being one of the few races that is cold blooded, reptilian tend to avoid colder climates as they very quickly feel its degenerating effects.

This species is most naturally resistant to diseases and poisons. (i.e. Grekk)

**Scythe**– A tool made for harvesting, normally a long wooden pole that is topped with an extended curved blade. A scythe is also rumored to be used by reapers who 'harvest' the living and escort them into death.

**Seed of Life**– A high level and extremely complicated recipe that has resurrection capable qualities when combined with healing magic. When prepared correctly, the seed will restore life to any creature that has been killed within 24 hours. If not created correctly, it may have no effect or extreme side effects. These side effects include, but are not limited to: blindness, coma, development of new allergies, paralysis, loss of vocal ability, fear of plants, cannibalism, facial numbness, psychosis etc.

**Senate House of Fornesio**- The nine senate members of Fornesio that act as one of the two parties of government in addition to the Duke. The Senate deals with civil matters, commerce, and all non-military budgeting. Stein refers to them as *the house of petty debate.*

**Shadowbane** – Also known as *lights kiss* or *sun wisp*, shadowbane is used to suppress the effects of dark magic and curses. For less powerful curses, shadowbane is capable of curing the disease completely. Some adventurers will consume it prior to embarking on a journey where there is known dark magic involved. Doing so will act as a preventative.

**Shaman** - a practitioner of alchemy, witchcraft, and other forms magic; typically given power from forces of nature, lesser deities, or pacts with darker entities.

**Shifter**- A race with the natural ability to alter their physical appearance to that of another race or even specific people. Their true form is rather plain and lacking distinguishing features. The typically possess white hair and skin with a metallic or sometimes mirror-like shine. The eyes are rumored to be the most difficult to transform and for most, any transformation results in retaining their eye color.

**Silvermoon**- City furthest south within the Radiant Empire. Renowned school of magic and training in the arcane arts takes place here. It is frequented by traveling that pilgrimage to the *Rim of the Clouds* and *Temple of Ancients.*

**Sky Sparks**– A rare ingredient of alchemy. It can only be harnessed by someone with magical abilities by containing the natural energy of a lightning bolt.

**Solihart**– Solihart was a brave dragonkin knight who battled the darkness of evil during the formation of the world. He was immortalized by the maker as a god and inspires courage, honor and ferocity in combat while remaining true to his cause. His followers, typically of paladin training, follow the doctrine of *The Wayward Warrior.*

**Sorceress/Sorcerer**- A person born with magical abilities, typically associated with an affinity towards a particular element (fire, ice, radiant, psychic, etc.)

**Spiral Currents**– All the currents of the seas meet just south of the Vian Kingdoms. These harsh conditions have protected their southern shores from invasion. Due to the vicious nature of the spiral currents, very few ships in the world are designed to withstand travel through it.

**Star-rod** - A small capsule, typically made of a flexible glass/gel and filled with alchemical ingredients. When force is exerted (such as snapping any part of the rod), the mixture reacts and will illuminate a dim light similar to a brightly burning candle. Being housed in a capsule allows for numerous uses (including underwater lighting) and is an extremely common component in any adventurer's pack. Its name is derived from the dim light being similar to that of starlight on a clear, moonless night.

**Star Serpent**– A mythical creature of the cosmos that is rumored to survive on the light given off by stars while swimming through the sky. Not much is known about these creatures since they have never come down from the night sky.

**Sucrape**–– A desert grape that only grows throughout the Vian Territories. The grape has rare flavors and possesses the ideal qualities to make wine. Because of its limited growing ability and supply, sucrape and the wine made from it is an exotic and expensive commodity.

**Sundale**– A small manufacturing town located within the Radiant Empire. The party claims to have defeated a hydra there recently.

**Tarasque**- A large creature of legend rumored to have similar size to that of a dragon. Its hulking, six-legged body is covered in fur and atop its head are large crystalline horns said to harness elemental magics. The tip of its tail, fangs, and horns are said to be sharper than swords.

**Tauros**– The legendary Minotaur warrior who was said to save of the last of their species from extermination at the hands of would-be 'heroes'. He inspired the formation of minotaur clans and instructed what each could contribute towards strengthening the brood. Tauros is believed to have been deemed worthy and given godhood for his feats of might. The Minotaur people have no written texts in his honor – it is their belief that the roar of valiant battle is his true tribute.

**Temple of Ancients**- Atop the *Rim of the Clouds* sits a massive temple of timeless origins. It is said to take form to the temple of whatever deity those who approach worship. If one should reach the temple, it offers an opportunity to be moved to their realm and converse with them. Often a destination of pilgrimage which proves most difficult and where many abandon or perish. There are very few who have been rumored to survive the journey.

**Tiaya**- (Tie-A-uh) The floren goddess of bounty, fertility, and natural beauty. She is said to visit the realm to enjoy the lands of her bounty in the form of a peacock. Followers have written and collected works of art and poetry in her name within *Le Plume*.

**Tomb Thirty-Eight** - An ancient, eternal, and impregnable entryway to the *Trials of the Champion*. It is said that as long at Vishnin holds faith in Tiaya that the tomb will exist.

**Trials of the Champion**- Once a Champion is declared in Vishnin, they are bound to the village and the people. The champion remains, even in death, and must create a series of magical trials in order to determine the worthiness of their successor.

**Tristian**– A large trading city located on the outskirts of the Radiant Empire. The port of Tristian is used for all imports and exports to the Vian Kingdoms as well as northern Gashimar. Lavi and Lee are believed to be from this city. Episode 1 begins here.

**Vampire–** Fabled creatures of the night, vampires require the blood of mortal beings in order to survive. They are natural predators with increased strength and agility. This is further enhanced with age and frequency of feedings. A vampire can't survive in sunlight and is susceptible to a variety of radiant magic. Due to the prior facts, vampires tend to be of a pale complexion (if applicable) and reside far from religious buildings and holy ground.

**Vetala–** Ghastly spirits that are capable of possessing cadavers. They are born by unnatural and evil acts of the living and develop power by possessing bodies and spreading their curse. The possession is generally limited to the dead, except in the case of a vetala lord or alpha.

**Vetala Lord– (i.e. Vulcan)** Also known as an Alpha. The vetala lord is a vetala who's power has become so developed within a being that it is self-sustaining and no longer able to swap hosts. It is powerful enough to be capable of spreading its curse even unto the living. Those that are susceptible to the curse are ones corrupted by greed and power while or those having a disregard for others. These corrupted are not all inhabited by the Alpha, and so they are not vetala. Instead they become corrupted, seemingly ordinary and unchanged, but submissive to the curse and will of the Vetala Lord and taking on some physical traits at will.

**Vetaless–** A female vetala. For unknown reason, females that are overcome by the curse of the vetala lord can be afflicted with incredible strength and reflexes vs. males which typically become corrupted. The vetaless senses are heightened to rival that of the Alpha, however they are still submissive to its will.

**Vian–** The northern island of the Vian Kingdoms, Vian is ruler by King Connero and is largely inhabited by dragonkin and reptilian. It is the most militaristic of the Vian territories and provided the greatest resistance against the Radiant Empires expansion.

**Vishnin-** The small continent south of Luray that is overflowing with natural beauty. It is home to a population of floren people and led by a Champion of great power.

**Vishnin the Strong-** Before his legend, the florens lived a hard life. The landlocked continent trapped them with all sorts of creatures, but none more terrifying than the *Tarasque*. Vishnin the Strong is the fabled hero of ancient florens who rid the country of the Tarasque and allowed the bounty of *Tiaya* to fill the land. It is after him that the land is named.

**Vian Kingdoms, The–** Three large, allied, island nations that remain independently ruled: Luray, Vian, and Fornesio. Originally operating as separate entities, the three kingdoms created a binding alliance to hold against the Radiant Empire's advancing military threat.

**Void, The–** Known by many names: the afterlife, spirit realm, the between, unknown, abyss, limbo, neutral plane, etc. Not much is yet revealed to this plane of existence, but it is believed to be a place where only the dead and gods can travel freely.

**Vorsolas–** An elven fighting style created by the Asra Clan. A primarily defensive style that favors utilizing the movements of an attacker to gain an advantageous position for retaliation.

**Werewolf**- A being cursed to transform into that of a humanoid wolf and become a feral, uncontrollable beast upon a full moon or other trigger.

**West Gate, The**– The final un-ruined section to the original wall that once fortified Luray from the invasion of the Radiant Empire.

**Wolftouched**- A humanoid wolf. Unlike a *werewolf*, a wolfouched would act and control themselves as they normally would. They would, however, be unable to revert to their original form. It is possible for a werewolf, with great mental fortitude, to tame their curse to take on this form.

**Yokai**- A creature in the south-western forest of Vishnin. Rumored to have been an ancient king of Ferece that was overthrown and exiled for his greed and disregard for his subjects. He was shipwrecked and lived the last few of his days in the woods before suffering a most grizzly fate. Now, he haunts the forest where he suffered the betrayal of his subjects. (also referred to as Oni)

**Yoshi**– A small, dwarven trading ship that the party acquired in the port of Tristian. It is able to traverse through many sea conditions at an average speed and has no noteworthy combat abilities as it possessed only a single cannon.

And more to come!